ARGOS

*The Story of Odysseus
as Told by His Loyal Dog*

RALPH HARDY

HARPER
An Imprint of HarperCollinsPublishers

Names: Hardy, Ralph, date, author.
Title: Argos : the story of Odysseus as told by his loyal dog / Ralph Hardy.
Description: New York, NY : HarperCollins Publishers, [2016] | Summary: Retells
 the epic tale of Odysseus, the ancient Greek hero who encounters witches
 and other obstacles on his journey home after fighting in the Trojan War,
 told from the point of view of the steadfast companion who never gives up
 hope of his master's safe return.
Identifiers: LCCN 2015029169 | ISBN 9780062396785 (hardback)
Subjects: | CYAC: Odysseus (Greek mythology)—Juvenile fiction. | Odysseus
 (Greek mythology)—Fiction. | Mythology, Greek—Fiction. | Dogs—
 Fiction. | BISAC: JUVENILE FICTION / Legends, Myths, Fables /
 Greek & Roman. | JUVENILE FICTION / Animals / Dogs. | JUVENILE
 FICTION / Classics.
Classification: LCC PZ7.1.H367 Ar 2016 | DDC [Fic]—dc23 LC record available
 at http://lccn.loc.gov/2015029169

Typography by Aurora Parlagreco
16 17 18 19 20 CG/RRDH 10 9 8 7 6 5 4 3 2 1

First Edition

*For Anu, who believed in me,
and George, who made it happen*

CONTENTS

BOOK II

BOOK III

ARGOS

The Story of Odysseus
as Told by His Loyal Dog

BOOK I

CHAPTER I

On the stupidity of sheep

Sometimes a new dog will ask me my lineage, for I look like no other hound on Ithaka, most of which are small and bred to shepherd livestock, if they are bred for any purpose at all. When I am asked, this is the story I tell, if the question is not put to me rudely, as often happens in this age.

My master, brave Odysseus—may the gods favor him—found me one day in early summer as he hunted a stag. Rain had begun to fall, and my master took shelter in a cave. Old men from the town claim that the cave served as a bear's den, but I have never seen such a creature on Ithaka, except Ursa in the summer sky. While waiting for the rain to stop, my master heard noises coming from deep in the cave's passages, but having no light, he waited near the mouth of the cave until the rain passed and then returned home, having lost the stag's trail.

The next morning, he returned with a burning torch to the cave and followed its dark tunnels until he found me, alone, gnawing on a boar's carcass. Next to the carcass lay the bodies of my mother, silver furred and wolfish, and three of my brothers, all black, like me. I alone in that cave lived. My master called me Boar Slayer that day, and later, Argos, and I am still called both. Sometimes when he has drunk too much wine, he will say that my mother was a wolf and my father was the last bear on Ithaka, and perhaps that is true, for my chest is sturdy, and no dog on Ithaka is my match in size. And while there are faster runners on this island, no hound can track as well as I or run as far.

I am Argos, the Boar Slayer, I tell the new dogs, bred of a wolf and a bear, loyal hound to brave Odysseus, guardian of Mistress Penelope, hunting companion to Telemachos, and there my lineage ends.

But tonight a storm comes and the Boar Slayer must guard the sheep. How is it possible for an animal to be so stupid that it does not seek shelter from a storm? They will stand in the most terrible weather, chewing their cuds, bleating on and on about how the grass on one side of the hill tastes better than the other, seemingly unaware of the rain that beats down upon them. Their wool stinks when it's wet. Don't they smell it? I can smell a wet ewe from twenty stadia, and so can a mountain wolf. And while there are no large packs near here, lone wolves, old and crippled, still roam the far pastures looking for stray lambs. And that is why I have to remain outside tonight in the storm. Because sheep are too stupid to come out of the rain.

Still, the mountain wolves will not feast on sheep tonight. Zeus, the father of the gods, hurls jagged lightning at Ithaka, our island, and that is the only thing they fear, besides my sharp teeth. The wolves will lie in their dens, sheltered from the rain, and wait for better days. Yet Telemachos, my master's son, is on edge. Marauders are about, stealing livestock because the island's brave menfolk left many winters ago with my master to capture the city of Troy, and although Telemachos is only eleven, I can tell he feels responsible for his father's estate. He sits with my mistress Penelope every seven days when the remaining shepherds report their livestock deaths, births, and thefts, marking these numbers on clay tablets, which even my master had never done.

I still remember that morning my master left. On the harbor, the mothers, wives, and daughters of the sailors beat their chests and tore their clothes, crying out for Poseidon, god of the vast seas, to protect their loved ones. My master's wife and infant son stood on the jetty as well, waving to him, blowing kisses and weeping. I sat beside them and felt my mistress's warm tears fall onto my back. But the gods have their ways; they seldom listen to humans. And no one has returned to fair Ithaka. So the marauders steal our sheep and break our fences, and there is no one to pick the olives, harvest the grapes, and shear the stupid sheep, which stand in the rain.

Ten years or more have passed since I last licked my master's hand. The kestrels speak of great armies with flashing shields, assembling from the corners of mighty Achaia, from Thessaly, Cydonia, Cythera, Ithaka, and more. The high-flying birds speak of heroes and villains, of Achilles and Ajax, Agamemnon, and Paris, the prince of Troy, who stole the beautiful Helen from Sparta and doomed many less foolish men. The chaffinches who alit in the open windows of Troy and gazed upon Helen no longer sing, so much were they in awe of her beauty. But about my master, Odysseus, I have heard nothing since his victory at that cursed city nearly a year ago.

Troy. It is there my master's reputation was made; it is there he became known as the city sacker and the Wily One. Who has not heard how my master had his men cut down the tallest trees in the wood, constructing a giant horse, a wooden statue as tall as Troy's walls, a noble and grand gesture of surrender? How the Trojans must have laughed at my master, mocked him as if he were a knave and not a king. They did not know my master as I do. He is indeed the Wily One. For as they taunted him, hurled rotten food at his men, and awaited his peace offering, he sharpened his sword deep into the night. So the great moonfaced owl told me last winter.

Once the horse was built, she was rolled up to the gate, which had withstood the Achaian siege without falling. Then the Achaian men who pushed it there retreated under insults and stones, returning to their ships and setting sail. Yet their crews were not full, but smaller by forty men. Nor did they sail far, only beyond the view of the lookouts, where they dropped anchor and waited.

I am told that a few Trojans were suspicious. One, a prophetess, cautioned them to reject the gift, but they did not listen to her admonitions. The Trojans rolled the great horse into their fort and celebrated the retreat of the Achaians late into the night. When all was silent, my master and his men slipped out of the horse and opened the gate for their comrades, who had sailed back under darkness. And so ended the siege of Troy, for the Trojans were all put to the sword. But the Achaians went too far. They destroyed temples to the gods and sacked the city, desecrating its altars and enslaving its women. Finally my master set sail for his home, unaware that the gods had been angered by his men's actions.

This every schoolboy knows, for some men did return to their homes from Troy to tell the tale. But my master and his men have not. The mountain eagles circle higher and higher, riding the rippling currents, looking for him as I have asked, but see him not. The seagulls I have ordered to fly over every ship to see if my master is enslaved report nothing. Even the vultures, which smell death everywhere, are silent. And so I believe he lives.

CHAPTER II

/©/©/©/©/©/©/©/©/©/©/©/©

Arrival of the suitors

Truly the gods are good. This afternoon mistress Penelope ordered the servants to leave her. Then she took Telemachos by the hand and, with no guard but myself, led us to a mountain meadow where they would make a picnic. It has been many years since I have seen my mistress so at ease, and so I believe she has heard from the oracles that my master returns soon. While Telemachos chases butterflies and my mistress picks mountain flowers, grape hyacinths, and scarlet anemones, I keep watch, as it is my duty and my joy.

Telemachos, seeing his mother happy at last, brings a wild iris to her. How they embrace! I sit down next to them, watching and waiting. Finally Telemachos says, "Argos wants a hug too!" and they fold me into their circle. When Telemachos lets go, he scrambles to his feet and grabs a small spear to practice his javelin throwing. I am tempted to run after him, but I must stay with my mistress Penelope, who weaves a garland of flowers.

Watching his son and wife, how can I not think of my master? He has been gone now for more than ten years. How we have all changed! Telemachos grows tall, but not yet broad, and his black hair curls in ringlets like his father's. Mistress Penelope is still radiant, outshining all the women of Ithaka, but sometimes the shadow of worry crosses her face, her green eyes sparkle less, and her lips forget how to smile. As for myself, I have seen just a few more days than Telemachos, but I have passed half my life, while he is still a pup. A pup who throws a javelin far.

Across the meadow I see movement. A doe, trailed by her fawn, steps carefully into the meadow, leaving the safety of the forest to graze on green grass and flowers. Mistress Penelope follows my gaze and sees them as well. She puts her hand on my shoulder, but there is no need. Today is not a day to hunt. Even Telemachos lowers his javelin to watch the pair. Then the trees move again. A buck steps into the meadow. The buck does not graze like the doe and the fawn but holds his antlered head high, watching over them.

"Three of them now," whispers Telemachos. "There is the father! Mother, the fawn has a father!"

"You have a father too," mistress Penelope reminds him gently.

"But he is not here on Ithaka, is he?" the boy says. "He is not here to watch over us."

"No, Telemachos, my son, he is not. But he left Argos here for that purpose until he returns."

I turn to lick Telemachos's hand, and when I do, I see him. A hunter. No, a *poacher*, on our land. He has a bow in his hands and is slowly raising it.

I bark. The buck turns its head. I bark again, and he sees the hunter. I hear a hum and the whistle of an arrow flying past us. But I have warned them in time. No animal on Ithaka has a faster first step than a deer. Before the arrow can strike, the deer are gone.

I turn back to the poacher and bark again, but after missing the shot, he retreated into the forest. I start to chase after him, but my mistress calls me back.

"Come, Argos, Telemachos. Let this day not be ruined with blood. The poacher's arrow missed, thanks to the Boar Slayer. Now it grows late, and the servants will be worried."

"What about the poacher?" asks Telemachos. "Should we let him get away?"

"I will send out guards when we return. If the poacher is still on our land, they will find him," my mistress says.

Or I will find him myself, I think.

Then mistress Penelope packs her sitting cloth and gathers the flowers she had picked. Telemachos throws his javelin one last time—the farthest he has ever thrown it—and we take the trail back to my master's house, Telemachos chatting happily about his new prowess, and his mother assuring him he will grow to be the finest javelin thrower in all Achaia.

But I can sense something is different on Ithaka; grim tidings are in the air.

I hear them first, and then smell them, for the wind is not strong: men. I climb the ridge that runs along the western side of my master's farm and look down at the road. A great throng of men, armed with spears, but using them as walking staffs, is heading our way. The fur on my spine rises and my lips pull back into a snarl. But I wait a moment before barking. Then I see several of them laugh and hear others singing. They are not on a raid, I realize. Is there a festival today? Then I wonder: *Is my master returning? Is this a welcoming party?* Despite my best efforts to control it, my tail begins to wag.

I watch the approaching men for a few more moments,

straining to hear word of my master, but I hear only my mistress Penelope's name on their lips. Then one of our servants comes running up the road to greet the men. After a few minutes, he turns and runs back to my master's palace, and soon all the servants are rushing around, stoking the cook fires and arranging chairs in the great hall, bringing great jugs of wine from the cellars and sharpening knives, and I hear the squeal of a pig being led to slaughter.

A moment later I hear barking, and soon after I see a pack of dogs, my herding pack, running toward me. They are led by Titus, a loyal but thickheaded mongrel, who guards the far pastures when he isn't scavenging food from the servants. The other dogs—curs, mainly, of dubious lineage—stand a few steps behind him, as befits their status, barking sporadically at the wind.

"Who are those men, Boar Slayer?" Titus asks. "Are they marauders? Thieves?" The fur along his back bristles at his own words.

"I know not their purpose, Titus, but thieves and marauders seldom travel by day, nor do they sing or dress themselves in fine tunics, I think."

"So it would seem. What should we do then?" Titus asks, sitting now on his haunches.

"Do? What is there to do?" I reply. "Return to your flocks and herds and tell your underlings to stop barking at shadows. The men approach my master's home and so I shall investigate their purpose." Behind Titus, a mangy-looking whelp barks again, and Titus spins around and snaps at him, biting his ear and sending him scampering away.

Truly, I think, *I must build a stronger pack.*

Just then I hear a whistle. Telemachos!

"Go, Titus. I will summon you if I need you," I say.

I leave the ridge and run back down to the palace. My master's son is outside in the courtyard. When he sees me, he claps his hands and I run up to him. He is blinking back tears and his fists are clenched. *Is he sad or angry?* Humans have such complex emotions!

"They are suitors, Argos," he whispers. "They think my father died after the fall of Troy and so they seek my mother's hand in marriage, as is the custom throughout Achaia, so one of them can inherit my father's land as I am too young to hold it."

My master dead?

I growl at these words, and again the fur along my back stands up straight. *How dare they! What proof do they have?*

"Easy, Argos," Telemachos says gently, stroking my back.

"They are many and we are few. My mother will send them on their way once we have fed them. That is her duty."

I sit on my haunches so he can pat my head, and we wait for the men to arrive at our courtyard. Since many of the island's bravest men left with my master years ago, the only men left on the island are poor farmers, shepherds, and traders, along with these men, who were too old to fight with my master when he left, too young at the time to leave home, or too craven to test their skills against the Trojans. None are worthy of my mistress.

I knew some of their names: Antinoos, Eurymachos, Agelaus, Ktesippos, Leiocritus, and more; even together, they are not worthy to enter our estate. When they reach the courtyard, they stop, stamping the butts of their spears down in unison as if they are trained warriors. Telemachos and I approach them. He has one hand firmly on my neck, but there is no need. They are guests, arriving with peaceful intentions, and it is Telemachos's role, as the only man in the household, to welcome them.

After he has done so, they enter the great hall, and there they remain for the rest of the day, eating and drinking my master's stores and insulting his servants when they are too slow to refill a cup or slice their meat. My mistress Penelope never comes down to greet them, and they leave when Luna is high in the sky. Antinoos's last words to Telemachos are that they will return the next day, and the day after, and the day after that, until his mother chooses one of them to marry.

Hearing this, I know one thing: woe has come to the house of Odysseus.

It is late now, and my master's house is quiet and dark. Even the guards are dozing, as it is the hour before rosy dawn comes to Ithaka. I make my way down to the shore, guided by Luna's face. The seagulls are asleep on the jetty, hundreds of them with their heads tucked behind their wings. I wake them all with a single bark. When they finish squawking, I say this: "You must fly higher and farther and find King Odysseus. If you fail, another man will become king and our fair isle is doomed. Go now, and do not return without news."

Their wings fill the sky.

CHAPTER III

/ɒ/ɒ/ɒ/ɒ/ɒ/ɒ/ɒ/ɒ/ɒ/ɒ/ɒ/ɒ/ɒ

Word of my master

This afternoon, while I am dozing in the sun—I had been up all night guarding sheep—a gull approaches me. I have one eye open and one closed, in the manner of most guard dogs, so I am both asleep and awake at the same time. The gull wakes me with a squawk next to my ear. I jump to my feet, jaws ready to snap his wing, but the gull is already hovering in the air, too high for me to reach.

"Are you the one called the Boar Slayer?" he asks, circling above my head.

"Yes, I am called that," I growl. "Come down so that I may introduce myself properly," I add.

"I think not, Boar Slayer. But I do come bearing news for you."

"News of what, orange beak? Nets full of fish? The lapping of the waves? The tide coming in and out?"

I do not like to be awakened from a nap, and truly the gulls are more likely to report a school of fish near the shore than news of my master. Still, this gull does not look familiar to me: his wings are darker than our gulls on Ithaka, and his accent is foreign.

"Very well. I will not bother you again. Perhaps we'll talk another time if you are busy."

The gull hovers higher and begins to arc its wings, then turns with the wind.

"Wait!" I cry, and sit back on my haunches. *Why would a strange gull fly up here to the highlands if not for important news?*

The gull circles lazily back toward me, dipping low above my head.

"Forgive my impertinence, high flyer. I was dreaming that my master had returned to Ithaka, and I woke to see that he had not, and so my temper was aroused. But what news do you bring? I will gladly listen to it."

The gull does not answer, but instead catches a gust of wind and soars high above me. "Brothers," he squawks. "I have found the Boar Slayer!"

A few moments later, dozens of gulls appear over the ridge and swoop down low over me, eventually landing beside the gull who had woken me.

"Could you not tell me the news yourself, white wing?"

"No, I could not, Boar Slayer. Truly, we gulls belong in flocks. That is how Father Zeus made us. If you see a gull alone, it is merely waiting for others to arrive, or searching for food to tell them about. We prefer to speak with our brothers nearby, to form a chorus of our words. We find this pleasing, though men who do not know our language complain about our noise, it is true."

"Your flock is with you now, so tell me then your news," I say. "What do you herald?"

"Only this. Your master's ships left Troy some months back, Argos, sailing toward Ithaka. I know this because I was following your master's fleet—or I should say, following a school of anchovies."

"Anchovies! Anchovies! Anchovies!" his flock echoes.

I cannot restrain myself from a loud bark. The gull's story echoes the owl's!

"Then he returns soon, whitest of birds! My master is returning with his men! How joyous the celebration will be!"

But the gull says nothing. He spreads his long wings and again hovers effortlessly above me. Then he lands on a fence-post.

"Have you ever eaten an anchovy, Argos? Truly, I would fly to faraway Crete for an anchovy. They are quite delicious."

"Delicious! Delicious! Delicious!" the gulls cry.

Seagulls are the most ravenous birds, thinking constantly about food, so I know I have to be patient with him before he will complete his tale.

"I shall have to try one sometime, my friend," I say. "But what of my master's ship? When will he arrive?"

"Some birds claim they are too oily, but I think not."

"When my master returns, I shall eat one in celebration with you."

The gull tucks his head in its wing for a moment and then turns one yellow eye toward me.

"There will be no celebration, loyal Argos. The winds drove your master's many ships to Ismaros, a small island by the Kikonians. There your master and his men sacked the city, killing the men and taking their wives and possessions, as men returning from war are wont to do. Still, your master was light of foot and wanted to leave, but his men behaved shamelessly and drank too much wine and slaughtered many sheep and cattle to feast upon."

"Shame! Shame! Shame!" the gulls cry in unison.

How unlike dogs men are, to kill so wantonly, I think. *Surely the gods made them like themselves, petty and cruel as often as noble and heroic.*

The gull suddenly spreads its wings and launches itself into the sky, flying a circle above my head. Seconds later his flock joins him, spinning gyres in the sky, making me dizzy.

"Ahh, the fishermen return to the dock. They will have nets full of calamari. We shall dine well this evening," he cries to his brethren, ignoring me.

"Sir Gull," I cry. "Is that all you have to say? Is my master sailing again toward Ithaka? If that is your story, I thank thee for your efforts."

Again he hovers above me; then he perches on a sea-pine branch, turning his head sideways to look at me.

"There is more to tell, Boar Slayer. Some men from the city escaped the slaughter and retreated to safety, summoning their kin from the interior of the country. These were hard, fighting men, with horses and armor, and there were many. They came early in the morning, and Father Zeus gave your master's men evil luck. The Achaians fought for hours and bravely, but eventually they were beaten back. Out of each of your master's fleet, six were killed, but some were able to board their ships and sail away, as the Kikonians are not sailors."

"But surely my master lives, bright-winged gull?"

"Aye, noble Argos. If only he had had a crew such as himself, he would have won the day. But he lived and was glad to escape death, I think. Now I must go. Calamari is best eaten fresh."

He lives. My master lives.

"We must go! We must go! We must go!"

"One moment, please," I beg. "So my master returns now, though with fewer men? Still, the gods will be praised when they return."

A third time the gull hovers and lands. Again, he turns his head sideways to look at me. "Boar Slayer, hear me out. Not long had they left Ismaros before storm-minded Zeus sent a foul north wind against their ships, and although they rowed hard against it, their sails were ripped and had to be stowed. For two days and two nights your master and his men laid up, bailing their ships and grieving for their lost friends. Then, on the third day, glorious dawn came, clear-eyed and dry, and I heard your master shout: 'Rig the sails and steer us home to Ithaka!'

"Ithaka! Ithaka! Ithaka!"

"How his men cheered that morn, Argos! But from atop the mast, I saw clouds scuttling by, as quick and silver as a school of tuna, and I knew that Father Zeus was not yet appeased. Once they rounded their swift ships past Maleia, the bitter winds changed course again and drove them for nine days until they made shore. That was when I left their ships, Argos, for the waters there hold few fish. I have flown for many days and nights, and now I must eat and rest. My mate will be laying her eggs soon, and she too enjoys calamari. Shrimp as well."

He smacks his beak as he says this, and then the gull launches himself into the air and turns into the wind. I bark once, and he dips his head to listen.

"Wait!" I cry. "Faithful friend, highest flyer of all the birds, what of my master? Where did he and his men land? Will they be returning soon?"

The gull circles twice and then flies low, low enough for me to hear his terrible reply. "Your master and his men landed in the country of the Lotus Eaters, noble Argos. Forget your master and tend to his son. No man returns from there alive."

Then, with an arch of his silver wings, he takes the wind and flies away.

"No return! No return! No return!" his flock calls back to me.

CHAPTER IV

~/~/~/~/~/~/~/~/~/~/~/~/~/~/~

The Boar Slayer

Tonight, as I lie down near the sheep paddock, I hear through the open window of her room my mistress crying. I had heard a servant girl earlier say that this was the twelfth anniversary of my mistress's marriage to my master Odysseus, and they had roasted a goat in their honor, but my mistress refused to eat it. Instead, according to the servant girl, she shut herself in her room and spent the evening praying to the gods. Now she weeps.

I enter the house and climb the stairs to my mistress's room. To the left I smell Telemachos in his bed, and I hear him snoring gently. He had spent the day practicing archery and wrestling, so I know he sleeps deeply. At the other end of the hall I hear the muffled sobs of a woman crying into her pillow.

It is my mistress, my queen. The hall is dark, but I can see that her bedroom door is closed. I lift my paw and scratch the heavy oak door. Three times I scratch, and then the door opens.

"Come, Argos," my mistress says softly. "I would enjoy your company tonight."

She is wearing a simple bed tunic and her long black hair is plaited, nearly reaching her waist. She has not cut it since my master left. Even in mourning, her beauty outshines every mortal I have seen.

My mistress no longer sleeps in her wedding bed, which my master carved out of a living olive tree as a gift to her. Instead she sleeps on a low pallet covered in thin fleece, which lies next to it. The pallet is hard, and many times I have heard my mistress's servants beg her to sleep on her own bed. "Your husband would want you to sleep on his bed, my queen," they say. "He carved it for you!"

"And does my husband sleep on a soft bed at night?" she would reply. "Or does he sleep on a ship's hard planks or beneath Luna herself, on a bloody battleground?"

To this they have no answer. So for more than ten years she has slept on this hard pallet, and tonight I lie down beside her on it.

"Argos," she says, stroking my forehead. "You think my husband, brave Odysseus, lives, do you not?"

I lick her hand. *My master lives. I am certain of it. Even that wretched seagull could not convince me otherwise.*

"I do also," she says. "But why have we heard nothing from him? Is he a prisoner of some terrible tribe of men? Is he stranded on an island, shipwrecked and thirsty? Does he lie wounded on some battlefield, surrounded by his fallen comrades? Every night I pray to the gods for a sign that he lives, but they answer me not. Every sound of thunder in the summer sky makes me think that Zeus is answering me, but what mortal can divine a thunderclap? I cannot. Outside my window a dove has built a nest. What does this portend, if anything? I know only that a dove mates for life, and I too shall never wed again unless by force."

She begins to weep again, and I nuzzle her cheek. After a few minutes she sighs and speaks again, but her tone is lighter, as if I have given her some comfort.

"If only you could talk, brave one," she says. "What stories would you tell? What fearsome beasts have you hunted? How is it that my husband, brave Odysseus, found you, the handsomest dog on Ithaka, in a cave?"

Then she rubs her fingers along the scars on my face. I *was* once a handsome dog, if I may be immodest, but now my muzzle is scarred, my ears are torn, and on cold days I limp. My fur, once as black as a volcano, is flecked with gray, as if snow had fallen on that black peak. The shield on my chest, a patch of white, is matted with burrs and nettles. Still, my teeth are sharp, my back is straight, and my tail curves like a flashing sword.

I grow drowsy under my mistress's caresses. How sweet it is to lie next to her, far from the braying of sheep and goats and the squawk of hens. I am nearly asleep when I hear a sound: footsteps. Quick and soft footsteps. I sit up. I know who is coming. Telemachos.

The boy knocks softly and enters the room. He is nearly twelve years old, neither a child nor a man, but simply a boy who misses his father.

"Mother, do you sleep?" he whispers.

"Come to me, my son," my mistress says, sitting up. "Were you having bad dreams?"

Telemachos sits on the bed next to his mother, and he also rubs my head and ears.

"I dreamed I was drowning, Mother," he says after a moment.

"I was swimming and Poseidon was angry and sent wave after wave crashing over me. Why would I dream this? What does it mean?"

Mistress Penelope puts her arm around the boy. "It means you ate too many figs for dessert, my brave swimmer, and your stomach is upset, that is all."

"But father is a sailor, is he not, Mother? Could this dream be about him? Perhaps his swift black ship is in a storm. What if he has been thrown overboard?"

My mistress hugs her son, who has begun to cry.

"Your father is a sailor, it is true, Telemachos, but he is also a warrior and a king. The gods would not let him drown at sea. His fate is not that of sailors and fishermen, but that of a hero. Did he not conquer Troy, my son?"

"Then why has he not returned?"

"He is on his way."

"Soon? He comes soon?"

"That I cannot promise. All we can do is pray to the gods and wait. And in the meantime, I must run the household properly, and you must be a good student and bring honor to our family by your deeds and actions. Can you do that?"

"Yes, and what of Argos? What must he do?"

"Argos has the most difficult task of all. He has to guard all the livestock and keep us safe too. Do you think he can do it?"

"Of course he can," Telemachos says, putting his arms around my neck. "He is the Boar Slayer, is he not?"

And then mother and son lie down and cover themselves in a warm fleece while I curl up beside them to sleep for a few hours myself. Even a boar slayer must rest now and then.

CHAPTER V

Among the Lotus Eaters

Along the beach I find what I am looking for: sea-turtle tracks. The gods favor these strange creatures with long lives, which they spend swimming across the blue sea, stopping to lay their eggs on the many islands that Kronos made before he was overthrown by Zeus. I knew that some sea turtles lay their eggs on that cursed land of the Lotus Eaters, and I thought perhaps one had seen my master. I find the turtle that night, digging with her strange paws in the moonlight, preparing to lay her eggs. But she had not seen my master.

"Others will come, Argos, who have seen that land," she says, flicking her black tongue. "On the next neap tide, return here, and you will find my sister turtle. She will know of your master's fate."

"Thank you, Mother Turtle. Good luck to you and your offspring."

She regards me for a long time with unblinking eyes.

"Argos, of the hundred eggs in this clutch, perhaps two will live. Most will die in their shells, eaten by seabirds. A few will hatch and point their beaks to the sea. In those cold waters swim sharp-toothed fish, which will swallow them whole. One or two will hide in the seaweed and live. That is our fate. Zeus has cursed us twice: we live too long and our children die before us. So speak not to me of luck. Now return when Luna wanes, and you will find your answer."

"Thank you, sister," I say gently. Though I have no offspring, her story tears at my heart. Then she resumes her digging and I take the trail that leads up to my master's home, more desperate than ever to learn of his fate.

Apollo's chariot has carried the sun through the skies twenty times while I herded goats and sheep. Some days I followed young Telemachos on long walks into the pine-covered hills. His servant, Dolios, knows that my master Odysseus would want his son to grow strong legs, so as a young boy, Telemachos spends many hours outside, running, climbing, and playing with the other boys from the nearby village. This will prepare him for the time when he will have to lead his companions into war, for there is no escaping that fate as an Achaian. I spend the evening snarling at the suitors, dodging their kicks, barking when they insult the servants.

In this way the days passed. Now is the evening of the neap tide, and I again take the path down to the shore and wait for the turtles to emerge from the waves. I wait for many hours, watching the endless waves come and go. Finally, when I am about to give up hope, I see three she-turtles blasting through the foam. I wait for them to crawl into the moonlight, and then I approach the one closest in size to the turtle from before, and it is confirmed: they are sisters. And she had laid a clutch of eggs on the island of the Lotus Eaters.

"Tell me what you saw there, Sister Turtle," I ask. "Were there six ships in the harbor? Was one black and swift keeled?"

"Aye, Argos," she says, stretching her wrinkled neck. "Your master was there. His ships had been docked for some days before I arrived."

"You saw him? My master?"

"Yes, I saw him. His fools nearly trampled my nest while they were carrying their shipmates back from the Lotus Eaters!"

"Was my master being carried? Had the Lotus Eaters stolen

his mind? Tell me, ancient one!"

"Patience, Argos. When one has swum the seas for as long as I, one learns to develop such a virtue," she says. "I am tired and hungry after my travels."

I watch as she unhurriedly chews a piece of seaweed, the slimy green grass slithering into her sharp beak. My master once said that a great ruler does not lead his people with force, but with patience and wisdom. And so I will wait; there would be no rushing her.

"Thank you for allowing me that brief respite, noble one," she says finally, with a long gulp that travels the length of her neck.

At last I will hear my master's fate.

"Your master is alive and as shrewd as ever, having sent his men ahead to meet with the Lotus Eaters. But no mortal man is as strong as the great Odysseus, and those he sent were weak and ate the sweet fruit they were given. Your master had to rescue them and bring them back. Oh, how they wept, those piteous men! But he tied them to the rowing benches, and soon they raised their sails."

"So he left the island! He returns soon?"

This news makes me twirl around on the sand like a young pup!

"But how is it that you, a turtle, arrived here before my master?" I ask.

"You have many questions, loyal Argos, and they are insolently framed, but I will grant you an answer. I swim day and night without stopping, whereas no man can row for too many hours, nor does the wind always favor a ship. That is why I have arrived here so swiftly."

"Pardon me, ancient one. I may appear rude, but I am only anxious for my master's return. Now that I know it is imminent, let me show my respect by guarding the eggs of your sisters here. I promise you that their offspring will encounter no predators as they return to the sea. I will guard them with my own powerful jaws, and no bird will dare snatch one in its beak, so I swear."

"So it shall be, loyal one, and I thank you. They will hatch in two moons' time. Guard them well on this lethal shore, and your pledge will be filled. I return now to the sea. I feel its pull, and I have many more miles to swim."

The ancient turtle begins her laborious trek back down to the shore. When she reaches the edge of the foam, she stops and turns her head to me.

"Farewell, Argos, and remember your pledge."

"I shall. And good swimming to you, sister. Mind my

master's ships as they approach Ithaka."

For a long moment she says nothing. Nor does she enter the sea. Then she turns to me and blinks her glassy eyes several times, as if she is trying to decide to tell me something or not. Finally she says, "Foolish pup! I never said your master's ships were steered toward Ithaka—only that they had left the land of the Lotus Eaters."

The fur on my back rises. "Where did they sail then, ancient one, if not back here to their home?"

"They were sailing toward the island of giants. The land of the Cyclopes, Boar Slayer," she says, making her way toward the crashing sea. Then she stops and turns to look me in the eye once more. "Only Father Zeus can save them now."

CHAPTER VI

ᘒᘒᘒᘒᘒᘒᘒᘒᘒᘒᘒᘒᘒᘒᘒᘒᘒ

The dread Cyclopes

Luna is round tonight, as she was when I last learned about my master from the deceitful sea turtle. I have never heard much of the Cyclopes, or of their ways, only that they are giants. Perhaps they are gentle, though, for often a small man is cruel and vicious, while a large man is careful and prudent with his strength. It is that way with dogs too: the small ones bite, while the large ones need only bark. Is this not so?

But I am not content to merely hope that my master is safe; I must know with certainty. There is a marsh in the south of Ithaka where flocks of teals lay their eggs after their long flights east from Aoia. *Surely they know of the Cyclopes,* I think as I make my way along a goat trail that winds its way toward that marsh.

After several hours, the terrain begins to change. The pine trees make way for junipers and the hills grow less steep. Soon I'm walking along flat earth, and I find a small pool from which to drink. After easing my thirst, I stop to listen. A thousand teals can drown an army's noise. Never have I heard such squawking and quacking!

The marsh is easy to find. My paws begin to stick in the muck, and soon I am trotting through reeds as tall as spears. After a few minutes I reach the small lake where the teals nest.

There are hundreds of them swimming in sharp deltas along the water, occasionally ducking their heads and lifting their bottoms out of the water. Near the shore, fledglings follow their mothers along the bank, learning to paddle their flat feet. I have come just in time. In a few weeks the flocks will have left Ithaka, flying farther south in their restless way.

I sit down at the shore and listen for a few minutes. Their language is incomprehensible. My worst fear has come true: I don't know their tongue. A large teal waddling along the bank approaches me as I sit wondering what to do.

"I am Argos, the Boar Slayer," I say slowly.

The teal says nothing.

"My master is Odysseus. He is known throughout the world as the Wily One. Do you know him?"

This time the teal quacks once, then stretches his curved neck, turning his head nearly around.

"Do you know the land of the Cyclopes?" I ask.

Again the teal quacks and twists his head impossibly.

"Save your breath, loyal Ar-Ar-Argos," a voice says from above me. "The teals do not speak the common tongue. After Father Zeus took Leda as his mate, no long-necked water fowl would speak it, and now they have forgotten it completely."

I look up. A crow is perched on a juniper branch. It was he who had spoken.

"Cousin Crow, wisest of birds," I call up to him. "I thank you for your assistance. Tell me, can you speak to them? Surely you know their language, master of all voices."

The crow hops down to a lower branch. "Yes, of course I know it. What do you wish to ask them?"

"I seek news of my master Odysseus. He was last seen sailing toward the land of the Cyclopes. I thought these high-flyers might have seen him and know his fate."

The crow alights on a fallen tree next to me so that we are eye-to-eye.

"I will ask them for you, Boar Slayer, but it may take some time to get the truth. These are the most disagreeable of birds, and they interrupt one another constantly. Go back to your master's home and return to your herding. I will seek you out tomorrow with the news, if there is any to tell."

"I thank you, Cousin in Black. It is true that while I am away, the herds wander afield, the sheep particularly."

The crow bobs its head. "They are-are-are quite stupid. I will come at dusk tomorrow," he promises.

Hearing these words, I turn around and begin the long run back to our home to the north. I arrive just as the sun falls below Mount Nerito and the shadows begin to creep over the fields. One ewe has wandered off, but I bring her back quickly to the fold. In my master's house torches are lit, and the nightly revelry of the suitors has begun. Oh, the shame they bring to the house of Odysseus! Surely my master will return soon and drive those hateful men away. Even the Cyclopes could not be worse than these insolent men.

At dusk the next day a shadow falls over my shoulder as I lead the sheep into their paddocks. How long this day has felt while I wait for news of my master! I cannot even be certain that the teals saw him, though they fly from the east, and giants and teals both need fresh water. If the land of the Cyclopes has lakes on it, then surely the teals landed there. Yet how flimsy my logic seems as the day passes slowly by.

Seeing the shadow, I look up and watch the winged crow alight on the roof of the paddock. When the sheep are bedded down, I rush back outside. The crow is waiting.

"Welcome to the home of Odysseus, Sir Crow," I call up to him. "Do you bring news of my master?"

"I do, Boar Slayer. If the teals can be trusted, I have your story, though it is a terrible one."

I feel as if a spear has passed through my heart.

"My master lives, does he not? Tell me that at once, crow!"

The crow lands on a low branch.

"Sit back on your haunches, Ar-ar-argos," says the crow. "I will tell you what I heard."

This is the teals' story.

My master and his men landed on a wooded island, as strange a land as any teal has seen. There the people of Cyclopes live not like other men, for they neither plow nor plant, and they live in the many caves that dot the island. They neither farm nor fish, because the immortal gods watch over them and give them their needs. There are many goats on the island and the wheat and barley and grapes grow with no hindrance, so the people of Cyclopes plan little and live apart from one another, needing no counsels, and each one is his own law, and thus they are lawless.

A short flight beyond this island was another island, where the teals saw my master and his men find harbor. It was full of wild goats and there was bright water to drink; yet again no men had farmed its pastures or planted crops, neither did they cast nets, so the ponds were full of fish for the teals to eat.

There brave Odysseus and his men from the twelve ships spent the day and the night, feasting on meat and drinking sweet wine. The next morning the Wily One took only the twelve men from his own ship and sailed round the island to learn of its natives, whether they were savage and violent or hospitable to strangers. The teals followed his ship, hoping to steal fish from their nets, but after my master had sailed a short distance, he spied a cave hidden with laurels, and there were great flocks of sheep and goats behind a high wall, built among large boulders strewn about. Herding the great flocks was a one-eyed monster.

The teals say this monster had but a single eye in the center of his face and was as tall as the peak of a mountain, so that my master and his men seemed to shrink in wonder at his great size. But brave Odysseus fears no one, and so he and his men lightly made their way to the cave.

When they arrived, the monster had left to herd his fat flocks on the range, so my master and his men entered the cave unbidden to see what manner of man this monster was. Inside the cave were giant baskets of cheese, and there were pens crowded with lambs and kids, as well as cisterns overflowing with milk. My master's men wanted to take the lambs and kids back to the ship and sail away, but the Wily One thought the monster might have more to give them. So they made a fire and waited for the monster to return.

He arrived carrying a heavy load of firewood, which he threw onto the floor of the cave with such force that it sent the men scattering into the dark recesses of the cave to hide. Then he brought in his giant flocks and put them in pens, and finally he rolled a giant boulder across the door to keep out intruders, though what manner of intruder would dare enter that cave, one can only guess. Then he milked his flock and built a fire, at which point he saw my master and his men.

"Strangers," he asked, "who are you? Are you lawless pirates, bringing evil to this land?"

"We are Achaians coming from Troy, driven off course by the winds, and making our way home as best we can," said brave Odysseus. "We are followers of Agamemnon, whose fame is great throughout Achaia. Through the will of Zeus, we have landed here, and we ask on bended knee that you give us a guest present, as men do in our land, in honor of Zeus. That is what the gods demand of all, O mightiest of men."

But the monster was pitiless to their plight. "Stranger, you are a fool. The Cyclopes do not fear Zeus or any of the gods, for we are better than they. I could kill you now and think nothing of it. But tell me, is your ship near or far off? I ask so that I may help you get aboard it and leave us in peace before my brothers learn of you, for they shall show you no mercy."

No man or monster is more cunning than my master, who replied, "Alas, no. Poseidon, shaker of the earth, drove my ship against the rocks, and we are stranded here for a time. Only my men you see here survived."

But instead of showing brave Odysseus pity at his tale, the monster suddenly snatched two of his men and hurled them against the ground, killing them. Then, to my master's horror, he tore them limb by limb and ate the remains, washing the terrible meal down with great buckets of goat milk. Brave Odysseus and his men cried out to Zeus in despair, but the god answered not, and they could do nothing but wring their hands in mourning while the monster lay down to sleep, sprawled out among them.

Once the monster began to snore with deafening rattles, my master took out his sword and thought to stab the great beast in the heart, but just as he was about to strike, he realized that the great boulder blocking the entrance to the cave was too large for his men together to roll aside, and they would be trapped in the cave. So they could do nothing that night except pray to the gods and wring their hands in mourning until the dawn came.

"But how did the teals know this?" I asked the crow when he told me his tale. "Were the teals in the cave with the monster and my master?"

The crow had asked that also. He said that the teals had told him that the monster kept chickens in his cave and the small ones passed in and out between the giant stone and the cave's entrance. It was they who told the teals of the events inside.

"But perhaps it isn't true," I demanded, fearing for my master. "Surely no such monster exists!"

Then the crow turned his head to look at me, and I could see in his black eyes that this was no lie.

The teal's story continued. As dawn's light crept through the cracks of the Cyclops's cave, the monster woke and made a fire. After that he milked his goats, and then, just as my master hoped he would roll aside the great boulder, the monster snatched up two men and ate them for breakfast, ignoring the screams of despair and outrage of my master's men.

After he had dined, the monster rolled aside the great boulder so that he could let his sheep out to graze, but he stood by the door watching to make sure that Odysseus and his men did not escape. Then he rolled the boulder back across as he left, leaving them trapped inside.

My master was left with his black thoughts of how he might avenge his men while the monster whistled to his flocks, guiding them to the pastures beyond the cave. Before the fire that had been lit could burn out, brave Odysseus found a wooden club the monster had left to dry. It was nearly as long as the mast on a ship of twenty oars, but my master and his men chopped it until it was the height of a man so that they could lift it. Then my master set to sharpening its end into a fine point while the rest of his men made it smooth.

When that job was done, the men, fearing that the monster might return at any moment, put the point of the spear into the fire to harden it. Finally, when the tip had turned black, they hid the spear and prayed to the gods they would have the chance to use it. As the men rested from their labors, they drew lots to decide who would help brave Odysseus spear the monster while he slept that night.

When the evening came, the monster rolled back the stone carefully so that no one could escape, and he brought in his goats and sheep from their pasturing. After that, he milked the goats and sheep, filling his great bucket, and when his work was done, he snatched two of my master's men and ate them. Then did my master approach the monster and say, "Here, Cyclops, now that you have committed so terrible a thing as to eat human flesh, drink this wine from our ship. I brought it for you as a gift yesterday, before your cruelty, but now drink of it and take pity on us."

So the monster took the great wine skins and drank them dry, and he was terribly pleased at its taste, for he demanded more.

"Give it freely," he thundered, "and tell me your name so that I may also give you a gift." But my master, the Wily One, did not trust the monster; instead he gave him more wine, until he was certain the monster's brain was addled with it, for no five men could drink that quantity and still stand. Then my master spoke. "Cyclops, you ask me my name and I will tell you, but you must then give me the gift you have promised. *Nobody* is my name. My father and my mother call me Nobody, as do all my companions."

So the Wily One spoke, but the monster was pitiless and

said, "My gift, then, is that I shall eat Nobody last, after I have eaten his men. That is my gift to you!" He laughed, and his joy was terrible to behold. And after he said this, the giant lay back and then slumped onto his bedding, asleep.

Then brave Odysseus brought out the great spear from its hiding place, and they heated the tip in the fire until it glowed bright. After speaking words of courage to his men, my master dragged the spear from the fire, and together they lifted it above their shoulders and charged, thrusting it into the monster's eye, where it sizzled with the sound of a crashing wave.

The monster gave a horrible cry and flailed his massive arms, but my master and his men ducked his grasp and hid in the shadows. With a groan the monster tore the timber from his eye, and it bubbled with blood. Then he cried out to the other Cyclopes who lived nearby, and they came running to his cave.

"Why, Polyphemus, do you cry out? Why have you made us sleepless tonight? Surely no mortal can be stealing your flock! Surely none can kill you by force!" they called from outside.

Then, from inside the cave, monstrous Polyphemus answered: "My brothers! Nobody is killing me by force! Nobody!"

"If, as you say, nobody has hurt you, then pray to your father, Lord Poseidon, to make you well!" they jeered at him. Then they left and returned to their caves, paying no more heed to the monster's cries, so the mighty Cyclops rolled aside the great boulder that blocked his door and sat down in the entrance himself, spreading his arms to catch anyone who tried to escape. But my master had thought of this and tied the rams together in groups of three, and his men clung to the belly of the middle sheep, and though the Cyclops felt all around the backs of the rams as they left the cave, he did not catch the men hiding beneath. Then, when his men had all escaped, my master seized the wool under the largest ram, and though the monster groped the ram's back, he felt not underneath, and my master escaped.

Hurriedly they made their way down the rocky trail to the beach where their ship was moored, driving the monster's sheep ahead of them. Once on board, they quickly gathered their oars and began to row. Through the rose-colored dawn, my master could see the monster standing at the entrance to his cave, turning his head from side to side, although blind he was, and bloody.

"Cyclops!" my master yelled. "Your evil deeds catch up to you who dared to eat his guests, so Zeus and the other gods have punished you!"

Angered by these words, the monster tore off the top of a mountain and let it fly, where it landed just in front of my master's boat, and the wave it made washed my master and his men back onto the shore. But my master, using a long pole, pushed the boat back into deeper water, and he urged his men quietly to lean hard on their oars, and they cut through the sea.

One they were past the shore, my master made as if to call out to the monster again, and his men checked him, crying, "Hardheaded one, why do you seek to enrage that monster? He nearly finished us with his last missile and he could break our ship's timbers, so strong is his throwing!"

So they spoke, the teals report, but my master had anger in his heart and cried out, "Cyclops, if any man asks you who it was that inflicted upon your eye that shameful blinding, tell him you were blinded by Odysseus, sacker of cities, son of Laertes, who makes his home in Ithaka!"

Hearing this, the monster groaned and answered him thus:

"Ah, a prophecy of old said that I would lose my sight at the hands of Odysseus, but I was on the lookout for a handsome man, endowed with strength greater than my own; not a little man, feeble and weak, making me helpless with wine. So come back, Odysseus! Let me give you a true gift, and together we shall pray for Poseidon, my father, to heal me and grant you safe travel home."

Then said Odysseus, "I would return only if I were certain I could kill you and send you to Hades, Cyclops, where you belong. Nor do I think Poseidon will heal you; you are blinded for life!"

Hearing this, the great monster knelt and lifted his arms to the heavens, crying out: "Hear me, Father Poseidon, who circles the earth. If truly I am your son, then promise that Odysseus, son of Laertes, who makes his home in Ithaka, may never reach that place. But if he does, let him come late, with his companions dead, on someone else's ship, and find his house in peril!"

And so he cursed my master. Then he tore off another great boulder and hurled it at my master's ship, but it landed just behind, sending the ship far out and onto the island where the rest of brave Odysseus's men were camped, waiting and grieving that their shipmates were dead. That night, after telling the story of the Cyclopes, my master sacrificed the giant ram he had ridden under to honor Zeus. Then, after feasting on the meat and drinking wine, they slept, and when rose-colored dawn came, they boarded their ships and dashed their oars into the gray sea, happy to have escaped death, but grieving still in their hearts for their lost companions.

So the teals told the crow, who told me.

I thank the crow, and he dips a wing and flies away. *If only my master could fly,* I think, *he would surely be home now.* But he does not fly; he sails, sails over the gray sea ruled by Poseidon, whose son he has blinded. O master, believe and perhaps the gods will give you wings!

CHAPTER VII

I keep a promise

I have heard nothing from the birds about my master for many days. Each afternoon the gulls fly over my head, screaming, "Argos! No news! No news!" before circling back to the sea. Now the evening has come when I see Luna, the full moon, rising over the ridge, and I must return to the shore to fulfill my promise. I wait for hours before I notice the sand move. Then I see a tiny flipper. Soon the sand all around me crumbles and shifts as flippers and soft beaks emerge. And then I see the birds. Only the glow from Luna reveals their white wings as they hover silently above me. Waiting. There are more than I can count.

The first turtle begins its clumsy procession toward the sea. How slowly it crawls! No wonder so few survive! Above me I hear a gull croak, and then I see a flash of silver and white as it dives toward the turtle.

But I arrive first! I snatch the turtle in my jaws just as the gulls' feet close on empty air, and I carry it into the crashing waves. I release the turtle there in chest-deep water and run back for the next one. By then, dozens of angry gulls are swooping and diving at me, pecking my head and neck, beating my face with their wings. But I am Argos the Boar Slayer, keeper of promises, and gulls do not frighten me. I find I can scoop two turtles in my mouth—along with wet, throat-gagging sand—at one time and carry them to safety.

Back and forth I run, from the beach to the sea. I save many turtles and lose but a few. Finally the last turtle emerges, and I carry it to find its sisters in the waves. Then I collapse on the sand. The beach is littered with eggs and feathers and black fur. My fur. As I lie there catching my breath, a circle of gulls forms around me, angrily squawking that I have stolen their food and betrayed our friendship.

"Why should we fly far out to sea to look for your master when you have done this?" one gull demands, snapping its orange beak. "You are a thief and nothing more. You are worse even than a harbor cat!"

"Yes!" they all cry together. "What has Argos done for us, we who search far and wide for his master? Thief! Thief! Thief!"

What have I done? Without the gulls to look for my master, how will I learn his fate? At that moment, though, Athena herself guides my tongue.

"Brother Gulls," I say. "It is true that I stole this meal from you, but I had a promise to fulfill. And think of this," I continue. "How many turtles return to this shore to lay their eggs? One or two? That is because you are such great hunters that few of them survive to lay their own eggs. Now, a hundred turtles or more will return to lay their eggs on Ithaka. Think how many more meals you will have when that happens. No longer will your flock fight over a few turtle hatchlings. There will be thousands to choose from. How your children will feast!"

The gulls say nothing. A few tuck their heads in their wings. A few more scratch the sand. Finally one speaks. "Aye aye aye! What the Boar Slayer says is true. We have hunted too well. Many of my brothers have never tasted the sweet flesh of a sea turtle hatchling. In the years to come, we will eat well because of this."

"Argos," another says. "Forgive our sharp beaks and claws. You have done well for us."

"Aye!" they shriek. "Aye! Aye!"

"Then you will still search for my master?" I ask.

"I leave tomorrow, Boar Slayer, following a fishing boat to the east," another gull, larger than most, says. "And I will not return without news of Odysseus."

"News! News! News!"

"I thank you, brothers. Now I must go to my home. Rosy dawn comes soon, and I must rest before I tend to the sheep."

And then I make my way back to the sheep barn, climbing the trail that winds up from the shore. Along the way I stop and look back over the sea. How strange it is, I think, that men build ships to sail over that dark and treacherous water. Why do they not stay home?

CHAPTER VIII

୧ଡ଼୧ଡ଼୧ଡ଼୧ଡ଼୧ଡ଼୧ଡ଼୧ଡ଼୧ଡ଼୧ଡ଼୧ଡ଼

My master returns

The cook fires had already been lit when I hear it: the bell from the harbor signaling the arrival of a ship. Boats of all kinds arrive almost weekly at the harbor, but the bell is rung only for ships bearing Ithakans. I sit and listen, my ears erect. From the harbor, carried by the western wind, I hear cries of "Ship! Ship!" And then the word I long most to hear: "Odysseus!"

My master has returned! I run to the courtyard and begin to bark. After a few moments Telemachos comes out, and he hears the cries too. Soon the servants appear from all over the estate, many of them crying or embracing one another as news of their master's imminent arrival spreads. A few of the suitors are already seated in the hall, and they too come out into the courtyard. What strange faces they make! They know they have to show joy at my master's return, yet this means that they can never marry Queen Penelope and inherit my master's land.

Finally my mistress Penelope herself descends the stairs and enters the courtyard. I have never seen her so beautiful, as she is wrapped in a silver tunic that reflects Apollo's setting chariot, and her lustrous hair hangs down in dark waves.

She takes Telemachos's hand and asks, "Is it true what the servants say? Has my husband and your father returned?"

Telemachos kisses her hand. "His black ship and others were seen by the harbormaster, my long-suffering mother. Noble Odysseus has indeed returned."

"Zeus be praised. Take Argos and trusted Eumaios and run to the harbor, my son. It would not be right that his family was not there to greet him."

"But my father will not know me, Mother. I was an infant when he left," Telemachos cries, sounding worried.

"He will know you, brave Telemachos. Every father knows his son. Hurry now! I must prepare the house for his arrival."

They embrace one more time, and then she calls the servants to her. Telemachos takes the shepherd Eumaios by the arm, and the three of us run down to the trail that leads to the harbor. Just before we begin our descent, we stop at a lookout point. There it is! My master's swift black ship, fully rigged, sails ever closer. Alongside it sail two more of his fleet. The ships are too far away for us to see men on the deck, but my master has the finest sailors from Ithaka on board, so we know they will have no trouble navigating the rocky harbor.

How swiftly we run down to the shore! Even Eumaios has wings on his feet. The trail we run along is bordered by low scrubs and trees, so we seldom have a clear view of the sea, but Telemachos stops once and peers through the branches of a pine, exclaiming, "It draws closer! My father comes closer!"

I look too. The ship is now near enough to see men on the deck, but I don't see my master. *He must be shining his armor,* I think. *The sacker of cities will not return looking like a worn-out sailor.*

Above us, a flock of gulls careens through the sky, flying east and west, and swooping down to the shore before climbing high above us again. *How strangely they fly!* I think. Then I realize that they fly strangely because the wind is shifting. But I think no more of it, because we finally reach the harbor.

Throngs of fishermen and sailors stand on the beach, watching my master's ship and companion boats come ever closer. They cheer and wave their arms, and flap tunics as flags. Children run along the jetty, screaming, "Odysseus! Odysseus! The king of Ithaka has returned!"

Then, just as the crowd's noise has reached its peak, there is silence. The children's words are lost; the shifting wind carries their sounds away. A tunic is torn from a fisherman's hands and is blown out over the sea. I look up. Above me, the gulls, which had been flying so strangely, are now fighting to stay aloft as the wind rips through their flock. Suddenly I hear a terrible whooshing sound and feel the sting of sharp pebbles scouring me. Sand chokes my nose. Telemachos shouts something, but even my ears cannot hear it. I look out toward the breakers and see that the wind is driving the waves back away from the shore. All around me, men lean into the wind, fighting to stay upright.

"No!" I hear Telemachos cry. "Father! Father!"

Through half-closed, sand-filled eyes, I see what made Telemachos cry. My master's ship, along with its small fleet, is being blown back to sea. I can see the flash of twenty oars, but the wind is too strong even for the finest rowers. There is no resisting it. Soon we see nothing but the wind-tossed sea.

I have seen storms lash Ithaka before with strong wind and rain, but this is not a storm. No clouds fill the sky, nor is there a drop of rain. There is only the terrible wind, unlike I have ever felt, and only the gods could have sent it.

"Father! Come back!" I hear Telemachos cry again, and suddenly he is running toward the sea.

"Telemachos, stop!" Eumaios screams.

I run after the boy. Just before he reaches the water, I leap on his back and he topples to the sand.

"No, Argos," he yells, pushing me off him and rising to his feet. Again he tries to dive into the sea, but I take his tunic in my mouth and pull him back.

"Argos," he cries. "Let me go! Let me go!"

By then Eumaios reaches us. He takes Telemachos's arm and leads the sobbing youth away. We find shelter from the wind by huddling next to the jetty, as do the gulls. After a few minutes, even the sharpest-eyed men on the beach lose sight of my master's ships, and they gather around us, trying to console Telemachos.

"The wind will die down soon enough, boy, and when it does, the Wily One will sail once again into the harbor," one old fisherman says gently.

"It's been more than twelve years, lad," another adds. "What's one more day?"

Telemachos says nothing; he just strokes my back while the darkness comes in around us. After an hour or more passes, Eumaios whispers, "Come, Telemachos. We must return home and tell your mother what happened. She will be worried about you. In the morning the winds will calm, as they always do, and we will see your father. I am sure of it."

We rise and make the long trek up to my master's estate. The wind continues to blow mercilessly around us, and at times we have to hold on to the trees along the trail to keep from being blown back. When we reach the courtyard, my mistress wraps Telemachos in her arms and weeps bitter tears. This time it is he who speaks words of consolation.

"Tomorrow, Mother," I hear him say. "He will return tomorrow, I know he will."

They go inside to escape the wind, but I have work to do. I spend the first part of the night calming sheep, and later, when a tree blows over and knocks down part of their pen, I keep the goats from escaping. Every time I think the wind might finally be subsiding, I hear a howl and the winds pick back up, blowing harder than ever.

Apollo's chariot passes nine times before the wind stops.

CHAPTER IX

⌒⌒⌒⌒⌒⌒⌒⌒⌒⌒⌒⌒⌒⌒⌒⌒⌒⌒⌒

An ill wind

On the morning of the tenth day, the wind subsides and I run down to the harbor to speak to the gulls. *Surely they will know what happened to my master's ship,* I think. I find the flock standing in a circle around a fallen bird. As I draw closer, I can see it's a small plover, a shorebird, and it is resting on the sand. Its pinfeathers are battered and one leg lies stretched out behind its body, broken and useless. The wind has nearly killed it.

A gull leaves its flock and flies up to me.

"What news do you have, Sir Gull? Did your family and flock survive the winds?"

"Aye, aye, aye, most of us, Boar Slayer. Others, caught in the storm, are just returning. And that one has a tale to tell," he says, pointing his beak at the plover.

"A tale about what?" I ask, feeling dread wash over me.

"Your master."

"Can she talk?"

"Yes, but her leg is broken, and she may not live long. Hurry."

I run up to the flock of gulls, and they part so that I can stand near the fallen plover. Up close, I can see the pink flesh beneath her damaged feathers. She opens her black-lidded eyes and regards me with a fixed stare.

"Sister Plover, I am Argos, loyal dog to Odysseus, sacker of cities. May the gods look down on you with benevolence."

"I know who you are," the bird says weakly. "And the gods are not benevolent."

"You know my master as well? And know you his fate?" I ask, ignoring her heresy.

"Yes. I was hatched on Ithaka, Boar Slayer, and know your master's entire family. Now, come closer so that I may talk more ea-ea-easily. I will tell you what you wish to he-he-hear."

I lie down beside the wounded plover, for her voice is weak.

"I normally stay close to the shore," she says, "but when I saw your master's ship coming ne-ne-near to the harbor I flew out to see-ee-ee if they had fish in their nets. I landed on the stern and saw your master slee-ee-eeping on the deck. I think a god or goddess must have closed his eyes, for he-he-he was the only man aslee-ee-eep. I wondered why this should be-be-be, so I listened closely to the other sailors, and I was able to piece-piece-piece this story together from them. It seems that for the last month, your master has been on the island where Aiolos rules, along with his six sons and six daughters. There your master and his men stayed in fine houses, fea-fea-feasting on fragrant food and watching glorious dances and musicians. At night the city sacker would tell stories of the war with the Trojans, and honor and glory were heap-heap-heaped upon your master and his men. Finally, rested and restored, your master asked for conveyance back here to Ithaka, and Aiolos gave him a bag made of ox skin."

"What was in the bag, dear plover?" I ask. "Coins? Spices?"

The plover shakes its small head. "Patience, Argos. I will tell the tale in full as long as I have breath. May I continue?"

"Pardon me, friend. Please do."

"For nine days and nights, your master's swift boat and his companion ships caught a steady western wind and sailed ever closer to Ithaka. Not once did his steersman even use the rudder, so straight they sailed. Then, on the tenth day, as you know, they rea-rea-reached the waters off our fair island and were see-see-seen by the harbormasters. That was when I flew to their ship. As I said, I found your master slee-ee-eeping on the deck. Then I saw one of the sailors carefully lift the ox-skin bag out of the ship's hold. A few other men gathered around while one kept an eye on your master in case he woke.

"'There must be gold or silver in this bag that Aeolus gave to the Wily One,' the man said. 'Why else would Odysseus guard it so closely?'

"Another man put his hand on the bag. 'Wait!' he whispered. 'Surely if it is gold or other riches, then brave Odysseus will share it with us, friends. Let us not betray him this way!'

"But that man was pushed aside.

"'Open it quickly,' another sailor said. 'Odysseus stirs!'

"And so they opened the bag. Oh, terrible day, the day of my death! I was perched right there when he untied it, relea-ea-easing all the winds of the earth. Such a force I have never see-ee-een, for who can see-ee-ee the wind, yet it wears down mountains, does it not? I was blown against the mast and pinned there, broken legged, as the ship's sail twisted round and filled with wind. How hard your master's men rowed, Argos! Odysseus himself lashed them all to their oarlocks before tying himself to the mast beside me so that no one would be blown off the ship. For nine days the wind blew us ea-ea-east. We ate nothing and drank only blessed rain that

65

fell into our open mouths, for to untie oneself to search for food meant death. How your master grie-ie-ieved, Boar Slayer! He cried out for Penelope and for his homeland, but his cries were drowned by the gale."

"Finally we landed back on the Aiolian island, and the winds died. We harbored there, and Odysseus untied his wretched men. He even picked me up and urged me to fly, but I was too wea-wea-weak. So he carried me with him as he and a few of his men climbed the steps from the harbor that led to King Aiolos's house."

"Aiolos himself rushed out to gree-ee-eet us. 'Why did you return, Odysseus?' he asked. 'The winds should have carried you straight to your homeland!'

"Then, Argos, your master fell to his knees and wept. Finally he said these piteous words: 'Alas, King Aiolos, while the gods induced my sleep, my greedy companions opened the bag of winds that you had warned me about. Now that we have returned, I beg you to capture the winds again and let us return once more to our dear homeland, for surely that is in your power!'

"But King Aiolos showed him no mercy. 'Most pathetic of living creatures, hated most by the gods, I have no right to thwart them and give you more wind,' he sneered. 'Truly they think you must be punished, and let it be so. Leave this island at once and never return!'

"So rising to his fee-fee-feet, the brave one took his companions back to the ship. Grie-ie-ieving still, your master and his men rowed and sailed for six days. Every night your master fed me with his own hands, Boar Slayer, and kept me alive. But that is all I shall tell today, for I grow wea-wea-weak. If tomorrow I still live, I will tell you the rest if I can, for truly it is a terrible tale that I have to say."

Saying this, the plover closes her eyes and tucks her head into her wing.

"We will stay with her throughout the night, Boar Slayer, and guard her from the harbor cats," a gull says to me. "Return in the morning if you can."

"Return! Return! Return!" his flock repeats.

I thank them and make my way back up to my master's estate. Inside the house I hear the wailing of servants, and I hear my mistress crying out to Zeus. I find Telemachos lying on his bed sobbing, and I lie down beside him and lick his face.

What else could I do?

CHAPTER X

⌒⌒⌒⌒⌒⌒⌒⌒⌒⌒⌒⌒⌒⌒⌒⌒⌒

Bleak morn

In the morning I run down to the harbor just as dawn's rosy fingers stroke the sky. The beach is empty. I run along the golden sand, searching for bird tracks. Instead I find gull feathers and the scent of a cat. Just then a shadow passes over me, and I look up. A gull swoops down and calls my name. I follow it and find a flock of his brothers standing under a small boat that rests on its side against the jetty. Around the flock I count three dead gulls.

"Brother Gulls, tell me who did this so that I can avenge you!" I cry. "Was it the orange harbor cat? I smelled his scent on the beach."

"Aye aye, aye, Boar Slayer," the largest of the gulls says. "That is the one. He came at us stealthily just an hour ago when the night was darkest. Most of us were able to escape his claws, but these three did not. They died defending the plover."

"Bleak is this morn! Bleak! Bleak!" the remaining gulls screech.

"I am sorry for your flock's loss," I say, lowering my head. "But the plover? She still lives?" I ask. My heart races as I wait for his reply.

"Aye-aye-aye, she does. Though how much longer I cannot say. Come, draw closer. She has been calling for you."

The gulls part and let me come close. The plover looks even weaker than before. Her eyes are hooded and dull, and her broken leg has turned black.

"Boar Slayer, is that you?" she asks.

"It is I, bravest of birds. I have come to hear the rest of the tale, if you are strong enough to tell it."

"I am, loyal one, for it is a short tale, though it is full of death. Let me-e-e tell it straight away. Your master and his men, after sailing for six days, arrived at the glorious harbor of Telepylos, home of the fea-ea-earsome Laestrygonians. There your master tied up his ship and ordered the others to as well. Then he sent two men and a herald to see-ee-ee who was king of the island and what manner of men lived there and if they eat bread. For several hours we saw nothing, no trace of men or cattle, and I heard your master wonder out loud who it was that had built this fine harbor nestled benea-ea-eath such high cliffs. Then, suddenly, we heard a shout, and two of the men your master had sent off to find the island king were running as fast as they could toward our ship!"

"'Where is the herald?' Odysseus asked, once they had boarded. 'Why do you run? Are we being attacked?'

"But the men could not spea-ea-eak, so terrible was their fe-fe-fear. Finally one cried, 'We must flee, brave Odysseus! Their king, Antiphates, is a giant and he has already eaten your herald. This land is cursed!'

"Just then we heard a deafening war cry, and thousands of giants appea-ea-eared from behind their houses, where they had been lying in wait! They fanned out along the cliffs and threw huge boulders down at us, smashing our ships before your master's men could untie them. Others threw long javelins, skewering your master's men like fish. Truly, I have never see-ee-een such doom."

The plover closes her eyes. For a long time she says nothing, and I fear that she is too weak to continue.

"But what of my master, fair plover? Tell me he lived!" I beg.

The plover slowly nods her head. "Your master took his sharp sword and cut the rope tying his ship to the harbor. Then he ordered his men to go below and lea-ea-ean their weight on the oars. Many of them were afraid to take their chances below the deck, and they dove into the sea-ea-ea hoping to escape; still, what hope did they have? The Laestrygonians hurled stones at them or speared them as they swam. But the men who went below on your master's ship lived. How they made the waves fly benea-ea-eath them! But theirs was the only ship that escaped, Boar Slayer. All the others were lost. Oh, terrible day!"

"All but one was lost?" I cry. "Tell me that isn't so!"

"Alas, Boar Slayer, that is true. I saw their destruction with my own eyes. But let me-e-e finish. Your master and his men sailed for another day, glad to have escaped death, yet grie-ie-ieving that they had lost so many companions. The next morning your master took me in his hands and said these words: 'Bird of my homeland, we are lost and know not how to return to Ithaka, but your fate is not ours. Fly now home to our island, so that I can say that at least one Ithakan returned from this dreadful journey.' Then he tied a small stick to my broken leg as a splint and tossed me into the open air. I don't know how many days I flew, but the gods smiled on me-e-e and brought here so that I may die on my homeland."

Around us the seagulls squawked at this sad tale.

"You may not die, yet, brave plover," I say. "My master's servant is skillful with all manner of animals and birds. I will take you to him, and we will see what he can do for you. But first, when you were high in the sky, did you see which way my master sailed? Was there land close by?"

"Yes, Boar Slayer. I looked back as I flew and saw they were sailing toward a fog-shrouded island. A tern from the island came up to me-e-e then, and I asked the island's name. He said it was Aiaia, the land of Circe, of the lovely hair. Then he flew off to find his supper, and I did not look back again."

I turn to the gulls who had protected the plover. "I thank you for your sacrifice," I tell them solemnly. "I will find a way to avenge your loss. Farewell."

"See that you do," the largest gull snaps.

"Avenge! Avenge! Avenge!" his flock echoes.

Then I gently take the plover in my mouth and carry the small bird back up to my master's estate. There I find Eumaios in the barn and lay the plover down beside him.

"What have you got there, Argos?" he asks. He lifts the plover and carefully examines its broken leg. After inspecting her, he shakes his head.

"There is only one way to save your friend before infection kills her," Eumaios says. Then he lays the plover down on a table and takes out his sharpest knife. With a quick stroke, he cuts the broken limb close to her thigh. The plover makes not a sound but lies there with her eyes closed as Eumaios bandages her stump. Then he makes a nest with a child's tunic and some straw, and places her there, along with a shallow bowl of water.

"If she is alive by nightfall, then she will live many more days," Eumaios says to me, stroking my head.

All through the day I do my work, herding the sheep and goats, and when I can, I race back to check on the plover. On my third visit she is sitting upright and the bowl of water is half empty.

"I shall live, Argos, I think. My strength returns and I can stand on one leg. See-see-see?"

She rises on one leg and stands there proudly.

"I am glad for you, Sister Plover. Wait a little longer, and then, when you are ready, fly back to your home by the shore. I must say good-bye now, because I have another task I have to complete."

I leave the barn and take the trail down to the harbor. Just as I pass the last tree that flanks the trail, a crow lands in front of me.

"Greetings, Boar Slayer," he says.

"Greetings, Sir Crow. Do you have news for me?"

"Only this," he says. "You seek the orange har-har-harbor cat, do you not?"

"I do. Do you know his whereabouts?"

"Alas, the cat knew you were coming for him, and just this afternoon he stole aboard a fishing boat leaving the har-har-harbor. He will not return for some time, I think."

In my mind I see the gulls he had killed, lying near the plover they had promised to protect. The fur along my back rises.

"You will let me know when he returns, will you not, Sir Crow?"

"Aye, Ar-Ar-Argos, that I will, for I love him not either. But it may be many days or even months before he comes back."

"What are days and months to me?" I say. "It is my destiny to wait on this island for my master's return. And I will wait for the harbor cat too."

The crow spreads his wings and hovers above me for a moment.

"Sir Crow?" I call, before he can fly away. "Do you know of the island Aiaia, where the goddess Circe lives?"

"I do" he says, rising higher. "Is that where your master is?"

"Yes, that is what I was told. That he sailed into its shrouded harbor a week ago."

"If that is true, Ar-Ar-Argos, then your days of long waiting are over."

I inhale sharply. *My days of waiting are over?* The crow circles around me until I grow dizzy.

"Why do you say that, most intelligent of birds? Is the island close by? Are the winds from there favorable enough?"

Finally, after flying another circle, he says this: "You cannot wait for that which never comes, Ar-Ar-Argos. No man returns from Aiaia. Dreaded Circe has your master now. Wait instead for the cat. He, at least, will return alive."

Then the black-winged bird flies away, leaving me to my misery.

CHAPTER XI

~~~~~~~~~~~~~~~~~~~~~~~~~~~~~~~

Titus is poisoned

One of my friends is dying. Titus, loyal pet of Eurylochos, who sails with my master, was poisoned last night, and lies panting beside me. Titus, who was whelped by Acacia and has hunted alongside me for hares, ate poisoned meat set out by one of mistress Penelope's suitors—meat that was intended for me. Of that I am certain, for it is I who guards my mistress's chamber when the suitors, pretending to be drunk, try to climb the stairs leading to her room. It is I who snarls and bites when a servant is mistreated. It is I who believes that brave Odysseus still lives.

This morning I heard Titus vomiting and ran to his den beside the goat shed. I found him pawing the earth, then turning in mad circles like one of Telemachos's spinning toys or a pup chasing his tail. Titus, son of Balthasar, does not chase his tail like a pup. He is an old dog, but the poison was entering his brain.

"Where did you eat last night, Titus?" I asked.

Titus would not look at me. He turned his back, ashamed. His black fur was dirty and matted with mud and burrs. He had no one to pull them from his flanks.

Finally he said, "One of your mistress's suitors put meat out by the kitchen hearth where you lie at night. Forgive me, Argos, but I was hungry. Since my master left, we have little food, and I grow too old and slow to hunt on my own."

"I would catch rabbits for you," I might have said, but Titus is proud and this would have stung him as badly as the poison. Instead I said, "You must drink, brother. Drink and eat grass. Come, I will take you to water."

He willed himself to stop spinning and said, "It is too late, Argos. They have killed me."

Still I led him to the stream beyond our western field and made him drink until his belly was round like a melon. I brought him grass and sweet herbs, but soon he could no longer swallow.

Now above us vultures begin to circle, calling their bird kin, and then perching in the pines, waiting.

"Stay with me, Argos," Titus begs through foaming lips. "Don't let the vultures have me."

"I go nowhere," I say. "Now, lie down, and perhaps the gods will smile on you today."

He lies beside me then, curling into himself, his pink tongue lolling out of his mouth.

"Does it grow dark, Argos?" he asks after some time.

"Yes, brother," I say. "But it is only the sun behind a cloud."

"Do the vultures come close?"

"No, Titus." I lie. "They know you have many days ahead."

"Do I smell a mountain wolf?"

"No, there is a den of foxes nearby, but they are harmless."

In truth, I can smell a lone, old mountain wolf, lying in the wood, waiting for me to leave. A mountain wolf will not eat the dead, but they will attack a sick animal.

Titus opens his eyes for a moment. They are glassy, and the spark of life is dim in them.

"Brother? Did you see the man who poisoned you?" I ask.

I don't think he hears me, but after some time, he says, "The one with the red beard and the limp. He put the meat in your bowl."

I know the knave. I have heard some men say he crushed his own foot to avoid the war with the Trojans. Being lame, he is most desperate to win Penelope's heart and often stays late to catch her alone.

Titus is panting mightily, the way we do after a long and good hunt.

"It grows cold, Argos, does it not?"

"Yes, Titus, there is a cold wind blowing," I say, though it is a hot summer afternoon.

I lie down next to him. The vultures leave their perches, spinning gyres above us, but they know not to come close. After some time Titus speaks.

"My master will come for me soon, Argos."

"Yes, very soon."

"We will hunt again."

"Yes, even the mighty boar will run from you."

But at that moment I feel Titus's body relax, and his panting stops. He is dead. After a few minutes I rise and trot over to the old mountain wolf, who has wasted a day waiting to attack my friend and is now feeling hunger. He is alone, and thus dares not attack me, for I am the larger.

"Cousin," I say. "Do not waste your efforts on my friend. I know where you can find fresh meat to ease your stomach's pains. Keep watch for me tonight, and I will bring you the prize."

The wolf looks at me with doubt in his yellow eyes but backs away into the wood. It's time to get rid of the vultures too. I return to where my friend lies, but as I do, I pretend to stagger. My tail droops and I hang my head low. I curl up beside my friend and wait. The vultures grow bold. They screech to one another and then, one by one, land on the small hill above the stream and teeter toward us. I close my eyes as if I too have been poisoned, and when they come so close their smelly beaks nearly make me gag, I leap to my feet and hurl myself among them, biting and clawing. I kill three before they can fly off, and rip the wings off many more.

"Feed not on this carcass," I bark at them, "or you will feel my teeth, most despised of birds!"

Hearing this, the vultures fly away, screeching their anger, but I care not. I return to Titus and sit beside him as the long evening shadows fall. Finally I hear Telemachos calling me. I bark, and after a few moments he comes running down the hill. He sees the dead vultures and then the body of my friend, and he knows I will not leave Titus unattended.

So my master's son picks up Titus and carries him to the edge of our vineyard, and he with his spear, and I with my claws, dig a grave for the body. Afterward Telemachos covers it with large stones so scavengers cannot dig it up. Then, together, we walk back to my master's house in the gathering darkness.

The suitors are leaving; my mistress Penelope has thrown them out, as she does every night, weary as she is of their promises and lies. The last to leave is the lame red-haired man. He looks about furtively, then lingers at the door, hoping for a final word with my mistress. This was a mistake, for now he has no one to protect him.

"Good widow," the man says, "we have tarried too long and now the road is dark. Perhaps there is room for me in your house tonight?"

My mistress shakes her head at his request.

"The moon is full. It will light your path," she says. "And I am not a widow."

Then, before he can utter another plea, Telemachos closes the door firmly.

And now I am alone with him. The man curses and starts back along the road. He is armed only with a long spear, which he uses as a crutch as well as a weapon. I trot toward him, and he points it at me while uttering another loud curse. I back away and then, pretending to ignore him, wander off toward the sheep stall where I sometimes sleep. From there I can track him as he limps along the path leading down the hill and through the valley toward his own miserable hut. After giving him a head start, I take a shortcut and pass him. Then I double back to wait.

At one point along the path, the trail narrows and there is a sharp turn overgrown with wild olive trees with low branches that block the sun—or the full moon. I wait for him there. And I smell my cousin. He lies hiding behind the boulders that have tumbled down from the mountains above us.

I can hear the man before I see him. He is singing loudly, as if to give himself courage to walk alone at night. He rounds the turn with his spear pointing straight ahead in case an attacker is poised to strike, as they often do at this spot. But still I wait in the shadows. Then, when he raises his spear again to use it as a staff, I jump from the shadows and clamp my jaws around it, wresting it from his grasp.

"You!" he screams, kicking at me with his lame foot. But I am quick and feel not the blow. With his spear in my mouth, I run down the path and then turn into the thick wood where he cannot follow.

"Cousin!" I call. "He is yours!"

Then I leave the man to his fate and the mountain wolf.

And thus do I avenge Titus.

CHAPTER XII

~~~~~~~~~~~~~~~~~~~~~~~~~

My master meets fair Circe

As I stand watch over a herd of sheep, a mountain sparrow, gray chested and with a black crown, alights on the sheep paddock and calls to me.

"Be you Argos, the Boar Slayer?" he asks me.

"I am he, little one. But please, draw closer. Your voice is small, and my ears are not as sharp as they once were."

Hearing this, the sparrow hops down from the paddock and perches on a fence rail, but he says nothing.

Perhaps he is resting, I think. Truly, though, I had never seen a sparrow remain so still, for it is their manner to remain in motion, alighting here and there, never stopping for more than a moment. Nor is a sparrow easy to converse with, for they seem to forget what was said a moment before.

"Gentle sparrow, you have found me, the Boar Slayer. Why did you seek me out?"

Hearing my voice, the sparrow lifts his tiny head, as if trying to recall his purpose.

"Why am I here? Why? Oh, yes, I remember. I was sent to find you."

"Sent by whom, agile one? Who sent you? Did my master, Odysseus, send you?" I allow myself to think this for a precious moment.

"No, it wasn't your master, Aptos—I mean . . . Argos. Your name is Argos, is it not?"

"It is. But who sent you then, little one? Try to remember."

I wait patiently while he thinks.

"Hermes," he says finally. "Yes, that's who it was. Swift Hermes asked me to send this message to you."

Hermes, son of Zeus, has a message for me? Truly, the gods are good. "What message, little flyer? What did the god say?"

The mountain sparrow hopped to another rail.

"I don't remember."

"Try, Insect Catcher. You must remember. You must or you will anger a god."

The sparrow hops to another rail and turns his head, as if in deep thought. Suddenly, although it is a cloudy day, I notice a ray of sunlight shining on his head, bathing him in gold.

"Oh, yes," he says. "I remember now."

I knew then that the golden light was Hermes himself. Hermes, who moves easily between the realms of the gods and those of men, was speaking through the sparrow. And so I sit next to him to hear his story.

The sparrow was from Aiaia, where lives the beautiful Circe of the golden tresses, who talks to mortals though she is the daughter of Helios, who lights the day, and her mother is Perse, who is the daughter of Ocean. The mountain sparrow had seen my master and his men arrive there, on her island, despondent and full of woe.

For two days my master and his men mourned their fellow sailors who had been lost to the Laestrygonians, but at dawn on the third day, my master took up his spear and his sword and set out to explore the island, to learn of its inhabitants, and to seek the way home to Ithaka. High on a cliff he saw smoke from the halls of a great building, and so he turned back, hurrying to his men to give them hope. Along the way, the gods took pity on my master and sent a great stag with towering antlers on his path, and my master slew the beast and carried it down to the ship.

"Dear friends," he announced, "sorry as we are, we are not

yet doomed to Hades until our day is appointed. Come, let us feast on this stag that the gods have provided for us, for we are worn out by hunger." And together they made a great fire and ate late into the night beside their ship. When the rosy dawn came again, my master roused his men and said, "Dear friends, now that we have eaten and slept, I tell you I do not know what course to take. When I climbed the highest point on the island, I saw nothing but the vast sea all in a circle around us."

Hearing this, his men groaned and pulled their hair with this sad news, but then my master said, "Wait, there is more. In the center of this island I saw smoke rising from a hall. Perhaps the inhabitants can tell us what direction to aim our prow."

"What if it's another Cyclops?" asked one man, and they all cried out in fear at that memory.

"We can never know until we find out for ourselves," my master replied. "Come, we will draw lots and divide ourselves. Half will explore the source of the smoke and half will remain here."

And when they had done that, and they were divided in half, brave Eurylochos was chosen to lead his group of two and twenty men to the center of the island, and the mountain sparrow followed them. When the men reached the great hall, they heard the spinning of a giant loom and the enchanting voice of the golden-locked Circe. Then Polites, one of the leaders of the men, said, "Friends, someone is singing sweetly inside, and I think there is no monster within. Come, let us call on her and see if she is a goddess or a mortal."

And when they called out to her, Circe opened the doors, revealing herself to them, and invited them into her hall. But Eurylochos, suspecting treachery, waited outside.

Once inside, Circe seated the men on chairs and benches and gave them a potion of wine and drugs, along with pale honey and barley and cheese. Such was the power of the drugs that the men forgot their own country and stared only in wonder at her while she drew forth a wand and touched them each on the shoulder, turning them into pigs. Then she herded them into pens and set them about eating acorns and small ears of corn, but they cried, too, for though they were pigs, their minds remained as before.

This did Eurylochos see with amazement, and then he stealthily crept back along the trail toward the black ship, to tell my master what had happened to his companions. But when he arrived, so great was his grief and despair that he could not speak, but only cry out in lamentations for many hours. Finally he managed to tell his tale, but my master did not console him. Instead Odysseus slung his great bow across his shoulder and sheathed his great sword.

"Guide me back there," he commanded, but stout Eurylochos fell to his knees and begged him not to go.

"Great Odysseus, do not take me there against my will," he pleaded. "Leave me here, for I know you will not return nor bring back our companions. Rather let us make haste with those who are left so that we may avoid the day of evil."

"Then stay, Eurylochos, if you will not guide me. For I am compelled to find my men and return with them."

And Odysseus left then for the glen, climbing high over a mountain to reach the valley where he hoped he would find his companions. Along the way he met a young man carrying a golden staff. This was Hermes himself, who had taken the form of the young man, and he took my master by the hand and asked, "Where are you going, grieving one, alone through these hills? Do you know your men have been captured by Circe and turned into the shape of pigs? Do you come meaning to set them free?"

"I do come for my men, though I knew not they were captured by Circe, golden youth," answered my master. "Nor did I know she had changed them to swine."

How like my master to never reveal everything he knows!

Then Hermes said, "You cannot get them out yourself. But come, I will help you with your troubles. Here, take this medicinal flower before you go into Circe's house. She will try to enchant you and put drugs in your food and wine, but this will protect you from her evil charms."

"Then I will take the medicine and pray to the gods that it is strong."

"There is more," the fair-haired youth said. "Once you have eaten her food and drunk her wine, Circe will strike you with her long wand. When she does, draw your sword as if to kill her. She will be afraid and invite you into her chamber. Do not refuse the bed of a goddess, but make her first swear an oath, that she will release your companions from their misery and that she has devised no evil hurt for you."

My master thanked Hermes, and after eating the black-rooted flower, which would protect him, he hurried on toward Circe's home in the glen. Once he reached her house, my master shouted for the goddess, and she opened the shining door and invited him in. There she bade him sit on a finely wrought chair and drink a cup of her poisoned wine. Then, when he had drained the cup, she struck my master with her magic wand and commanded, "Go to your sty now and lie with your friends there!"

So she spoke, but my master, drawing his sharp sword, rushed toward her as if to kill her. The goddess screamed aloud and ducked under the sword, falling to her knees and crying out for mercy.

"What manner of man are you, and where did you come from?" she demanded. "Who are your parents? No other man beside you could have withstood my drugs once he drank them."

"Release my men," my master demanded, "and I will tell you my name."

The goddess shook her head. "You must be Odysseus, of the black ship," Circe said. "I was warned that you would come my way, and now you have."

"I *am* Odysseus, son of Laertes, on my return from Troy," my master said, and demanded again that his men be released.

"I will release them," the goddess said. "But first let us retire to my chamber so that we have faith and trust each other."

So she spoke, the mountain sparrow said, but my master trusted her not.

"Swear a strong oath," he demanded, "that you will release my men from your magic and that you will not seek to unman me, nor devise evil against me."

And the goddess swore a great oath and led him into her room, where her servants bathed my master, washing away the weariness of his journey, and then anointed him in oil. When he had bathed and dressed in a fine tunic, the servants brought food to my master, but he touched it not.

"Brave Odysseus," Circe said. "Why do you touch not food or drink, but look like a man eating his own heart? Do you suspect me of treachery? Did I not swear an oath to you?"

So she spoke, and my master replied, "O fair Circe, how can a man eat when his companions are not free?"

Then Circe walked out through the palace, holding her wand in her hand, and entered the sty where my master's companions were kept, and touched them all with her wand. Soon where there had been bristles and curly tails stood tall the fine men of my master's black ship, and they ran to my master and clung to his hand, begging him to take them back to where their ship lay in harbor.

But Circe spoke and persuaded my master otherwise. She told him to return to the ship and drag it onto land, stow their possessions, and then return with the entire crew.

And so my master left the citadel in the glen and returned to his fast black ship where his crew wept tears in lamentation, thinking their companions dead.

"Weep no more," he said to them. "Your companions eat and drink their fill in Circe's hall while we tarry. Drag the ship up onto the beach and stow your goods. Circe has bid us all to her citadel."

The men did as my master ordered, except for Eurylochos, who addressed the men thus: "Poor wretches! Where are you going? Why do you seek evil in Circe's palace? She will turn us all into swine or wolves or lions so that we can guard her great house."

My master, upon hearing this, nearly drew his sword, but instead his men obeyed him and not Eurylochos. When they had finished their tasks, they left Eurylochos alone by the hollow ship, but he soon followed after.

When they reached Circe's hall, she bathed them all with loving care, anointed them with oil and put about them mantles of fleece and tunics. Then when they entered the room where the rest of their companions were feasting, they burst into tears, so happy were they to be together again. But Circe said, "Cry not, for I know of your suffering on the sea and the damage done to you on land. Eat your food and drink your wine until the spirit returns to your chests."

"Fair Circe will nourish them, will she not?" I ask the mountain sparrow when he says this.

"Aye, Boar Slayer. She knows herbs and potions that will restore your master's men, it is true."

The mountain sparrow says nothing for many minutes. Never have I known a sparrow to not chirp incessantly until this one. I watch as he hops onto another rail, in the shadow of a branch, and the golden light no longer shines on him. Hermes has gone, but there is more I must know.

"Tell me, bravest of birds. When will they leave Aiaia? What is the rest of Hermes's message?"

"What message do you speak of, strange dog?" the sparrow asks, and he begins to fly away.

"Mountain sparrow!" I snap.

He pauses midflight.

"I know where there are fields of grasshoppers waiting for your sharp beak," I say, hoping he will stay longer. "But you must first return to that rail yonder and finish your tale."

After a few moments the sparrow returns to the rail and the light reappears.

"They may never leave that island, Argos," the sparrow says finally. "Circe's potions will cure their bodies, but steal their minds. Already they have forgotten their homeland. Some do not even remember their names. You should forget them too. Even your master, Odysseus. That is Hermes' message to you.

Now, where are those grasshoppers?"

"Three stadia over to the west is a newly threshed field," I whimper. "You will find them there."

"I thank thee, Aptos," he says, and flies away.

Now I stand on my hind legs and place my paws on the rail where the golden light had shown, hoping that Hermes has more to say, but alas, the light is long gone, and I am alone.

CHAPTER XIII

Telemachos learns to hunt

At first I did not believe the mountain sparrow, but as the days pass and no black ship is sighted at the harbor, I begin to fear the worst. Odysseus, sacker of cities, would not forget his homeland, his beloved wife, his valiant son, and his loyal dog unless a goddess had emptied his mind.

My mistress Penelope weeps every night by the sea. When the suitors leave, she takes her torch, and she and I climb down the narrow trail to the rocky beach, and she lays her hand on my shoulder and cries to the gods for the return of my master. Great is her despair and terrible are her lamentations. Most nights she holds the torch up as high as she can, waving it in great arcs above her head, as if my master's sleek black ship is bearing toward us, and the lookouts, perched high on the mast, on seeing the torch, will guide the black ship safely home to Ithaka. The ship never arrives.

Then, when the torch is nearly extinguished, I guide my mistress back to our house, walking slowly so she doesn't stumble along the path. At the door I step aside and let her enter, while I begin another night of sentinel duty, patrolling the sheep pens, guarding them from the mountain wolves, and human thieves too, until at dawn, when Apollo begins his journey across the sky, I curl up next to the barn and sleep for a few minutes until the roosters crow. Such is my fate now.

As the months pass, Telemachos grows into a young man. His voice no longer squeaks when he talks, and hair has begun to grow on his face. Every morning tutors come from the village and work with him. How hard he studies! He has learned all the gods by name and what prayers to say to them. He practices his letters and reads poetry. Sometimes he reads it to me, and I confess, it puts me to sleep. Then there are the numbers! I do not understand the marks he makes, but he must understand it well because the tutors no longer strike him on the wrist—although perhaps now they are afraid to. Then, in the afternoon, there is wrestling and spear throwing, archery, and boxing. On days when there is wind, he goes to the harbor and practices his sailing. A king must know all these things, and one day Telemachos will be a king.

But now he is a boy who misses his father.

Now, in his thirteenth spring, Telemachos has turned even more inward, for there is no man about to teach him the ways of the hunt, as boys learn at this age. And so Telemachos broods. I know he wishes to hunt, because he spends long hours practicing with his bow and hurling his spear at gourds, but he knows nothing of tracking game, of staying downwind from the fearful doe; he knows not the footprint of the wild pig, nor where the hares make their warrens. Neither does he know to strike a pair of antlers with hard wood to taunt a buck into showing himself, nor does he know where the point of the spear must go if a boar charges. In short, he knows nothing about how to hunt like a man, and so I will teach him to hunt like a dog.

This morning Telemachos rises early to practice with his bow. I follow him out to the pasture, where he sets up a gourd, and when he sets down his bow to lift the gourd up to the fencepost, I take his bow in my mouth and trot away. He runs after me, calling my name, but for once I disobey him and continue to lead him away from the house and toward a stream deep in the wooded valley where the deer come to drink. But humanfolk are so loud! How to get him to stop calling my name?

I stop and let him catch up to me, and I put the bow down at my paws. When he stoops to pick it up, I take one end in my mouth and begin to tug, leading him farther into the woods. He follows me, curious to play my new game. But it is not a game. To hunt is to live. I crouch down and slowly creep up a hill, sniffing the air to make sure the wind has not changed. Telemachos, as smart as his father, soon realizes what I am doing and crouches low alongside me. Together we slither into the wood, barely disturbing a leaf. Every few minutes I stop to sniff the air, and Telemachos sniffs as well, although humans have pitifully small noses. Then I rub my face in the dirt, and the boy does too, darkening his shiny face, which animals can see for leagues.

We pass a tree where a young buck has rubbed off the bark with its antlers. I stand on my hind legs and lean against the tree, showing him the missing bark. I think he understands. Farther along the trail, where it grows wet, I see the footprints of a deer. Telemachos walks past it, so I growl softly until he turns, and then I put my nose next to the footprint and growl again. He sees instantly what he'd missed. Now he knows we are close to our prey.

As Apollo carries his chariot higher, we reach the hidden stream. There we duck under a laurel and wait. First one small doe appears, then another. Soon they are joined by as many deer as there are whiskers on my snout. I look at Telemachos and lick his bow hand. Slowly he notches an arrow and raises his bow. Then, as often happens in the morning, the wind shifts, bringing our scent to the deer. Several raise their heads, alert, ready to flee.

Now! I think.

I hear the hum of his bowstring and see the arrow take flight. He has aimed for the largest buck, a proud deer that did not test the wind when it shifted and brought new scents. That costs the deer his life.

Telemachos, who is not a boastful boy, whispers his gratitude to the gods and then hugs my neck. Together we clamber down to the stream. Telemachos ties a leather cord to one of the buck's legs, and we drag the carcass back to the farm until one of the servants comes out to help us the rest of the way. Later, that servant shows Telemachos how to dress the deer so that none of it is wasted. The skin is hung to dry, the hooves are boiled for a jelly, the entrails given to the lesser dogs after a priest reads them. That is our way on this island.

Now it is late afternoon and the suitors have arrived, as they do almost daily, to vie for my mistress's hand and my master's estate. Although they come day after day, month after month, they are guests and cannot be refused hospitality. To do so would bring shame and dishonor on the house of Odysseus throughout Achaia, which my mistress would not allow. Nor do we have enough servants and shepherds to drive them away when they are rude or insolent, though they hear my growls when they berate a servant or complain to a shepherd that his sheep are not fat enough.

Just as I am about to head to a far pasture to bring in a flock, one of the suitors sees the deer Telemachos has slain, dressed and ready for the spit. He orders the servant to prepare a fire and to cook it straightaway, for the men were growing hungry, complaining that "Fair Penelope offers us little meat."

"No," declares Telemachos firmly, stepping between the suitor and the servant. "The deer is my kill, and it is for my family and servants to eat. Not for men who should hunt for themselves."

The suitor draws back his hand to cuff the insolent Telemachos, but I leap between them, baring my teeth. Behind me, I hear Telemachos draw his xiphos, a small sword, but sharp enough to sting. The suitor, who had left his spear at the door to the main house, turns and walks away, uttering oaths at Telemachos for his rude behavior. Later that night the suitors are sent home, cursing and hungry, but the family of Odysseus, son of Laertes, dines well.

Throughout summer and autumn we continue to hunt. Telemachos misses many kills and makes many more. Such is hunting. We trap hares, his arrows find more deer, and he spears a feral pig. The boy grows strong; his spear arm fills out with muscle, and his legs grow stout enough to carry his kill many leagues. But of his father, my master Odysseus, the boy and I hear not, despite my pleas to the seabirds to bring back news, and sadness descends on the house of Laertes as another winter approaches.

CHAPTER XIV

A reminder of home

Winter comes fierce and unforgiving to Ithaka. The livestock grows lean and huddles together against the cold winds; mountain wolves grow bolder, encroaching on nearby farms—but not my master's; and few ships enter our harbor, so we hear no news. Then early this morning, while I am making my rounds, the mountain sparrow returns! Again, he seems bathed in a golden drop of light.

"Boar Slayer," he calls down to me. "I leave for Aiaia when rosy dawn comes. If your master and his companions still live, though madness has seized them, I will tell you of it when I return in the spring and winter has left our island."

Hearing this, I have an idea. My master is known as the Wily One, but I am clever also.

"Wait, Sir Sparrow," I call. "Can you take something to my master, something from Ithaka? Perhaps it will jar his mind and the madness will leave him!"

"What can I carry, Argos?" the sparrow asks. "I am small and my wings will not support any great weight. Even a grasshopper in my claws soon becomes too heavy, and Aiaia is a long journey from here."

I say nothing. Instead, I sit down and pull up my rear leg and begin to scratch my neck. In winter I do not shed, so I claw mightily. Soon a clump of my black fur falls to the ground.

"Take this," I say to the mountain sparrow. "Surely my fur is light enough for your journey, and your claws can easily grip it. When you reach Aiaia, leave this fur where my master can see it. If the gods are good, then he will remember his life here."

The mountain sparrow flies down and grasps the fur in his claws. "It might work, loyal one, for sometimes the gods *are* good if we act without their help. When I return, I hope it is with good news!"

Then, clutching the tuft of fur in his claws, the mountain sparrow flies away. I follow him as he darts among the junipers along the edge of the estate, and then he turns south and east, flying into the dawn, and I can see him no longer. Then I return to my rounds.

Spring comes and Ithaka turns green again. Meadow flowers bloom, and the shepherds spend long nights delivering lambs and kids. In the warm afternoons, Telemachos and I take long walks along the goat trails that cross this part of the island, and he complains bitterly about his tutors or the latest insult from the suitors. Not once does he mention his father.

When we return in the evening, Telemachos strokes my face and scratches my ears, and then, reluctantly, joins the suitors for dinner. A few of the suitors, realizing that he no longer speaks of Odysseus, have tried to befriend him in order to win my mistress Penelope's favor. They sometimes offer him choice cuts of meat and give him small gifts such as soft sandals and flutes, which he accepts graciously, as his mother has taught him.

Tonight, as the suitors are feasting, one of them, Ktesippos, a balding fat man with the swollen belly of a giant sow, offers to teach Telemachos how to wrestle.

"I am the greatest wrestler on Ithaka," he boasts. "No man has thrown me, nor remained upright in my grip. Here, let me show you."

He stands up and comes around to where Telemachos sits. I rise to my feet, but Telemachos puts his hand on my shoulder.

"Come, boy," Ktesippos says. "Stand up and face me. Let me see your stance."

And Telemachos does stand up, but he wrestles Ktesippos with words, not muscle, saying, "You may be the finest wrestler on Ithaka, Ktesippos, since only schoolboys and old men are left on this island. But when my father, the city sacker, returns, he will break your arms and throw you on your back, and you will regret the day you sought to replace him!"

Then, hearing these stinging words, Ktesippos swings his right hand to cuff Telemachos, but Telemachos ducks, and then punches the clumsy suitor in his ample gut. The big man falls to his knees while the other suitors laugh and hurl food at the groaning man.

"Come, Argos," Telemachos says. "These craven men do not deserve to sit at the table of brave Odysseus with his son."

A few of the suitors hear these winged words and stand up to protest, but Telemachos and I turn and leave the room. From there we walk to a hillside shrine for Zeus, and there Telemachos makes an offering to Zeus asking that his father return soon, and he swears then to the father of the gods that never again will a day pass without his father's name passing his lips. I will help him keep that promise.

A week has passed since the night the suitors behaved so disgracefully, and the birds have begun to return to Ithaka. I watch each flock, hoping it brings the mountain sparrow, but none do. And then, this evening, I hear a familiar voice.

"Boar Slayer, I return bearing news of your master," the mountain sparrow calls as he alights on a branch near the sheep pasture where I stand guarding spring lambs.

"Greetings, loyal friend," I reply, my heart tumbling like a newborn lamb trying to walk. "Do you come from Aiaia? Did my plan work? Did my master remember his land and his family? Tell me at once!"

"What plan was that?"

"Sir Sparrow, you took a clump of my fur and were to give it to my master!"

Suddenly a ray of light appears, shining on the bird's tiny crested head.

"Of course! That plan! Yes, your plan worked, Argos! Brave Odysseus saw your black fur and a veil was lifted from his eyes. How piteous were his tears and those of his men when he spoke to them. Even fair Circe was moved by his suffering."

Oh, what joy I feel then! I leap into the air twisting and turning, unable to restrain myself.

"So she will let him leave now, will she not, friend?" I ask, once I can stand still. "My master sails soon?"

But the sparrow dips his head and says softly, "Argos, the gods give and then take away, is that not so?"

"What do you mean, Sir Sparrow? Surely the goddess will release my master! What more could she want?"

Then the sparrow flies down from the branch so that I will not miss a word.

"Let me tell you straightaway what happened, loyal one, before I forget. When I reached Aiaia, I flew directly to your master. I found him carving a small flute, but his eyes were mindless, Boar Slayer, as if he had no thoughts in his head. I landed on his knee then, which took great courage, I must say, because we birds do not enjoy a man's touch, and I dropped your fur onto his lap.

"After a moment he lay down his carving knife and picked up your fur, studying it with great intensity. Then I saw a smile creep across his noble face, and his eyes grew bright—as bright as twin stars, Argos. Then he leaped to his feet and began to seek out fair Circe. He found her in her garden and approached her, saying, 'Goddess, it is time to think again of returning to my own country, if truly it is ordained that I shall return. Accomplish now the promise you gave. See me on my way home. The spirit within me is great, and my men and I wish to see our home.'

"Then fair Circe nodded, as if she had known this day would come. 'Son of Laertes and seed of Zeus,' she said sadly, 'you shall no longer stay at my house if you wish to leave. But first there is another journey you must undertake.'

"'And what is that journey, fair Circe?' your master asked."

"'You must sail to the house of Hades, the land of the dead,' the goddess answered. 'Once there, you must slaughter your sheep and make a pool of their blood. When the spirits of the dead drink this, they will become as flesh and speak to you. But let the prophet Teiresias drink first, for his is the tale most worth knowing, for the dead speak only of the past, while Teiresias knows how your fate will spin, as he, though blind, can see the future and help you return to Ithaka.'"

And then the sparrow begins to weep.

"I left then, Boar Slayer," he finally manages to say. "I could not follow your master to Hades. I was too afraid."

"Sir Sparrow," I say gently. "I thank you for what you have done in the service of my master. Now it is spring and you must build a nest. Go and fashion a strong one for your family. You can do no more for me. Nor can anyone, I think."

CHAPTER XV

/◎/◎/◎/◎/◎/◎/◎/◎/◎/◎/◎/◎/◎/◎/◎/◎

Come the mountain wolves

For several months a tutor, Callius, potbellied and bald, has arrived at my master's house daily to teach young Telemachos the subjects every future king must know: astronomy, geometry, philosophy, and history. These are subjects that do not concern a dog, so I usually fall asleep next to my young master or find a shady place to scratch my ears and rub dirt on my fleas. Why do humans worry about the stars when to scratch an itch is the greatest pleasure the gods can give?

I do not like the tutor much. He is also said to be a healer, but I do not believe it. If he had talents, then he would not need to offer services as a tutor, for there is much illness and infirmity among the people who live in the villages. I have heard rumors that he has poisoned more people with herbs than he has cured. Moreover, he smells unclean, and he is rude to the servants. Worse, he is sharp-tongued toward Telemachos, insulting him when he misses a question, and more than once I have seen him strike the boy on the hand when Telemachos made a mistake with his silly numbers.

After a few weeks of his tutelage, I heard Telemachos ask my mistress why she had chosen Callius, of all tutors, to give him lessons.

"Telemachos, my son," she said, "Ithaka is full of farmers, fishermen, and sailors, but there are very few philosophers on our fair island. Your father sat under the tutelage of Callius's father, and now his son teaches my son. Do you not think that is the way it should be?"

"But he smells, Mother," Telemachos protested. "He smells and he is cruel and he calls me stupid."

"Students always say their teachers are cruel, and no one would dare call the son of mighty Odysseus stupid. Now, you have much to study and learn if you are to rule Ithaka wisely one day. Be a good boy and try your best, will you not?"

And then she embraced the young boy and ruffled his curly hair. Telemachos said nothing about the whippings Callius gave him when he missed a question. Or when he answered one correctly.

Two days ago, the tutor struck Telemachos thrice on his palm with a leather strap. The first time he did this because he claimed Telemachos made a mistake with his geometry. The second time he struck him because Telemachos showed the tutor that he had not made a mistake; the tutor had instead. And the third time he struck him because Telemachos refused to apologize for correcting him. Still, I did nothing, though the hair along my back rose when I saw this. Telemachos will one day be a king, and I cannot fight his battles for him, and I have greater worries that concern me.

On the west side of our island, fair Ithaka, a pack of mountain wolves grows large. With few men on Ithaka to hunt them and keep the pack small, they have multiplied in number over the years, and large packs need more and more food. The land there is rocky and barren, so few men have built farms or raise sheep. Only fishermen and bandits live there, and they are afraid of mountain wolves, so the pack's leader has become bold. In order to feed his growing pack, he leads his fellow wolves closer and closer to our side of the island, where the sheep are fat, and they are guarded by small dogs and young boys with short spears. Friends of Telemachos. And no match for mountain wolves.

My master would know what to do. He would rally the men from the farms and villages, arm them with bows and spears, and go mountain wolf hunting. "Kill the leader and the pack dies after," I have heard him say, speaking of mountain wolves—and men. But my master is far from home, and the men from the farms and villages sailed with him but for the cowardly ones who come daily to try to steal our land and wed my mistress Penelope.

They are afraid of the mountain wolves too. When they leave my mistress in the evening, they band together, spears level, as they make their way along the narrow trails that lead to the nearby village. No one lingers for a quiet word alone with mistress Penelope, a final plea for her charms. To do so risks being alone if the wolves come.

So I must find the pack leader and tell him to stay away from our village and this rich, sheep-filled side of the island. Or kill him if he will not.

Apollo's chariot passes six times before I hear again from the shepherd dogs in the valley that the mountain wolves are nearby. Two ewes are missing, and then yesterday a shepherd boy found one of them torn asunder. The boys in the village have been pulled from their schools and made to stand guard over their family's livestock because dogs alone do not frighten these wolves. And they grow more bold daily. Boys in the village speak of mountain wolves seen when the sun is high, brazenly stalking a calf separated from its mother. One of the boys said the lead wolf is the size of a small horse, gray as the slate rocks that tumble down from the hills. And just last night, in the distance, I heard them howl. They have come now to our side of Ithaka.

Apollo's chariot has passed again, and now an old shepherd from our farthest pastures is speaking to loyal Eumaios, who is charged with caring for all of my master's sheep. The old shepherd says that thirteen sheep were killed overnight by the pack of mountain wolves just west of here. Three goats are missing on the south of the island, and he thinks they too will not be found alive. I cannot pretend otherwise: the mountain wolves will soon be at our door. My master's estate is the largest on Ithaka, with more sheep, goats, and oxen than I can count, and all Ithaka knows this. Even the mountain wolves.

This morning I spoke to an elder magpie and asked him to fly west and relay this message to the mountain wolves. "Tell them," I said, "to remain west of Mount Nerito, to fill their bellies with wild hares and feral pigs, or else face my wrath."

The magpie has returned with their reply. "The whole of

Ithaka now belongs to their pack, their leader said, and they will kill anything that tries to stop them. Those were their words, Boar Slayer."

"How many are there?" I ask the magpie.

"I counted twelve males, Argos," he says. "But many of them are young, not more than two years old. They are brash and full of themselves, I think."

"Twelve males? That is indeed a large pack."

"And what of their pack leader, Lykaon?" I ask. "Is he as big as the shepherds say?"

"He is, Boar Slayer. I have never seen a wolf so large. In size he is your match."

"I thank you for your efforts," I tell the magpie. "A time will come, and soon, I think, when I may need you again. With your intelligence and my brawn, we make a formidable team."

"Formidable indeed, loyal one," he says, and bobs his black head at least twelve times. Then he flies away into the trees, and I begin to ponder how to kill a wolf.

CHAPTER XVI

@@@@@@@@@@@@@@@@@@@@@@@@@@@@@@

Tales of Hades

Just as evening is about to fall, a crow alights upon the sheep paddock where I am guiding the sheep into their stalls. He watches me for some time and then says, "You are Ar-Ar-Argos, the Boar Slayer, loyal companion to Odysseus, are-are-are you not?"

"That is what I am called, friend. Who seeks to know my name and master?"

"I do not know his name, but in the cave on the east side of Mount Nerito a bat hangs, waiting for night to fall. He has news of your master. Go to him, for soon he leaves for other lands."

"News of my master? From whence does the bat come, most clever of birds?"

"From Hades itself," the crow says. "Hurry, night falls soon."

Then the crow flies away. I rush the remaining sheep into their stalls, nipping the last few on their fat rears to get them to move quickly, and then I run as fast as I can toward the mist-shrouded mountain that juts out of the earth in the middle of our island.

I reach the mountain as black night falls over Ithaka. I know the cave where the bat hangs upside down, sleeping through the long hours of the day. Telemachos and I waited out a storm there only last summer. Then, just as I arrive at the cave's mouth, a thousand bats fly out into the night. Have I arrived too late?

"Greetings, Stag Hunter," I hear a shrill voice from over my head say. I look up and see the tiny creature clinging to the stone above me. Truly, he is no larger than a mouse—a mouse that flies.

"Greetings to *you*, Night Flyer. I will not detain you long from your insect hunting. The crow said you had news of my master, Odysseus. Is it true? You have seen him?"

"Yes, I have seen him," the bat says. "I was on Circe's island while he was there, and then I followed his swift ship on its mission to Hades, for I too visit the underworld to see my kin."

I whimper out loud when I hear this. *It is true. My master has been sent to Hades!*

Regaining my composure, I call up to him. "Tell me, then, what you saw, O winged one. Do not me spare me the truth, for I have suffered many years to hear my master's ultimate fate."

"I will tell you what I know, loyal one. But it is a hard tale, for men do not go easily into the underworld and return unchanged."

I sit on my haunches and crane my neck upward to hear his story.

"All day, Argos, your master's ship with full sail sped north as Circe instructed. Soon they reached the deep ocean and the land of the Kimmerian people, hidden in fog and cloud. There they harbored, and Odysseus and his men sacrificed many sheep and made offerings to the gods and said prayers to Hades and Persephone, the queen of the underworld, as they were instructed. The blood from their sacrifices made a giant pool, and toward it the spirits of the dead were drawn, just as Circe had said, but your master would let no one near it until Teiresias came.

"Terrible was that night, for many spirits gathered around

your master and his men. They were the hordes of the perished dead, brides and unmarried men, elders and tender children, and many fighting men, still splendid in their armor. They swarmed about with an inhuman noise, filling the men with terror, but your master drew his large sword and would not let the spirits of the perished come near. Don't move!"

"Is that what my master said?"

"No, brave one. A mosquito flies near your left shoulder. Don't you hear it?"

"No, winged one."

With a flash of leathery wings, the bat swoops down and a moment later is hanging above me again.

"Delicious. Now, as I was saying . . . Then a familiar soul approached—Elpenor, one of your master's men, who had fallen to his death while drunk in Circe's palace just before they left. Your master had not buried him, so quickly had they left for the underworld. Seeing him, your master wept piteous tears.

"Elpenor, the phantom, spoke thus: 'Son of Laertes and seed of Zeus, I pray that after you leave the house of Hades and set sail for Aiaia, you set me on a pyre there and burn me with my armor, then heap up a grave mound on the beach and plant the oar with which I rowed for your black ship. Do this for me, or I am cursed for eternity.'

"And your master promised this. Then more souls came—most tragic of all, your master's mother, Antikleia."

I know that my master's mother had died, but to see her spirit in Hades must have been terrible for him. My *poor master*.

"What did my master say when he saw his mother, Night Flyer?" I ask.

The bat is silent for a moment.

"Never have I seen such sorrow on a man, Boar Slayer," the bat says finally. "He wept and wept, but still he could not go to her, for his duty was to find Teiresias first, or else his prophecies would be lost. But then, emerging from the shadows, the blind prophet Teiresias appeared, carrying his golden staff. Ahhh, the moths are thick tonight, Boar Slayer."

"Moths? But . . ."

"One moment."

Up, down, around, he darts. Never have I seen such flying agility. My neck becomes tired just following him. And then, a few moments later, he returns to his perch.

"Truly the moths on Ithaka are among the finest in the world, Argos."

"That may be, cousin. But what did Teiresias say?" I demand.

"Patience, four-legged one. A bat must eat many times its

weight in food each night. That is our curse and our delight. Now then. Returning to my tale, Teiresias said, 'Son of Laertes and seed of Zeus, how is it that you are here in this cursed place, far from sunlit Ithaka? Sheath your sword and draw back so that I may drink this blood and speak to your fate.'

"Hearing this, your master sheathed his sword, and the prophet drank deeply.

"'Glorious Odysseus,' he began,' you seek to return to your home, but one god is against you. Poseidon, the earth shaker, bears you ill will because you blinded his son, Polyphemus of the Cyclopes. But even so, you might return, though after much suffering, if you obey my instructions and contain your desires and those of your companions.'

"'Tell me then, perfect seer, what I must do and I will follow it closely,' your master begged.

"'First, when you return to your fast ship, sail over the blue waters, escaping its grasp if you can, to Thrinakia. There you will find fat cattle and sheep pasturing, but touch them not, for they belong to the god Helios, who sees and hears all things. Keep foremost in your mind your sweet homecoming and leave those beasts unharmed, and you might reach fair Ithaka, after much suffering. But if harm comes to them, then your destruction is foretold, for your ships and your men will perish, although the gods may smile on you alone.'

"'I swear to you, then, we will follow your instructions,' Odysseus promised."

"And he will, Night Flyer," I say. "Of that I am certain."

"Perhaps, perhaps not, Argos, for I saw the briefest smile cross Teiresias's lips when your master said this."

I ignore this remark, for what does a bat know of my master's will? Still, the bat is silent for a moment, and I begin to think I have insulted him. Or he still hungers.

"Please, continue, winged one," I say. "I will interrupt no more, and then you may eat your fill."

"So be it," the bat replies. "Then Teiresias drank again and continued his prophecy, for he was nearly through reading the thread of your master's fate."

"'If you return to Ithaka, City Sacker,' he said, 'yours will not be a joyous homecoming. Your companions will all be dead, and your ship will be lost. On a borrowed vessel you will arrive to find strange men in your house, eating away your wealth, and courting your wife.'

"'Steadfast Penelope would marry again?' your master cried.

"'No, brave one,' Teiresias answered. 'Godlike Penelope is ever loyal, but the men make her suffer and insult her honor. You may avenge this insult if you can, by bronze or trickery.'

Your master then gripped his sword tightly, Argos, and I knew that he would use bronze to defend his house.

"'Do I die then, perfect seer?' your master asked after his rage subsided.

"Teiresias shook his head. 'No, Odysseus, if this thread is followed, Death will come to you, as it does all men, but it will be in old age, and it will come from the sea. Fear it not, then, for there is much more suffering and death to come sooner.'

"Then your master asked, 'May I speak to my mother now, blind one? I would know of her sad fate, for when I left Ithaka, her health was strong and death seemed far away.'

"Teiresias nodded. 'Let her drink this blood as I have, Odysseus, and her words will come, as will the words of all the souls here.'

"And saying that, Lord Teiresias turned and disappeared in the gloom of Hades.

"Then Odysseus's mother, who, before, could not to speak to your master, such was her lamentation, spoke to him in winged words.

"'My child, how did you come here into this gloom and darkness?' she asked. 'Are you still alive? Why are you not in Ithaka with your wife and son?'

"Your master answered, 'Dearest Mother, I came to speak

with the soul of Teiresias. It was a duty I had to obey, even though I have not been to Ithaka in many years. Indeed, I have been wandering since the days I helped defeat the Trojans alongside the great Agamemnon.'

"'I know of your battle with the Trojans, my son. Many great warriors are here because of it,' she replied.

"For a moment they were silent while Odysseus contemplated what he had done. But then he looked to his mother and said, 'Now that I have answered, I have many questions for you, for I have not set foot on Achaian land for many years. Tell me, how did you die, swiftly or with a long sickness? And what of my father and the son I left behind? Do they know I still live? And tell me about Penelope, my loyal wife. Does she need anything? Does she believe I live?'

"So your master spoke, and his mother answered quickly, 'Your wife endures many hardships and spends her nights weeping by the sea. Telemachos administers your lands as well as he can, but he is still just a boy, though he grows strong, and he has a faithful companion, a fierce and loyal dog. Your father lives on, but he is poor, for he cares not for anything but your safe return and he grows old harshly. As for me, I died not quickly nor from illness, but rather the sweet spirit of life left me over my longing for you, your cleverness and gentle ways.'

"Hearing this tale of woe, your master sought to embrace his mother, but three times she fluttered away as his arms encircled her, like a dream or a shadow. Then your master cried, 'Mother, will you not wait for me? My arms long to touch you! Even though we are in Hades, is there not relief from this dismal mourning? Or are you nothing but a ghost that Queen Persephone has sent my way to make me grieve even more?'

"Odysseus's mother answered thus: 'O my ill-fated child, this is what happens when we die. The sinews do not hold us together once the spirit has left its cage of white bones. The soul flitters like a moth and flies away. That is why you must leave. Go back to the land of light as fast as you can, back to your good wife Penelope, but remember what you have seen here.'

"But while she said this, other souls gathered round, the souls of wives and daughters of gods and princes, all sent by Persephone, and each one spoke of the sorrows of the perished. Then the soul of great Achilles, noblest of the Achaians, approached, and soon Minos, too, came forward, glorious son of Zeus, and the giant Orion too. Beyond them struggled Sisyphos, trying to push the great stone up the mountain, and when he had nearly reached the summit, the pitiless boulder rolled back down to the plain. Your master watched him try and fail again. He would never gain the summit; that was his fate.

"More of the perished gathered about Odysseus, clamoring to hear news of the living, but their noise was too great, and your master, fearing that Persephone might send some monster of the underworld after him, left that place as fast as he could and boarded his ship. Apollo's chariot could be seen in the east, so I did not fly to his ship, though I heard him cry, 'Cast off the cables and set your oarlocks!'

"That was the last I saw of them, loyal one," the bat says. "I do not fly by day, and so I did not follow their swift boat on its way back to Aiaia. I found a dark cavern in which to hide until the next night, and then I flew toward this land."

For a long time I cannot speak. Finally I say, "How can I thank you, winged one, for your endeavors?"

"There is nothing you can do for me, Boar Slayer. We bats are not like other creatures fashioned by the gods. We fly, yet we are not birds. We eat insects, yet we are not reptiles. We are blind, yet we see all. That is our fate. Go now, back to your home and sleep. Your master sails ever closer, though as long as he sails over water, he faces the wrath of Poseidon. Pray to your gods for fast winds. That is all you or anyone can do."

Then the bat unfolds its wings and flies out of the cave, darting right and left, up and down, as is their way, until he is swallowed by the darkness completely.

CHAPTER XVII

A trap is laid

There is a cleft between two ridges on the south side of Ithaka where a small berry shrub grows. The berries that grow on it are plump and bloodred, oozing sweet, sticky juice, but even the insects avoid it. I have heard the birds warn one another that the berries are poisonous; to eat just a drop of their red juice means agonizing death. I am going to find it.

I travel at night, while the flocks are safe in their barns, following the deer trails that bisect the island. Selene, goddess of the full moon, guides me deep into the valleys, lighting the path for me.

"What do you seek in this valley, Argos the Boar Slayer?" a hedgehog asks, emerging from the underbrush, when I find myself lost.

I tell him what I seek.

The hedgehog nods once and then stares at me, unblinking, from beneath a tree root for a few moments. "Pick me up," he says. "I will take you to it."

He curls up and I take him gently in my mouth, avoiding his barbs, and follow his directions until he says we have arrived. Then I set him down, and he uncurls and stretches his spiny back.

"There is the bush you seek, Boar Slayer. The stem is safe to put in your mouth, but do not let your tongue touch the berries or lap their juice. If you do, I have heard that goat's milk will ease the poison, but you must drink it soon after, or you will die."

"Thank you, Brother Hedgehog," I say. "Good hunting to you."

"I thank you. Where is your master, Odysseus? Does he return soon?" he asks.

"I have heard that he sails back to Aiaia, but he will return home soon if the gods are willing."

The hedgehog nods. "Few men return from that island, I think, loyal one. But if any man should, it will be your master."

Then he waddles off to hunt for an ant mound. I don't dwell on his dispiriting words about Circe, for I have to return to the farm. I circle the bush and find the stem with the most berries on it. Placing the stem between my jaws, I bite through it and twist it off, careful not to break any of the berries. Then, with the stem firmly in my jaws, I turn around and retrace my steps home. Selene casts her silver light in front of me, and I return to my master's land just before she sinks beneath the hills.

Noble Telemachos has left the leg bone of an ox near my bed and I crack it open, digging out the marrow with my teeth. I need to draw strength from that bone, the strength of an ox, for tomorrow night I may be fighting mountain wolves. I gnaw it for an hour, sharpening my teeth to fine points. Then I rest until I hear the dull bleat of a sheep. It's time to take them to the fields.

I bury the stem of berries to keep the goats from eating it—they will eat anything—and trot down to the sheep stall. A shepherd boy is there, and he unties the gate. The sheep come streaming out, and I lead them to a fine, grassy hill where, from the crest, I can watch them easily. All day long while they eat their grass, I rest and rehearse my plan.

The suitors arrive in midafternoon, but this day I don't growl at them as they approach the house. I remain high above on the hilltop, watching. Only my eyes move. Later, I see Telemachos leave the house and take the path that leads down to the harbor. He whistles for me, but for once, I don't run to him. He whistles again.

Oh, the sting of that whistle! Menfolk will never know how a simple whistle from their master cuts into a dog's heart. It is born into us. We freeze! We listen! Our hearts race! Our tails wag! Every instinct I have told me to run to him; he would praise me, rub my back, and scratch my ears. Some dogs live for this. A silly barnyard dog does. A weak housedog does. A clumsy puppy does. But I am Argos, the Boar Slayer, and tonight I must kill wolves. I whimper once, softly, then I cover my ears with my paws and lie perfectly still while Telemachos gazes out over the fields looking for me. Finally he turns and heads down the path that will lead him to the harbor. Alone.

What if robbers waylay him? No, I tell myself, he is godlike Telemachos, and he is armed with a sword. *What if a wolf sees him walking alone and attacks from behind?* No, I think, there are no wolves that close to the shore. He is going to the harbor to ask if any sailors have seen his father's swift boat while they sailed the islands. He does this every week, hoping to hear news that my master lives. I know the answer. He has been among the dead, but he still lives.

Finally the shepherd boy calls my name, and I begin to round up the sheep. I had kept them close together, much to their dismay, so in a few minutes I have them streaming down the hill toward their stalls, where they will drink and ruminate their cuds, for they have no real thoughts. At least one will be taken for dinner this day, if the suitors have their wish.

Then I run to the place where I buried the berries and dig up the stem. Grasping it firmly in my jaws, I take the trail that leads west into the pine-covered hills beyond Mount Nerito. The wolves will reach it tonight coming from the other direction. Along the way, I stop at the goat barn at the far end of my master's land.

Several goats stand along the fence, chewing the grass between the rails. I drop the berry stem and trot over to them. I find a doe that has recently given birth and push aside its nursing kids until my own belly is full of goat milk. If my plan fails and I swallow poison berry juice, perhaps it will save me.

After several hours I reach the spot I've chosen for my plan, an overgrown valley with a small clearing surrounded by large rocks on two sides and a steep drop-off into a ravine on a third. A small creek trickles some distance away. Many deer come there to drink. And so do their hunters. But the location suits me: a mountain wolf pack cannot surround me here. Best of all, the place smells of boar, for it once served as the lair of a boar sow. Telemachos himself had killed it, with my help.

Luna has fallen, and rosy dawn is an hour away. The wolves will be stirring, hungry after a long night. It's time. I take the stem of berries and place it on the flat grass in the clearing. Then I lower myself onto it, crushing the berries with my chest, staining the white shield of fur there bloodred. Then I roll over and over on the berries, spreading their juice on my sides and back. I even, carefully, smear some of the juice on my muzzle, taking care not to lick it. Then I lie on my side and begin to whimper.

After a few minutes, a magpie lands on a tree above me. *Not now!* I think. I know him; he had been my messenger to the wolf pack earlier. Now I'm afraid he will spoil my plan.

"Noble Argos," he calls down. "Are you wounded?"

"Yes, friend. A boar tusked me."

I can't tell him the truth. Magpies are notorious gossips.

"Can you walk?" he asks.

"No," I say. "I think not."

"You must try, loyal one. The mountain wolves are coming. Get up, if you can, and flee!"

"How many are there?"

"Ten or more. It is the new pack from the west. They travel together. Hurry, Argos. Try to run! Their scouts will be here soon."

"Let them come, magpie. I do not fear death. But I would not have you see it. Fly away and return when it is done."

Then I close my eyes and wait, lolling my tongue, making myself pant. Finally, just as I hear the wolf pack scouts entering the clearing, the magpie leaves his branch.

"Die well," he calls back to me.

I close my eyes and whimper loudly. *Oh, the shame of that sound.* But it works. It draws the wolves close. There are two, I think. I keep my eyes closed tight, but I hear them approach. They circle me in opposite directions, growling softly. Finally one of them finds the courage to speak.

"You are Argos, are you not?"

"I am," I groan.

"Who has killed you?"

"A boar did this. He pierced my chest. I will die soon."

"Sooner than you think, dog of man. My brother and I will tear your throat, and you will not threaten our pack again."

I open my eyes. They are a skinny, mangy-looking duo, both dirty gray and barely two years old, with no status in the pack.

"You can kill me, it is true, brother. But what will your leader say when he finds that you robbed him of this glory? He will bite off your tails and then you will never mate, will he not?"

"He speaks the truth, brother," the smaller one says. "There

133

is more glory in finding him and telling Lykaon. He will reward our loyalty with more food, and we will grow stronger. And we will keep our tails."

I whimper again. "Go quickly, brave pups. I will not live long enough for your debate. And finding a corpse will not help you."

"The Boar Slayer is right, brother," the small one says. "We must hurry."

"Live a bit longer, Argos," the older wolf says. "To die like this, alone, would bring shame to your descendants."

"He has no descendants, brother! All Ithaka knows that!"

They laugh madly.

I will rip out their hearts right now for that insult, I think, *but I cannot do it now.* Instead, I whimper again and roll my eyes.

"He dies! We must hurry!"

I hear them run off. Apollo's chariot rises higher over the tree line. *Soon,* I think. *Soon.*

Mountain wolves—even a pack of them—move silently in the hunt, but this pack is not hunting. They are seeking glory. I hear them howling and snarling from several stadia away. Only when they draw close do they stop their yelping. I open my eyes and wait. Their leader, Lykaon, shows himself first.

He is the largest wolf I have ever seen; his diamond-shaped head is as massive as a bear's, and his eyes glow with an evil intelligence. The rest of the pack clusters around him. The two scouts run up to me. The smaller one, showing off, nips my tail, and I lift my head, snarling and snapping my jaws. I just miss, and the smaller one squeals like a puppy.

Then I close my eyes as if exhausted.

"He still lives, Lykaon, as we said."

"I can see that, fool. But he still has a bite to him. That is good. There is no glory killing a half-dead dog. Even one such as Argos."

The wolves draw closer, but I have chosen my location carefully. Because of the boulders and the ravine, they must either stay behind their leader, where there is room, or squeeze in close to me and risk my sharp teeth. They choose to hide behind Lykaon.

I raise my head. "I die soon, Lykaon. Are you a buzzard that eats what is already dead? Why do you linger? Let me die with honor, with my throat in your jaws."

Hearing this, he attacks, lunging for my neck.

But I am Argos, the Boar Slayer, and I am ready. I leap to my feet and meet his charge. Lykaon tries to stop and rears up on his hind legs in surprise. Then I pounce, locking my jaws on his throat, and pulling him down. He's very strong, though, and he gets his legs under me and pushes me off, but I flip him onto his back and bite again. We roll over and over on the grass, biting and clawing, both of us trying to get a death grip.

Finally we separate for a moment, and then Lykaon charges again. This time I go in low and find his windpipe between my jaws and crush it. When I know the bite is mortal, I release him from my jaws. Suddenly, another wolf charges. He bites my flank, but I wheel away and send him spinning. Then I charge him and he retreats to the safety of the pack, which stands watching their pack leader die.

"Attack him, brothers," Lykaon cries. He is nearly dead; his eyes have grown glassy, but his wolves obey him. First, a black wolf, a three-year-old with yellow eyes, rushes toward me. He is fast, and I feel his jaws on my chest. But I jump back in time and leave him with only a mouthful of fur. Poisoned fur. He begins to gag immediately. Another wolf leaps, a gray shadow, but I duck and he sails over me, landing near the ravine. I charge him and he stumbles over the edge, clawing with his paws at the rocky earth, trying to gain a hold. I bite his leg, and he falls.

"Avenge Lykaon!" a wolf behind me cries. Suddenly I feel two of them on me, biting my ear, my shoulder, my flank. But they are smaller wolves, low in status, and not trained to fight. I spin round and round and they fly off, taking some of my flesh with them. I kill the one with half my ear in his mouth first. The other wolf is already sick from the poison berry juice I spread over my fur.

Then I throw myself into a knot of three wolves preparing to charge me. I bite and claw at them. They run away, back along the path they had taken. Four more wolves slink toward me, two from each side, cutting off my escape. But instead of charging them, I turn and run toward the largest boulder. One of the wolves tries to cut me off, but I cuff him with my paw, just before I leap to the top of the boulder. Then a silver-colored wolf scrambles up the boulder toward me, teeth flashing. I kick a rock down onto his face, and after that, he stays on the ground. I stare down at them. Three are dying from the poison; only four remain, and they are all wounded. I am panting and bleeding, but I have won the day.

"Wolf pack!" I cry. "Your leader is dead and only four of you remain alive. Return now to your hunting grounds on western Ithaka and remain there. I will not hunt you down if you stay on your territory, but will allow you to mate and raise your pups on this condition: you must hunt only wild game henceforth. You may not separate sheep from the flock or a kid from its nanny. These animals belong to the men on this island, and the men owe their allegiance to my master, brave Odysseus, who returns soon. Keep this pledge, or I will hunt you down, one by one."

The four mountain wolves turn to one another and appraise their many wounds. After a few moments, the largest one says, "We yield, Argos, slayer of boars and wolves. There is mercy in your terms. It was Lykaon, after all, who led us to this cursed part of Ithaka. Now that you have killed him, we can return to our dens and we will trouble you no more."

"Well spoken, cousin," I say. "Good hunting to you and your kin."

They each lower their heads as they pass under the boulder, then they trot away, heading west. For a moment—just a moment—I feel like following them. I would be their new leader, and I would spend the rest of my days hunting and raising litter after litter of strong pups. But that is not my fate. I belong to the house of Odysseus, and there I have to return. I must see my master again, if he lives, as the birds say he does. And Telemachos still has much to learn from me.

Just as I think this, the magpie returns, alighting on a branch above me. He says nothing; instead, he looks down at the destruction below him and whistles.

"You still live, Argos?" he asks.

"I do, clever magpie."

"You have your master's cunning."

"Perhaps. Now, do this for me, most eloquent of birds. Spread the word throughout the forests of Ithaka, what I have done here. Tell the mountain wolves on the north and the south to keep their packs small and to hunt only game. Tell them Argos the Boar Slayer has tasted wolf blood and found it to his liking."

"So I shall," he says. Then he spreads his wings, and in a few moments he is flying north, cawing loudly now that he has something worthwhile to say.

I leap down from the boulder and begin the long run back to our land. I am bleeding from many bites, and my left ear is shredded.

I am no longer the handsomest dog on Ithaka, I think.

CHAPTER XVIII

ᖆᖆᖆᖆᖆᖆᖆᖆᖆᖆᖆᖆᖆᖆᖆᖆ

What the owl says

A gull has circled twice overhead, and then when I bark at it, the bird lands on the ridge overlooking the path down to the harbor. A moment later, a dozen or more gulls land near him.

"What news do you bring from over the sea, Shell Eater?" I ask the first gull when I reach him.

"Only this, loyal one. An owl has arrived on your island. He has news of your master, whom I followed for three days after he sailed from the underworld without stopping to anchor, finally landing again on Aiaia. I left soon after, but you must find this unblinking one, for he knows Circe and will tell you more."

"More, more, more," cry the other gulls.

"How will I find him, White Wing? The forests here are

thick and owls are difficult to see, even for a tracker such as I."

"Go to the tallest tree on the island, Boar Slayer. This owl is vain, having lived with the goddess, and always seeks to occupy the highest perch. There, I am sure, you will find him."

"Find him, find him, find him," they repeat.

"Thank you, fair gull," I say. "I wish gentle winds for you and your brethren."

"One cannot control the wind, Argos. Now hurry and seek the owl before night falls and he begins his hunting. If he leaves his tree, you will not find him."

"Hurry, hurry, hurry!" his brothers call.

The gull spreads his white wings and rises above me. Then he dips one wing and circles away, flying effortlessly down to the shore, where the retreating tide has left glittering shells exposed. The flock follows a moment later. I turn and run the other way, deep into the piney woods. I know the tallest tree on Ithaka, a juniper to the north of my master's farm. I had tracked a stag there once, and Telemachos's arrow had found its heart. I reach the place just as Apollo's chariot sinks below the western hills. I stand on my rear legs and brace my front legs against the trunk, looking up through the branches.

"Father Owl," I call, "are you there? I am Argos, the Boar

Slayer, loyal dog of brave Odysseus. The gulls told me I'd find you here."

Several moments pass, and I am fearing the owl has already left for its hunt when I hear a rustling sound high in the branches above me. I jump back just in time, as a thick excrescence explodes on the ground beside me.

"Did I hit you-you-you, Boar Slayer?" the owl calls down to me.

"Nearly, Mouse Hunter," I called back. "But I shall not stand so close next time."

"See that you-you-you don't. Now that you-you-you have awakened me, what do you-you-you want? Be quick, for my belly growls."

"I seek news of my master, Odysseus, Sir Owl. I hear that you were on Circe's island, Aiaia, when he returned from the underworld. Is that so?"

"It might be. But why should I tell you-you-you what I know? What can you-you-you do for me in return?"

"What could a fierce hunter such as yourself desire? Is there not enough prey on this island for you?"

"The hares here are easily caught, it is true-true-true, as are the smaller rodents. What I desire tonight, though, is fowl. But not tough old biddies. Tell me, on your farm, are there young chicks, newly hatched, scratching for seeds? If so, show me where I might find them, and I'll tell you-you-you of your master's return to Aiaia, for I was there when his ship arrived."

I do not hesitate to answer.

"Yes, Sir Owl. On my farm there are chicks, hatched not three weeks back. I will drive them from their coop tonight if you tell me truthfully what you saw on that cursed island."

Then I hear a great beat of wings, and suddenly the owl swoops out of the juniper and alights on the lowest branch of a tree next to me. Its black tufted ears stand straight up, and its round eyes stare at me unblinking.

"Hear these words, then, Argos, for I was there with Circe when your master arrived, still pale from his journey to the underworld and lamenting his fate."

"Once Odysseus and his men beached, he sent men to retrieve the body of Elpenor from the house of Circe, so that he might be buried as he asked. When they had done so, and planted the oar on his funeral mound, Circe appeared, along with her servants, bearing meat and shining red wine. Glorious in her gown, she addressed Odysseus and his companions: 'Unhappy men, sent alive to Hades, so dying twice, come eat and rest here all the day. Tomorrow, before you set sail, I'll show you the way home so that no more unhappiness follows you.'

"Hearing this, I think your master's heart was gladdened, and he and his men feasted on the unlimited meat and never-ending wine until night came, and all of your master's men fell asleep on the beach. But I was awake and saw Circe take your master by the hand and lead him away from his men. She bade him to tell her of his visit to the underworld, and when he had done so, she said, 'You did what I asked, so now I will tell you all.'

"'Brave Odysseus, your journey will not be easy, for many of the gods are with you, but many too are displeased. So you must listen carefully and do exactly as I say. The winds will carry you east for two days, and you will reach a sea flecked with foam and dark as wine. There by this sea live the Sirens. They are enchanters of all who are human, and no sailor who has heard them has ever returned to delight his wife and children.'"

Did my master think then of his wife, Penelope, and his fine son, Telemachos? I wonder, but I say nothing, and the owl continues with Circe's warning.

"'Truly, the beach where they sit is piled high with the bone heaps of men who sailed too close so that they might listen to their enchanting melodies. So you must sail straight on past or you will perish there, and your bones will be added to the pile.'

"Then your master asked, 'But how can we sail past them, fair goddess, for we are men and yield easily to temptation? And I would willingly listen to their songs, for I have heard they are as beautiful as has ever been sung.' Circe shook her head and then clasped your master's arm.

"'If you wish to see your wife and son, you must do this: before you reach the Sirens, melt beeswax and stop your companions' ears so that none can listen. But if you yourself want to listen, have your men bind you to the mast, hand and foot, with knots you cannot untie. Then tell your men that no matter how much you beg them to untie you, they must not, for if they do, you will surely leap from your ship and drown. And if you implore them further, they must bind you with more lashings until you have passed the enchanters. Will you do this, brave Odysseus?' Circe said.

"'I will do so, Goddess,' your master promised."

"Surely my master will follow her counsel, Sir Owl!" I cry.

"Interrupt me not, Boar Slayer, if you-you-you wish to hear the tale." The owl snaps his fiercely crooked beak.

I bow my head, and after a few moments the owl clears his throat.

"Then Circe continued. 'There is more to tell, I fear,' she said. 'After you have passed the Sirens, you will come upon a giant rock, which divides the sea into two courses. You must decide then which course to take, but I will tell you first what you will encounter on each side. On one side, there are giant swells and overhanging cliffs, which not even a sparrow can pass through. Of all the men who have tried to sail this way, only Jason and his ship passed safely through, and that was with the aid of a goddess. Now, on the other side is a high peak covered always in cloud, and halfway down that towering rock, there is a cave. Inside that cave, the monster Skylla lives, whose howling is terror.'

"At those words, your master shook his head. 'Monsters can be slain, fair Circe,' the Wily One said.

"'No one, not even a god, would want to face Skylla,' Circe replied. 'She has twelve feet and six long necks upon her. On each neck, there is a hideous head with three rows of teeth, full of black death. Her body from the waist down remains hidden, holed down into the cavern, and from there she fishes, looking for dolphins or dogfish or anything larger. Never has a ship passed her without losing men, for she snatches at least one sailor with each of her heads and carries them off.'

"'Then I should choose the other course, fair goddess,'

your master said grimly.

"'Brave one, the choice is more difficult than that. If you choose the second course, you pass by a lower cliff adorned with fig trees.'

"'And what monster resides there?' Odysseus asked.

"'No monster, brave Odysseus,' the goddess said. 'But instead a black whirlpool called Charybdis. Three times a day she sucks the sea down into her black hole, and not even Poseidon could rescue you if your ship is caught. So hearing this, I urge you to steer clear of Charybdis and instead make for Skylla's rock, for it is better to mourn six friends than lose your entire ship and all its company.'

"Your master thought deeply on this for some time and then said, 'Come then, Goddess, answer me truthfully. Is there not some way to sail around Charybdis and then fight off the monster Skylla when she attacks my companions?'

"Fair Circe shook her head, her tresses rustling like the leaves in a storm.

"'Intrepid warrior! Your mind is forever full of fighting and battle. Will you not give way even to the gods? She is not mortal, but an *immortal* thing, monstrous and bloodthirsty; there is no fighting against her, nor is there any defense. Your only hope is to run from her, for if you waste time arming yourself and slowing your ship to aim your spears and arrows, she is likely to attack twice, thus killing twelve men and not six.'

"Truly then, Argos, your master sighed and covered his face in his hands so that the goddess could not see his grief. Then, after he had composed himself, he said, 'I have heard you, Goddess, though your advice pains me dear. Tell me more, though. After we escape dread Skylla, what travails await us then?'"

"More hardship awaits my master?" I cry out.

"Foo-foo-foolish pet," the owl says. "You-you-you who-who-who have never left this island know nothing of life beyond its shores. The gods play with man as you-you-you would a pup, teasing him and allowing to think himself brave and power-ful, only to strike him with a sharp claw. That is the way with gods. Now, let me continue, for I grow hungry, and you-you-you have promised me soft-boned chicks for dinner.

"Here is what the goddess said: 'Good Odysseus, after you have sailed clear of the monster, you will, after a few days, reach the island of Thrinakia, where you will see pastured on the meadows there fat cattle, sheep, and oxen. Teiresias him-self told you this, did he not? So if you obey him and leave the flocks alone, keeping your mind fixed on your return to Ithaka, you will all make your way home, after much suffering.

But if you disobey Teiresias and harm his flocks, then I will allow the gods to take their revenge, and though you might still reach Ithaka, none of your companions will.'"

I jump to my feet and growl. "He will lose all his companions? That cannot be! Surely you misremember what she said, wise owl!"

"I misremember nothing, dog! That is my curse. Now sit and listen; my story is nearly done, for just then golden Eos herself came, bathing your master and fair Circe in her light. I left when Eos appeared, as owls may not be seen in daylight without bringing bad luck, so I know not what your master said in reply to Circe. That is my tale, though it be one of woe to you-you-you and your master."

For a moment I say nothing. How could I, after hearing my master's fate? Finally, though, I speak. "I thank you, then, for recounting your tale, Father Owl. Now, as to my end of the bargain, give me time to return to my master's farmland, and I shall drive the chicks out into their open coop where you will find them defenseless against your sharp talons, though I risk a beating for doing so."

"Who-who-who would lay a hand against Odysseus's hound, Boar Slayer?"

"In truth, there is only one who would dare it. His name is

Melanthios and his charge is the lesser animals, the fowl and some sheep. But think nothing of it, Night Flyer. My sharp teeth will find his flesh soon enough."

Saying that, I make my way back to my master's land and do as I had promised. But the owl does not come, nor does he appear on the next night. On the third afternoon, a magpie tells me that a great owl had been seen flying north toward shrouded Mount Nerito, and I wonder then if I had spoken to a goddess instead of an owl, for they often take the shape of animals.

CHAPTER XIX

/ᴑ/ᴑ/ᴑ/ᴑ/ᴑ/ᴑ/ᴑ/ᴑ/ᴑ/ᴑ/ᴑ/ᴑ/ᴑ/ᴑ/

The blind philosopher

A strange dog is trotting up the road leading to my master's estate. I can see him from the ridge near the sheep paddock, and I follow him as he draws closer. He is sturdily built, although his ribs show through his fur, and he holds his head erect. His short fur is a mottled mix of brown and black, and his tail is not more than a stump. Truly he is a mongrel, yet oftentimes, they are more intelligent than well-bred dogs, which do no work, but eat from the hands of their noble owners. When I approach him, he rolls onto his back, as is the custom everywhere.

"I am Argos, the Boar Slayer," I tell him. "Please rise."

"I am called Epirus," he answers after he stands up.

I do not recognize his accent.

"Well met," I say. "What brings you to the estate of Odysseus? We do not need shepherds or guard dogs. Are you hungry, for you look poorly fed?"

"Alas, Argos, it is true. I am hungry, but so is my master, Galenos. We arrived here on your island not long ago from Samos to see a healer, and already we are destitute, having been robbed twice."

"Twice! That is two times too many, Epirus. Tell me what happened. You said you came to see a healer?"

"Yes, a man who is said to have knowledge of herbs to cure many things. My master's eyesight is failing him, so we came to your isle with the hope that the healer would offer relief. Instead he charged my master all his coins before applying the cure, a paste that burned my master's eyes and has rendered him blind. So now my master has been robbed of his possessions and his sight. Surely he has been stolen from twice, would you agree?"

"Yes, he has been doubly aggrieved. But tell me, what was the healer's name?"

"A name I shall never forget, Boar Slayer. His name is Callius."

I knew he would say that name. And I know what I have to do.

After a moment to think, I say, "Epirus, return here with your master, Galenos, later today. My mistress is kind to supplicants, and she will feed you both. Of that I am sure."

Epirus smiles and licks his lips.

"I thank you, Argos, and we will come as you suggest. But what of tomorrow and the next day? My master is a philosopher, not a beggar. He knows many things, but not how to live as a blind man with his hand out."

"Alas, it is true, Epirus. If we do not eat every day, our stomachs pinch, and then even a philosopher cannot think. But tell me, does your master know numbers and letters, stars and stories, and all the things that wise men should know?"

"Yes, he does, Argos. On Samos he was a famous philosopher and tutor, and much loved by all his pupils. But here he is just a blind and hungry man."

"Friend," I say, "you need tell me no more. Bring your master back today when Apollo's chariot is past its meridian, and we shall see if the gods are good."

"I will do so, Argos. I leave now so that I can return soon with my master."

The dog turns and lopes away, back toward the village, and I check on the flocks, which are grazing happily on tender spring grass.

Apollo's chariot climbs higher and soon passes overhead. The tutor Callius arrives, late as usual, and enters the house. I follow him inside. He smells of stale wine and garlic and immediately scolds the servant girl for not bringing him cold water to drink. In his hands he carries a scroll for writing and his leather strap. When he puts them down to take his cup, I snatch up the scroll in my jaws and carry it away. The fool runs after me.

I run slowly, looking back to make sure he stays close enough to think he can catch me. Twice I put down the scroll, only to snatch it in time to run away again. Eventually I lead him to the sheep's barn. The door is open, as I knew it would be, and I run inside. Callius follows me, and once I am inside, I drop the scroll. How he curses me then! What vile things he says! Still, I let him pick up the scroll before I show my teeth. He retreats to the back of the barn, afraid of my jaws, and then I run out and push the door closed with my nose. And then Telemachos, who has seen it all, bars it.

I hear a bark and look up the path. Epirus and his master, a white-bearded old man with a cane, are making their way slowly toward my master's estate. Telemachos runs over to the old man and offers his arm. Soon the blind man is seated at our table, and servants are bringing him barley soup and thick bread, and Epirus is chewing on an ox bone. While he eats, Galenos tells Telemachos stories of great warriors and poets and the names of Achaian kings long dead and forgotten. After some time my mistress comes in, bows, and touches Galenos's feet, as is the customary way to greet an elderly philosopher.

Then, rising, she turns to Telemachos and says, "Son, where is your tutor? Should you not be with him now?"

"He is late, mother," Telemachos says. "He is always late. But Galenos is also a tutor."

Then he begins to recite the stories that the old man had told him. "You see? He knows many things that Callius does not."

At the sound of the tutor's name, Epirus raises his ears and Galenos turns his head, blinking his sightless eyes.

"His tutor is Callius, my queen?" asks Galenos. "Bald, fat Callius?"

"That is he, and he *was* my son's tutor," my mistress says. "But he is no longer, if you will take his charge."

"I would be honored to do so," the old man says, smiling. "May I start immediately? This Callius fellow has filled the boy's head with nonsense and errors, and there is no time to lose. Fortunately, young Telemachos is very intelligent, and so it will not take long to set him right, with words and not straps."

Telemachos jumps up and embraces my mistress.

"You see, Mother?" he whispers. "Not every tutor is cruel. Galenos is kind and smart too!"

Later that afternoon, as Apollo's chariot passes over Mount Nerito, Telemachos lifts the bar on the barn door, and Callius staggers out into the open. Epirus is waiting for him. My new friend chases Callius down the trail that leads to the harbor, and I do not bother to learn his fate. There are some things not worth knowing, the philosophers will tell you.

CHAPTER XX

/@/@/@/@/@/@/@/@/@/@/@/@/@/@/@

The Sirens' song

With the owl having left, I am desperate to learn my master's fate after leaving Aiaia, but what birds fly near there? I wondered, for the fish near Aiaia swim deep below the surface.

"There is only one bird who might," a gull tells me one morning. "Seek out the black sea raven, whom some call cormorant, and who dives deep and feeds near that island, where other seabirds do not. There is a nesting colony of cormorants south of here. Perhaps they will have news. But tread carefully near their nests, loyal one, for they are fierce mothers."

"Fierce, fierce, fierce," his brethren echo.

I thank the gull, and now that the sheep are put to pasture, I have time to run south and seek the cormorant colony. Hermes himself puts wings on my feet, and I run fast along the shore until I see a secluded cove, protected from the harsh wind, and I hear the squawking of a hundred sea ravens. I approach them slowly but try not to appear stealthy and arouse suspicion. I do not wish to feel a hundred beaks pecking on my head.

When I am close, I bark once and sit down to wait for their nest mother to come to me. A few moments later, I hear the beat of powerful wings, and a large black-winged cormorant alights near me. Her underside is as white as a cloud, and her bright eyes shine like embers.

"Greetings, Deep Diver," I say. "I hope your nests are full."

"They are indeed, Argos," she says, snapping her long, pointed beak.

"You know my name?"

"Of course. We have been waiting for you."

"You know then what I seek? To learn of my master's fate upon leaving Aiaia?"

"Yes, I know his fate, for I perched on the prow of his ship myself. I would have come to you sooner, but I could not leave my eggs. Now that you are here, I will tell you what I saw, but you must promise to keep your hackles down and growl not, for I won't have you upsetting my sisters."

"So I promise, Nest Mother. Tell me and spare not my feelings, for I would know the truth."

The cormorant stretches out her black wings and begins.

"On the deck of the great ship, your master's companions wound the stern ropes waiting for his command, but before great Odysseus could give the order to row, fair Circe sent a following wind that filled the sails, and soon their black prow sliced through the sea, with the steersman holding her steady. Then did your master address his companions sorrowfully.

"Standing at the bow, he said, 'Friends, it is not right that only I know what the goddess has divined, so I will tell you all that we can escape destruction.'

"'Tell us everything, brave one,' one man cried, 'for we are your stalwart companions and have suffered much, though without you we would all have perished.'

"Hearing this, your master told his companions about the Sirens.

"'Tie me hard, in hurtful bonds,' he commanded, 'for I would hear them sing. Your ears, though, will be stopped with wax, for to hear their voices would lead to calamity.'

"Quickly the men did what your master said, some lashing him to the mast while others melted the wax. Fair Circe slowed the wind so that the preparations could be made, and just as the last man's ears were filled and the final knot was tied around his feet, the sweet song of the Sirens could be heard above the wind.

"'Come this way, honored Odysseus,' they sang. 'Stay your ship so that you can listen to our singing, for no one has ever not stopped to hear us, the songs that spring from our lips, without being well pleased. We will sing of the war with the Trojans and your mighty feats.'

"So they sang in sweet melodies, and your master was enthralled, begging his men to slow their oars and steer toward the island. But noble Eurylochos and loyal Perimedes rose up straightaway and fastened more bonds to him and urged their companions to row the harder. Soon they had passed that haunted island and lost the sounds of the Sirens' enticing song. Then, and only then, did they untie their brave leader, who was bruised and bleeding from straining against the lashes, yet he thanked his men and called them noble.

"Then, after a short time, a lookout cried that he saw smoke and heavy surf. So frightening were the sea swells that the hardened sailors dropped their oars and prayed to their gods. With no one rowing, the black ship stilled, and your master had to go up and down the ship admonishing his men and urging them to be brave.

"'Dear friends,' he cried. 'Did we not face that most terrible evil, the Cyclops, together? Did I not lead you safely from him? I think that this day you will also remember how I lead you from harm! Dip your oars deep into the breaking water and stay away from the smoke of the cauldron and crashing waves. Row toward the sea rock. That is our best way.'"

"But surely he told the men about Skylla?" I ask the cormorant. I can't believe my master would lead them unknowingly into grave danger.

"No, Argos," the cormorant replies. "Of that plague he said nothing. What could he do? Since the monster cannot be killed, his only choice was to lose six men, or risk losing the entire ship."

Poor master! What terrible lives men lead in order to amuse their gods.

"So steering clear of the dread whirlpool, they rowed toward the sea rock. And there terrible Skylla swooped her long sharp arms down toward the black ship and snatched six of your master's finest men, his best rowers, who were stationed at the stern, and hurled them down onto the rocks. Then, as they cried out for your master to rescue them, she ate his fallen men. It was the most pitiful scene I have ever looked upon."

Deep in my chest a growl begins to form, but I do not make a sound.

After a moment, the cormorant continues.

"After finally escaping Skylla, as Circe promised, they sailed swiftly toward the island of Thrinakia, ruled by the god Helios, where his fat sheep and oxen bleated and mewed. Your master's men begged him to stop and purchase or steal at least one of the beasts so that they might offer a sacrifice to their fallen comrades, and feed themselves fresh meat as well.

"Then did Odysseus repeat to his crew Teiresias's warning that they must not touch the flocks belonging to Helios, for the gods would punish them if they did. But led by Eurylochos, the men pleaded to be allowed to harbor on Thrinakia, promising your master they would not slaughter any ox or sheep. Odysseus relented, and so they rested in the harbor and ate the food Circe had given them, then mourned their lost companions before settling down to sleep.

"During the night a storm came, and then after, the next day, the winds blew in from the south and east, hard winds that kept them from sailing. The winds came the next day and the next day after, and did not stop for thirty days, pinning your master and his men on the island, and eventually their food ran out.

"I would have brought them fish, loyal one," the cormorant says, "but even I found little food in the water, and so I could not help them."

I nod my head to thank her and ask her to continue. Slowly

I feel my hackles rising as I sense where the story is heading, so I urge her to be quick.

"After their provisions were depleted, your master's men turned to hunting and fishing, but the island had few animals except for livestock, and the rocky coasts tore their nets and left them empty. Soon hunger pinched their stomachs and left them too tired to hunt. One morning Odysseus left his men in order to find a quiet place to pray to the gods for mercy, to still the fierce winds and give them a course to sail. But instead of answering his prayers, the gods laid a blanket of sleep on him. While he was gone, Eurylochos called the rest of the men together and gave them evil counsel.

"'Listen to me, companions,' he said. 'Surely no death is worse for wretched mortals than to die of hunger. Yet all around us, sheep and oxen grow fat in the meadows, while Odysseus prays to the gods for direction. Come, let us slaughter one of Helios's oxen; there are many and one will not be missed. Then, when we return to Ithaka, we will build a temple in Helios's honor and ask for forgiveness. But if this angers him and he dooms our ships to sink, I would rather eat waves than eat nothing, growing ever weaker on this desolate island.'

"Hearing this, the men agreed and selected a handsome, horn-curved ox and slaughtered him, burned his entrails, and made libations to Helios, before cutting the meat and cooking it on spits. Late in the evening, when sleep had left your master's eyelids, he rose and made his way back to where his men were camped. As he drew closer, he saw the cookfires and the wind brought him the scent of cooked meat. I heard your master cry, 'Father Zeus, why did you lull me to sleep? Now my men have committed a deed most monstrous, and we are cursed again!'

"Just then, although the night was clear, a bolt of lightning split the sky," says the cormorant. "Zeus was angry, and Odysseus knew they were doomed. He woke his men, crying, 'Faithless men! Why did you break the one promise I asked of you?'

"But none of his men answered truthfully, instead blaming the other, until Eurylochos said, 'What is done is done, brave Odysseus. Surely the gods will not punish us for eating the food they put before us! We have promised to build a temple for Helios when we return, and we will do so. Eat with us, regain your strength, and with Zeus's help, we will soon leave this cursed land.'

"But before Odysseus could answer, they all heard the bellow of an ox, though there was none close by. Again they heard the sound, and one of the men who had been watching the cookfires cried out for Zeus's mercy, for the sound of the oxen was coming from the meat on the spit, and they knew then they would not be forgiven.

"For six more days your master and his companions remained on the island, filling their bellies with meat and praying at night for mercy. On the seventh day, the hard eastern winds died, and the men made their black ship ready, hoisting its white sails to catch the western wind. I perched myself on the prow again, and later that morning they departed."

"Soon they were on the open water, and the cheer in them rose as their sleek vessel put the dread island behind them. Then, late in the sun-filled afternoon, the sun disappeared and a dark cloud hovered over the black ship. The peaceful western wind grew hard and bitter, and then a terrible wind snapped the forestays and sent the mast crashing down on the steersman, pounding him dead. But before Odysseus's men could take their oars, Zeus hurled a bolt of lightning down upon them, throwing all the men from their ship into the gray water, where they bobbed like sea crows until they drowned.

"Thus did the gods punish them all, save your master," says the cormorant. "He was able to cling to the broken mast and float above the waves while his companions met their fates."

I whimper now, like a young pup first weaned, and I am not

ashamed of it. I cannot bear the thought of my master alone on that cold black sea, clinging to the shards of his swift ship.

"But he still lives, does he not, Sea Flyer?" I ask with dread in my voice. "What happened then? Did help arrive?"

"Alas, Argos, I could do nothing but give him hope. I stayed near him, flying circles above him by day, and at night. I perched on the mast itself, so your master would not be alone. When he hungered, I caught small fish for him, which he ate as we birds do, in one swallow."

"I thank you for staying with him," I say, and she nods her head in acknowledgement. "But tell me, where did the currents take him then?"

"The currents took your master back toward Skylla and dreaded Charybdis," she replies, "but this time Zeus protected Odysseus, and terrible Skylla did not swoop down with her fierce claws, and Charybdis only spun your master and threw him back into the open sea still perched on the mast. I followed him for nine more days, bringing him fish to eat, and on the tenth night the currents brought him to the island Ogygia, home of the lovely nymph Kalypso, who talks with mortals. There she oiled his flesh and fed him meat and figs. But she laid a trap for him, as well."

How much more can one man suffer?

"What kind of trap, black-winged one?" I ask, feeling my hackles rise again. "Surely the nymph will protect him!"

The cormorant does not answer. Instead she turns over shells strewn along the water's edge, as if looking for food. I press her more firmly. "What manner of trap was it, sea raven?"

Finally the cormorant lifts her beak. "Remember your promise to me, Boar Slayer," she says firmly. "Raise not your voice again."

I clamp my jaws shut and wait. The cormorant lifts her long neck to look back over to her colony and then says these words.

"While your master slept, exhausted from clinging to his mast for ten days, cunning Kalypso had her servants chop down all the large trees on the island and burn them!"

But I am puzzled. "Why would she do this?" I ask. The cormorant stares at me with her yellow eyes until I answer my own question.

"With no trees on the island," I say finally, "my master cannot construct a boat. He is trapped!"

Then, despite my promise, I race through the cormorant colony, barking and snapping, spilling nests and crushing eggs beneath my feet.

It is the most shameful moment of my life.

CHAPTER XXI

Stag hunting

Galenos, the blind tutor, has taught Telemachos well. Tonight, now that the cowardly suitors have left for the evening, the youth comes to me and bids me to follow him. We climb a hill overlooking the shore and sit together in the gathering darkness, with only the night-flying bats to keep us company. Telemachos has brought with him a woven mantle, and he spreads it out on the grassy hillside for us to lie upon. Then he rests his head on my flank, and after a few minutes—during which I think he has fallen asleep—he asks, "Argos, do you know how the universe began?"

Of course dogs have no use for this type of speculation, so I remain silent, though I lick his ear so that he will continue.

"You see, according to Galenos, when the universe was born,

there was only Chaos, the void of emptiness between heaven and earth. Then Erubus was formed, the place of unending death and night."

I whimper as he says this, but Telemachos adds hastily, "Not night like this, Argos, but ceaseless, silent blackness. Then Eros was formed from their union, and she separated night and day, and then Gaea appeared, our mother earth. She was joined by Uranus, who made the heavens, like those above us."

I confess now that I am growing drowsy. The mantle on which I lie is soft, and this story of the gods is not like the rousing adventures that Telemachos usually tells me. But Telemachos continues his tale, and so I remain awake, as a dog must do, but with one eye closed.

"Then Gaea and Uranus created the Cyclopes, the hundred-armed Hecatoncheires, and the twelve Titans," the boy continues. "But Uranus was threatened by his children and forced them back into Gaea's deepest canyons and gorges, which angered her. She convinced the youngest Titan, Kronos, to help her overthrow Uranus and he did, but he too, after marrying his sister Rhea, became cruel and jealous of his offspring, and swallowed them as they were born."

I growl hearing this, and Telemachos pats my head to comfort me before continuing.

"Let me finish, Boar Slayer." He laughs. "You see, Rhea hid her sixth-born child, giving it to the nymphs to raise, and wrapped a stone in its place, which Kronos swallowed instead. Do you know who that child was, Argos?"

I lick the boy's ear again. The child was Zeus. Every dog knows that.

"That's right. Zeus. And once he was grown, he returned to Mount Olympus and tricked Kronos into swallowing a magic drink, which made him heave up Zeus's other siblings from his stomach. Then there was a great war, greater even than the one my father fought against the Trojans. Kronos recruited all but three of the Titans to his side, while Zeus freed the Cyclopes and the Hecatoncheires from Gaea's caves to fight alongside him. After many terrible battles, Zeus, armed with lightning bolts, prevailed. Then he exiled his foes, except for the Titan Atlas, whom he punished by forcing him to hold the earth on his shoulders."

But who or what holds up Atlas? I want to ask, but I do not do so, because then Telemachos begins to name the constellations glittering above us, and that is something no dog can remain awake for, and so I fall asleep.

Sometime later Telemachos sits up, and I spring to my feet with a snarl. I sniff the wind and find no threatening scent of wolf or man, but still the fur along my back rises. Someone or something is on the hill with us; that I know. Telemachos senses it as well.

"Who's there?" he calls out. "Announce yourself!"

Telemachos draws his xiphos, but it is I who see it first: a large stag standing over the ridge, looking down on us. Even in the darkness I can see its enormous antlers, as wide as a spear, perched high above its head. For a moment I think I should give chase, but something tells me not to—a voice in the wind, perhaps. So I remain beside Telemachos, who now sees it too.

"Leave it be, Argos," Telemachos says softly. "This is not a night for hunting."

Then the stag leaps to the crest of another hill and disappears from view. After a few moments Telemachos rolls up the mantle, and we begin to make our way down to my master's house. Several times we stop and look back from whence we had come. The stag appears again, high on the ridge, watching us. Surely, I think, the stag is an omen sent by the gods. But what does it portend, fortune or misfortune? How does one know?

Then I remember something Galenos had said to Telemachos when the boy asked a similar question. The tutor said, "An omen may be good or evil; we know not which until after the moment has passed and the deed has been done, and then we make our claim to have known all along."

Tonight one of the suitors claims to have seen a giant stag grazing near Mount Nerito. "Its antlers were as broad as a man is tall," he announces, but the rest of the suitors jeer at him. "There are no more giant stags on Ithaka," one sneers. "Our forefathers killed the last great deer a generation ago," he continues. "And the mountain wolves got the rest," another suitor adds. Soon they are discussing other matters: the swiftest ships, the greatest javelin throwers, and the best grapes for winemaking. But Telemachos looks at me with raised brows, and I know we will be hunting tomorrow. Hunting for giant stag.

We leave before dawn's rosy fingers reach my master's estate. My mistress is awake and bids us good hunting, and Telemachos kisses her and then touches her feet to show respect. She has raised him well. When we reach the top of the ridge we turn around, and she waves to us one last time before entering the house. *How lovely she looks in the dawn,* I think.

Telemachos carries a knife, his bow, and a quiver of arrows; that is all, except for some dried meat and honey. We are to travel light and fast. I think we both had the same thought:

a few of the younger suitors had seemed interested in the stag sighting also. They wanted its antlers to prove their merit to my mistress, and so we must kill it first.

Telemachos is young and strong, and together we run swiftly along the goat trails that lead to Mount Nerito. We stop only so that I might sniff the air for our quarry's scent, but as we reach the mountain pastures, we slow our pace and approach stealthily. A stag does not grow large if it is not watchful for wolves and hunters. I lead Telemachos to the stream that feeds a small pond on the west side of the mountain. There we both drink our fill, and then, near the pond, we find a laurel-covered perch in which to wait for our prey. I know many deer stop at the pond to drink during the heat of the day, and that is our best chance to see the stag. As we wait, we see many smaller deer approach the pond—deer we would have taken any other day. But we hunt only the giant stag, so Telemachos lets them live.

Apollo's chariot is high in the sky when I hear branches breaking. In such stillness the noise echoes as loud as an army striking their shields. Telemachos hears it too. He puts his hand on my shoulder to steady himself while he readies his bow. We both see it at the same time: our prey. The stag's swooping antlers appear first, followed by his handsome head, then his powerful shoulders. He stops at the edge of the clearing to sniff the wind, and then he slowly steps toward the glistening pond, turning his proud head side to side, ever watchful.

Truly, I had never seen such a magnificent creature! Now that it is daylight, I can see that his pelt is nearly bloodred and his antlers are as long and sharp as a javelin. His neck is thicker than a man and his hindquarters ripple with muscle as he walks. But it is his eyes that give him away. They are the eyes of a god. Telemachos knows it as well.

"That is not a stag," he whispers as he slowly lowers his bow.

Just then we hear the twang of a bowstring. I bark a warning, but it is too late. The stag leaps, but before he lands, an arrow protrudes from his shoulder. The stag bellows and begins to run, twisting and zigzagging through the underbrush, as two more arrows pierce the air. But they miss.

"Come, Argos!" Telemachos whispers. "We must find the stag before the other hunters do!"

We back away slowly until the laurel leaves close in behind us, and then we run in the direction that the stag has taken. It is easy—too easy—to follow its bloody trail, but even a wounded stag can outrun a man for some distance, until it must lie down to die. After a few minutes I realize where the stag is running—to the summit of Mount Nerito. I know a shorter way to get there. I bark and change direction; Telemachos follows me. Soon, we are climbing up steep cliffs and clambering over boulders, but straight up is the fastest way.

My only fear is that the stag will collapse before it reaches the summit, and the hunters will find it before we do. Telemachos knows what I do: a god in the form of an animal can be killed. Neither can it change back into a god with a human object in its flesh. We have to find the stag and remove the arrow lodged in its shoulder, or the god will die. And then the other gods will punish us.

Below us, I can hear the cries of the hunters running up the trail that leads to the summit. We both know their voices; they are the young suitors who ate at our table the night before. If they catch us with their stag, they will think we intended to claim it as our own, and they will kill us. And Telemachos has no shield or javelin, only his bow and knife. As we near the summit, the brush and small trees begin to thin, leaving us exposed to the hunters, so we climb even faster. At the top of the mountain is a small clearing surround by a ring of boulders. It is there I know we will find the stag. And it is so.

The stag is lying on his side. Foam covers his mouth and neck, and blood still seeps from the arrow, which has worked its way deeper into his shoulder. He tries to rise and run, but there is nowhere for him to go, and he is too weak to stand very long. Telemachos runs up to the stag and tugs him gently to the ground. Then Telemachos withdraws his knife. The stag's eyes widen in fear.

"Lie still, immortal one," Telemachos says gently. "We seek only to help you."

I stand guard by the trailhead from which the hunters will soon emerge, so I do not see Telemachos cut the arrow out, but I hear him whisper, "I have it," when he has done so. Then I hear him cry, "Goddess, have mercy on us!"

I turn and see Artemis herself.

She stands taller than a man, but her face and build are slender and lovely to behold. In one hand she holds the arrow that felled her, and the other hand cups Telemachos's chin.

"I thank thee, Telemachos, son of Odysseus, for coming to my aid," she says, with a voice that rings like a golden bell. "In return, I will grant this: that your arrows shall never miss their mark, whenever you draw your bow."

I bark a warning. The hunters are coming close.

"Goddess, we must all flee!" Telemachos whispers.

Artemis smiles and brings her hands together. Suddenly a fierce wind rises up, swirling the leaves around us, and then I hear the harsh squeal of a boar. He appears out of a small cave and charges toward the trail where the hunters are climbing up to us. We watch the boar disappear, and a few moments later we hear the screams of terrified men. I turn back around, and Telemachos stands alone. He is rubbing his eyes, and the goddess is gone.

I run up to him and tug at his bow, leading him away from the summit. Soon his head has cleared, and we are bounding down the slope. We don't stop running until we reach my master's estate. Tonight, when the suitors arrive for their customary dinner, three chairs are empty at the table.

And they will never be filled, I think.

BOOK II

CHAPTER XXII

/ʘ/ʘ/ʘ/ʘ/ʘ/ʘ/ʘ/ʘ/ʘ/ʘ/ʘ/ʘ/ʘ/ʘ/ʘ

A strange dog

Nearly seven years have passed with no news of my master, although I have asked every bird and sea animal that alights or lands on Ithaka if they have news for me. They report nothing, yet I think he lives, as does my mistress, for nearly every night she sends servants to the harbor seeking news from incoming ships. I have much to do here: the flocks need my vigilance, my mistress needs a guard, and Telemachos needs a companion.

How tall he has grown! How handsome and strong! In the summer his skin turns to bronze, and his curly dark hair becomes like gold ringlets. Truly he is his father's son. But he has few companions. The other boys his age have gone to sea or become apprentices to winemakers and blacksmiths, farmers, and merchants. But except for hunts, Telemachos remains close to home. He is the son of a king and will one day rule Ithaka, but he cannot leave his mother, for the suitors would dishonor her if he did. So he waits for his father, Odysseus, to return.

The years have been hard on me. My muzzle is now flecked with white, and my hearing is not as sharp as it once was. In the cold mornings, my joints are stiff and my hips ache. I have reached the age when I should remain inside, lying on a fleece rug curled up next to a fire. But that is not my fate. So I too wait for my master, Odysseus, to return.

Daily the suitors come and insult the servants and eat our stores of food, olive oil, and wine, so there is no end to the misery on Ithaka. Our house grows poorer; the suitors, fatter. I seldom see my mistress; she has become a prisoner in her own home. If she goes to the village, the other women spread false gossip about her; they cannot believe a wife can be so loyal to a man considered dead. Moreover, while the suitors pursue my mistress, the other women in the village are left unmarried and resentful, for she is the prize the greatest men on the island seek. So she remains inside the estate, hidden away from the quick tongues and hard stares of the village folk, with only her servants, her son, and a dog for company.

As for me, I find my way to the harbor every day or so, in case there is news from the gulls. This morning I am at my usual post near the harbor when a mangy cur approaches me. I know the dog by sight only—we have never spoken, and she is newly arrived on Ithaka. But she is known around the harbor as a fish eater, and most dogs do not eat fish. Moreover, her lineage is suspect. She is at least ten shades of gray and brown, and her fur is not sleek and thick but wiry and sparse. Pink, scaly skin shows through along her hindquarters, and her eyes are small and runny. Truly, she is misbegotten. So when she says she has something to tell me, I am skeptical. What could a fish-eating mongrel have to say to me? Still, I let her approach.

"You are Argos, loyal servant to Odysseus, are you not?" the dog asks, without lowering her head or rolling onto her back as a lesser dog might.

"I am. What do you have to tell me, stranger? And what is your name and lineage so that I may call you properly?"

This is cruel of me and I regret my words instantly, but the gulls have not come for several days, and I am worried and anxious about my master, so I am not in the frame of mind to be interrogated by a mutt. But she seems to take little offense.

"You need not know my name nor my lineage, sir. This matter concerns you, not me," she says without reproach.

I look at the dog more closely. Her ribs show through her skin and her stomach is shrunken. She is not a handsome dog, to be sure, and she smells as if she slept in fishnets, yet she carries herself well, and her eyes, although no doubt infected, are bright with intelligence.

"Forgive my manners, friend," I say. "I am much concerned about my master and forget myself sometimes. Now tell me, what do you wish to say?"

She steps closer, and it takes all my will not to wrinkle my nose in disgust. "Your master's son, Telemachos, is in danger," she says.

And then she runs away.

"Wait!" I cry. I bark several times, but she doesn't stop. Instead, she disappears in the alleys that bisect the harbor. I start to chase after her, but just then a gull flies over my shoulder and lands on the jetty. I run to him. Soon more gulls arrive.

"What news do you bring, High Flyer?" I demand, keeping an eye on the alley where the dog disappeared. "Have you seen my master?"

"Not I-I-I, Boar Slayer, but another gull may have. A few days ago, a sister said the fog covering Kalypso's is-is-island lifted for just a few moments, and she saw a man there, staring out at the sea. Then the fog closed in again, and she saw him no more."

A whimper escapes my lips.

"Be brave, loyal Argos. Your master is the Wi-W-Wily One, is he not? Did he not conquer Troy itself with his cunning? He will escape that i-i-island one day, for surely his fate has yet to be written."

"Fate! Fate! Fate!" screech the other gulls.

"Thank you, White Wing. I will take your counsel. Now, I have another question. You saw me speaking to that dog that just ran away. Can you fly high and look for her? I do not know why she left so suddenly, but she has much to tell me, I think."

"I-I-I know where she is, Argos. While you were speaking, a fishing boat came in on the other side-side-side of the harbor. No doubt she heard its bell and ran to meet it. She is a strange dog and eats only fish; the boat brings her dinner. You will find her there, poking through the nets, I-I-I am sure of it."

Saying this, the gull spreads its wings and rises above me.

"Farewell," he cries.

"Farewell! Farewell! Farewell!" his flock repeats, pummeling the air with their wings.

I bark once and then run down along the beach to the other

side of the harbor. The gull was right: I find the fish eater gobbling down a baby squid. Fishermen mill about, so I say nothing to her. While I watch, the dog eats two squid and several small fish, including fins and tails. Truly, I have never seen such a thing. Then, when she is satiated, the strange dog looks at me once and then trots back to an alley. I follow her to the entrance of a small temple for a goddess, though I know not who. Finally the dog sits back on her haunches and waits for me to speak.

"You said my master's son was in danger, sister. How do you know this? What kind of danger does he face?" I demand.

But instead of answering me, the strange dog enters the temple, which is just a small building held up by eight columns. In the center lies a bronze bowl for offerings, but there are none. The dog sniffs the bowl and then turns to face me.

"Please, friend, tell me what plot concerns Telemachos! If he is in danger, I must be there to protect him. That is my duty."

"Do you know who this temple is dedicated to, Argos?" the dog asks, ignoring my plea.

I shake my head, trying to remain calm.

"I thought as much. It is dedicated to Amphitrite, the sea goddess. Yet no one comes to it, even though the island has many fishermen and sailors. Why is that, Boar Slayer?"

Her questions are maddening and for a moment my lips curl into a snarl. Was Telemachos not in peril?

"I do not know, sister. There is a larger temple for Poseidon along the shore. The sailors and fishermen go there to make their offerings to the earth shaker."

The strange dog sneezes, and a wave of fish breath sweeps over me.

And then I know who she is.

"Yet, this is also a beautiful temple," I say. "It is not right that no one comes here. I shall lead Telemachos here this very evening, and he will make an offering, I am sure."

The strange dog smiles and licks her lips. Her tongue, though, was not pink, but as green as the sea.

"Goddess," I say. "Take pity on me, your loyal servant, and tell me who threatens my master's son. I must know."

How that dog's eyes glow when I say that.

"Hear me then, Argos, most loyal of dogs," she says. "There is a suitor by the name of Akakios who plans ill for young Telemachos. Akakios owns many ships, and his plot is to kidnap Telemachos and send him far away by sea. Thinking her son dead, your mistress Penelope will have to choose a husband, since she has no heirs."

"How will Akakios ensure that my mistress marries him and

not another suitor, for there are many to choose from, cursed be they all?" I ask.

"The evildoer will tell Penelope during his courtship that he has heard from a sailor that Telemachos lives. If Penelope promises to marry him, then he will send out his entire fleet to find him. What choice will she have?"

The fur along my back rises, and my ears flatten. Already, though, a plan begins to form in my thoughts.

"Thank you, Goddess," I say. "I will keep my promise to you. If I can save Telemachos, many offerings will be made in your honor."

I lower my head and lick the dog's strangely shaped paw. There are webs between her claws.

"Go now, and quickly, Argos," the dog goddess says. "Akakios strikes soon."

I turn to leave, then stop.

"Goddess, why do you concern yourself about Telemachos? It must be more than just your empty temple that brought you here to Ithaka, is it not?"

But the dog is not there. Instead, while my back was turned, she has changed into the shining goddess Amphitrite herself. She is glorious to look upon, and I have to close my eyes.

"The ways of the gods are not for you to know, Boar Slayer," she says. "But I will tell you this. My husband, Poseidon, the earth shaker, hates your master and seeks to destroy him. Yet I love my husband not and would see his plans thwarted. I cannot save your master at this time, but I can save his son. That is why I came to you. Now hurry."

I turn and run. In a short time I reach my master's estate, and there I catch my breath and begin fleshing out my plans. Soon I have it. Not for nothing am I the Wily-One's pet; I will use my master's trick against my foe.

CHAPTER XXIII

What the goose heard

Last night Father Zeus stormed. Never have I seen such arrows of lightning nor heard thunder as if a thousand bronze shields were struck at once. The servants in the house extinguished all the candles, not wishing to provoke his anger with their light. The animals bedded down in the barns, and even I took shelter in a cave while I waited for Zeus to find appeasement. Finally rose-colored dawn has come, and the last roll of thunder has abated. Outside I hear a goose calling, so I leave the cave and take the trail down to the harbor. I find the goose perched on the dock. His head is folded under his wing in the manner that birds have, and I have to bark twice before he straightens his long neck.

Although they are dull-witted, of all the winged creatures,

none flies higher than the goose, and that is why I have sought him. *Perhaps he has flown over Mount Olympus and knows why Father Zeus was angry*, I think.

"Greetings, Cloud Flyer," I address him. I stay some distance away as I say this, for it is commonly known that geese are the foulest-smelling bird.

"Greetings to you, loyal Argos," he replies. "Come closer. I have much to tell you."

Reluctantly, I step closer. "What news do you bring, Sir Goose?"

"Closer, Argos. My voice is tired from calling my brothers, and I must leave soon."

Before stepping closer I ask, "Do you have news of my master, noble goose?"

"Aye, Boar Slayer. That is why I have stopped here. The gods spoke your master's name last night."

Hearing this, the fur on my back stands up, and I approach him with my head low in respect and to avoid his breath.

"Please," I beg. "Tell me everything."

Before speaking, the goose curls his neck three times and then belches loudly.

"Ahh, much better," he says. "Now, what was I talking about?"

"You said the gods spoke of my master," I remind him, stepping back a little.

"Yes, of course. Well, I was leading our flock last night and decided to take us over Mount Olympus. My brothers and I saw the gods holding counsel there, so we stopped to listen. Most of the gods were present, Argos, and Olympus shone with their glory. Fair Athena was in attendance, and she addressed her father thus: 'Father Zeus,' she spoke. 'I beg you to remember your servant, noble Odysseus. For seven years he has been constrained on Kalypso's island, suffering with a heavy heart, longing to see his son, Telemachos, now nearly grown, and his long-enduring wife.'"

My master spoken of in front of Father Zeus himself!

"What did Lord Zeus say then?" I ask the goose, who again is curling his neck.

He belches a second time and says, "Truly Athena is wise, loyal Argos, for this plea is what angered Father Zeus, just as she intended. Never have I seen such lightning or heard such thunder!"

"Indeed, noble goose, Ithaka herself shook like leaves on a tree. But tell me, what did Zeus say after he hurled his lightning?"

"Boar Slayer, what Father Zeus said will bring joy to your

heart. He ordered Hermes to fly to the nymph Kalypso with this message: that she of the most lovely hair shall not forestall the homecoming of enduring Odysseus any longer, but allow him to construct a raft and leave her island immediately. She must direct him to sail to the island of the Phaiakians, who will provide him with a fast and steady ship, for it is fated that he return to the land of his fathers."

"O most noble of birds and highest flyer of all, truly your words give me hope! What can I do to reward you for your loyalty? Tell me, and if it is in my power I shall do it."

The goose spreads his wings and belches a third time before answering.

"This I ask of you, loyal one. Young Telemachos has grown to be a fine hunter, and none can outfly his straight arrows. Lead him not in the direction of our nests for two winters, so that our flock can grow, for we have suffered much from his prowess. Do this, and you shall owe me nothing else."

I nod and say, "I swear to you, then, Sir Goose, I shall do as you ask. Soon your flocks will blacken the sky."

"And I shall fly at the front," the goose says, burping yet again.

"Indeed. Farewell, Sir Goose. May the gods be good to you."

Then I run back up the path leading to the stable, where even the smell of goats and sheep are welcome to me. The goatherd is calling my name just as I come over the hill, and I spend the rest of the day chasing the yellow-eyed kids, pretending to be a mountain wolf so they will learn to stay together and not wander off alone as their stupid cousins, the sheep, do.

CHAPTER XXIV

൙൙൙൙൙൙൙൙൙൙൙൙൙൙൙

Deadly wine

Akakios, who plans to kidnap Telemachos, is a vain and stingy man who loves his wine as much as his ships. Since his home is near the shore and the soil there is too poor to grow grapes, he has his wine brought to him in large wooden barrels. The winemaker who sells it lives on the south of my master's estate, so I have seen his ox-pulled cart every week pass through our land on his way to distribute his wine to the noble families that live along the shore. At each stop he picks up the empty casks and delivers full replacements. Tomorrow is a festival day, so he will be making his rounds this afternoon, when Apollo's chariot is over the western sky and the cool winds blow in from the sea. That is when I will take my revenge.

The day drags slowly by, as often happens when one

anticipates the unknown. Finally I hear the lowing of an ox, and I know the winemaker approaches. I let the oxcart pass and then follow along behind it, hiding in the scrub while the winemaker delivers his barrels to every fine estate along the shore. He and his servants bring back empty barrels and stack them next to the full ones, and then he covers the cart again with sailcloth and continues on his way. Luna is nearly overhead when he reaches Akakios's estate, and I know his servants will be in a hurry to finish before darkness falls and it is unsafe to travel.

When the winemaker nears Akakios's estate, I jump into an empty barrel, curl up, and wait. How tight the fit is, but the gods make my old bones supple again, and I can bear the pain. The barrel, with me inside, weighs as much as a wine-filled one. Now I must pray that I am carried inside. A moment later I feel my barrel being lifted and carried into Akakios's house. I think of my master then, imagining what he felt when the Trojans wheeled his giant horse into their own fortress, sealing their doom. I am now also inside my enemy's gate.

Once the house is quiet, I topple my barrel and crawl out. How my bones ache! How my black coat smells of rotten grapes! But I am inside now. I stop and listen. His servants have gone to bed, and Akakios has not yet returned from my master's house, although I know he will arrive soon. Then I smell it. A guard dog. And he will smell me.

I creep out of the storeroom and make my way to the courtyard, where I see him. The dog is tied by his neck to a tree. Even in the darkness I can see he is a large beast; his coat is either brown or black, I cannot tell which. His neck and tail droop pitifully.

"Brother!" I call softly. "Do not bark! I bear you no harm."

"There is no food here, friend," the dog replies. "Come back tomorrow after the festival. There will be scraps on the ground then."

I move closer to the dog so that he can see my face.

"I do not seek food. What is your name, brother?"

"I am called Cadmus. And yours?"

"I am Argos."

"The Boar Slayer?"

"I am also called that. Tell me, Brother Cadmus, does Akakios tie you up every night?"

"Yes."

"Why?"

"Because he knows I will run away if he doesn't."

"Why would you run away? Are you not loyal to him?"

"Loyalty must be earned, should it not, Argos?"

"Indeed," I say. "He beats you?"

"Aye. He is a cruel man. He has no wife nor children, only wine to keep him company. And I have often felt his strong foot and stinging strap. But why are you here, Boar Slayer?"

"To kill your master."

"Why? What has he done to you?"

"He has threatened to kidnap my master's son. For that he cannot live."

For a moment Cadmus says nothing. I wait for his warning bark. It never comes. Instead he says, "You have shamed me by coming here, brother."

"Why? That was not my intention," I say.

"Have you not found me tied like a slave to a stake by my own master? Have you not come to destroy the man who has been cruel to me my entire life?"

Truly, I see that my words have stung him. Proud Cadmus's tail hangs low and his ears lie flat.

I quickly gnaw through his rope. "Go now," I tell him. "You are free. Your duty to your master has ended."

Cadmus shakes his head. "No, loyal one. My duty begins now. Leave with haste and return to your master's son. Akakios will trouble the house of Odysseus no more."

We touch noses, and I leave. As I climb a ridge, I see Akakaios arriving in his cart. Sometime later I think I hear a man cry out, but it might be the wind, which blows from the north this time of year, bringing sounds from far away.

The next day I meet Telemachos outside his tutor's home and make him follow me to Amphitrite's lonely temple. Somehow he understands me, and the following day when we return to the temple, Telemachos brings an offering, and he vows to continue to do so every week.

Thus the goddess will be appeased.

CHAPTER XXV

~~~~~~~~~~~~~~~~~~~~~~~~~~~~~~~~

Kalypso makes an offer

Many days passed before I heard news about my master. Had Hermes spoken to Kalypso? Would she obey Zeus, her father, and release him? How could he leave the island with no ship to convey him? Every evening I took the path down to the docks to eavesdrop on the sailors arriving from distant lands, to hear if they spoke of a man sailing the sea alone on a makeshift boat. I heard nothing.

Then, as dawn spreads her rosy fingers, I hear a dove cooing from the eves of the sheep stall, and I trot over to greet it, as doves are not common on our island.

"Are you Argos, the Boar Slayer?" the dove asks when I reach the stall. She is as white as the sea spray that licks the docks on a stormy afternoon.

"I am called that," I say. "What wind brings you to Ithaka, fair dove? You will find eagles here, but not your brethren."

"If you are indeed Argos, then I will not remain long. Lift your head so that I may see if your chest is white, like a shining shield, for I have a tale to tell you if it is so."

I lift my head high and stand on my back legs, revealing my chest.

"Ah, you are indeed he," says the dove, bobbing her shapely head.

"From what isle did you come, fair dove?" I ask. "And what news do you bring?"

"From the island where lovely Kalypso lives, loyal one, and which your master has called home for seven years now."

I put my front paws in front of me and lower my head in respect. "Please, most revered of all birds, tell me your tale. Did Hermes come to your island as Father Zeus commanded?"

The dove flies down from the eaves and takes a perch on a pine stump so that I can hear her clearly, for her voice is soft and low, as doves never shriek or caw as many other birds do.

"Aye, Boar Slayer, Hermes arrived on winged foot four days ago. Fair Kalypso was spinning cloth of the most lustrous silk, and your master, famed Odysseus, was staring out at the sea, lamenting his fate, as he has done every day since I was a hatchling. Seeing Hermes, beautiful Kalypso said, 'How is it, Hermes, with your golden staff, that you have never visited my island until now? Speak what is in your mind, and it shall be accomplished if I can do it. But first let me offer you repast. I have ambrosia and sweet nectar for you to eat.'

"When she had set this out before him and he had eaten his fill, Hermes said, 'Goddess, you asked me what brought me to your island, and this is my answer: Father Zeus sent me here across this endless saltwater. He says you have with you a wretched man who longs for his homeland after sacking Troy and then losing all his companions before washing ashore here. But it is not his fate that he should die far away from his people. It is ordained that he return to his own house and the land of his fathers. So I have come this far to tell you this.'

"Then, loyal Argos, did beautiful Kalypso weep, for she had fallen in love with your master. Oh, the sound of her weeping broke my own heart, for we doves mate for life, and we die when our companion dies. That is our destiny."

The dove coos softly and closes her opaline eyes. I am not interested in the romantic life of doves, but again I lower my head to show respect. After sufficient time, I say, "But surely, noble dove, fair Kalypso agreed to Zeus's command, did she not? She agreed to let my master leave?"

"Nay, Boar Slayer. It was not so simple, for to give up what one loves is no easy task, even for a god. Seeing Hermes unmoved, her tears dried, and she became angry.

"'How hard-hearted you gods are, and how jealous!' she cried. 'Why can I not find happiness with a mortal? Did I not save his life? I found this man clinging to the mast of his ship, a ship that Zeus himself destroyed with a bolt of lightning, killing all his companions, and I brought him here, nursing him back to life! I cherished him and I loved him, and now Zeus commands me to send him away?'

"But Hermes said, 'Goddess, be careful not to defy your father, lest he rage against you and drive you from this enchanted island.'

"Then gentle Kalypso picked up a stone and threw it at Hermes, but he dodged it, and the next one too, and the next, until my fair Kalypso fell to her knees, sobbing piteously. Seeing this, the messenger god took pity on her and said gently, 'Loveliest of nymphs, ask Odysseus himself if he wishes to leave. If he chooses to remain here with you, then I shall return to Olympus and tell Father Zeus to change his destiny.'

"So fair Kalypso rose to her feet and walked down to the beach where your master sat on the seaside rocks, staring far out into the horizon as if he could see his homeland instead of the endless water. With such tenderness she placed her jeweled hand on his shoulder. Argos, how it broke my heart to see such love she had for him! Then she said, 'Bravest of mortals, for seven years you have remained on this island, spending nearly every hour staring out to sea. In this time I have grown to love you, but now I ask . . . is there love in your heart for me as well, or is it too full of longing for your home and family?'

"Then your master turned his tear-swollen eyes to the goddess and said, 'Why do you ask, shining nymph? I am cursed to remain here until the end of my days, am I not? There is no way for me to escape my fate, as no ship has ever come near, nor are there any trees for me to construct a raft of my own.'

"Then my lovely mistress wept again. 'Cursed?' she cried. 'You have answered my question, fearless one, with that word. So let me tell you this. Father Zeus has commanded that I release you from this fate if you desire it. I know now that your heart belongs on Ithaka, and there you must return.'

"Hearing this, your master rose to his feet and took my mistress's jeweled hand.

"'That is easily said, fairest one,' he said. 'But how will I leave this place? I have not the wings of yonder dove, nor can I swim like the fish that leap from wave to wave.'

"Then my mistress in all her shining radiance said, 'Wretched man, do you not know that in these seven years you spent staring out into the sea, the trees I burned upon your arrival have regrown tall and straight? Chop them down and fashion a raft for yourself, and I shall spin you a sail. Father Zeus has promised you fair winds, enough to carry you to the land of the Phaiakians, where they will give you a fast ship for the rest of your journey.'

"Oh, how your master embraced my mistress, and then together they climbed the path up from the shore, where he saw, for the first time, the trees he could fell for his raft. For four days and nights he labored, and finally it was seaworthy. He attached my mistress's sail and carved a paddle to steer his craft.

"Just as your master was about to launch his boat into the tireless waves, my mistress fell to her knees on the sandy shore and begged piteously. 'Brave Odysseus,' she cried, 'although I cannot make you immortal, if you remain here, the gods will give you a long life. No sword will ever sting you, nor will age cripple your legs and bring you misery, so I promise.'

"Then, Argos, I saw your master weep, for surely he knew that my mistress would never love another man. 'Fairest of all,' he said, 'you know my answer. I would not break your raw heart if there were another way, for truly you are the most

beautiful of women. Still, my longing for my own wife Penelope and my son weighs even heavier upon me. Let me go now,
and I will honor your love with tales of your generous spirit
when I reach Ithaka.'

"Hearing these words, my mistress gave your master bread
and wine for his journey, and he pushed himself into the crashing waves, where soon a favorable wind took him out to sea.
And then I flew here, loyal one, to tell you this, that you might
know your master's fate."

Oh, such joy runs through me now! My master will soon be
sailing home, and I will be there to greet him! "I thank you,
purest one, for coming here and relieving me of my burden!" I
cry. "Though I am an old dog, you have made my heart young
again!"

But the dove says nothing in response to my gratitude, but
hides her head under a white wing.

Seeing this, I say, "Forgive my overweening joy, shining dove,
for I know your mistress is alone now on her mist-shrouded
island. Return to her and give her comfort, I beg you."

The dove lifts her head. "You misunderstand me, loyal one. I
hide my face because I have not told you everything, and truly
the words are difficult to speak."

"What words are these, White Wing? Did not Zeus himself

send a fair wind to convey my master to the Phaiakians? Surely no harm can befall my master now!"

"Still your pink tongue, Boar Slayer, for you have nearly answered your own question. Give me a moment and I will tell all."

Hearing this, I sit on my haunches and wait for the bird to gain her courage. Finally she says what I am most afraid to hear.

"It is true that at the council Zeus himself promised to send a fair wind to steer your master to the Phaiakian land and so appease gray-eyed Athena. But not all the gods were at the council, Stag Hunter, as swift Hermes told me that fateful morning."

The fur along my back rises, and a snarl forms on my lips.

"Tell me, kind dove, what god did not attend, and who is he that he could stand up to Father Zeus?"

"There is only one, Argos. He is brother to Zeus himself. He is Poseidon, the earth shaker. And your master killed his son, Polyphemos of the Cyclopes."

Then does my heart break.

CHAPTER XXVI

The color of goldenrod

This morning I heard a ewe was missing from the neighboring farm. The shepherd dogs have been out all night searching for it; I heard their sharp barks growing more desperate as the sky changed from black to gray. Soon Apollo's chariot will begin its crossing, and the ewe will be found dead. Of that I am sure. By now an eagle has found it, or it fell into a crevasse while grazing beyond its pastures. These things happen to poorly watched flocks. When they find its carcass, the ewe's owner will beat his shepherd and then the shepherd will kick his dog. It has always been thus. Of course, my master never struck me. No man has. And lived.

The ewe has been found. Alive. I hear the excited barks coming from across the valley, so I leave my own flock to see it for myself. And one of the barks is unfamiliar to me, further piquing my curiosity. When I reach the neighboring pasture, I see three of my brother shepherd dogs standing in a circle, tails pointed toward the center, yapping happily to anyone who will listen about how the ewe was found. As I approach them, they roll onto their backs—as they should—until I tell them to stand up. "Which one of you found the sheep?" I ask. "And had the stupid creature fallen into a crevasse?"

The dogs lower their heads and will not meet my gaze.

"None of you found it? It returned on its own?"

The youngest among them, a mongrel with a brindle coat, finally answers. "A stranger dog found it. The ewe had escaped its fence and wandered near the goat path leading to the village. A thief walking along the path saw her and put a rope around her neck, with the intention of selling her at the market. The new dog followed his trail and caught up to him where the path narrows before the bridge."

"Then what happened?" I ask. I know the place where the path becomes confined by a band of trees. There is ample room for a dog to attack straight on, but hardly room for a man to swing a staff.

"She jumped the man from behind, biting his leg so he couldn't chase them. Then she took the rope in her mouth and led the ewe back here." The mongrel finishes the tale by lashing his tongue across his muzzle. Despite his own failure to catch the ewe, he seems quite proud to retell the events.

"She attacked a man? On her own? What if he had struck her with a spear? A dog is worth more than a ewe!"

"The thief was drunk on wine," a female's voice says from behind me. "I could tell by his footprints that he could not walk straight and so probably could not throw a spear."

I turn to see her, although I had smelled her approach. She isn't very large, but she has a fine straight back and long legs. Her coat is the color of goldenrod, and her eyes smolder like volcanic rocks set deep in a well-shaped head. Her teeth glisten as she speaks.

"What does your master call you, Sister Shepherd?" I ask.

"I answer to Aurora," she replies, lowering her head slightly. She is an alpha female, and so she does not roll onto her back.

"You did a brave thing, Aurora," I say, making sure to glower at the other dogs, who would never have dared to attack a man, even if they had been able to track the ewe. "But now you must be careful. The thief will return, claiming to your master that you attacked him for no reason. He will demand a ewe as recompense. And he might demand your death too. That is the law on Ithaka when a dog attacks a man."

"The thief did not see me, I think. And before I bit him, I tracked him for some time, howling like a wolf. I even rolled in ash to change my coat to gray. He will think I was a mountain wolf, and he will brag to his friends that he survived a wolf attack."

When she finishes this tale, my brothers sit on their haunches and howl. What imbeciles!

"And what are you called, sir?" Aurora asks.

Before I can answer, she saunters up to me and rubs her nose against mine. Perhaps this is custom elsewhere, but not on Ithaka. Still, her nose is soft and wet, and she smells of wild flowers. For a moment I forget my own name!

"He is Argos, loyal companion to brave Odysseus," the brindle answers for me.

"Argos. I have heard that name even on my former home of Samos. You are the great boar killer, are you not?"

I nod. Words finally come to me. "Yes, I have killed many boars. The last one was as tall as a half spear, and he weighed more than two horses. Yet I have never covered myself in ash, tracked a thief, and returned a ewe to my flock. Your deed was brave as mine. But tell me, when did you arrive from Samos?"

"Two moons ago my new master bought me from my former owner, who had given up his farm on Samos and was sailing to Carthage. When he stopped here for provisions, he sold me, thank the gods. I had already killed all the rats on the ship, but I am a shepherd, not a rat killer."

"That is a task for cats, anyway," I say. "We are meant for nobler pursuits."

"Indeed, brave Argos. But now I must return to my flock. They are poorly trained and stray the instant I turn my back."

"Where is your farm?"

"North of here, where the river makes its turn, in the shadow of the mountain Nerito. My master is called Okylaos. He is poor, but he treats me kindly so far."

"I know that farm. There is an old olive tree there—the oldest on Ithaka, so I am told."

"Yes, that is the one. It is a fine tree to lie under when Apollo's chariot is high and the days are long. Now I must return there. Farewell, sir."

Before she can leave, I step close to her and bite her gently on the ear. That is the custom on Ithaka, and now the other dogs know that Aurora will one day be my mate. Then she trots off, looking back once, at the top of the ridge, before disappearing from view. The other dogs, most notably fat Thenos, forget their place and begin to tease me. With three snaps of my jaw, though, I have them running back to their farms, tails tucked between their legs.

I am Argos, the Boar Slayer, and I do not suffer fools.

CHAPTER XXVII

∾∾∾∾∾∾∾∾∾∾∾∾∾∾∾∾∾

A wounded gull

Each day for seventeen days, a different seagull has landed at the harbor with news that my master and his craft sail ever straight toward the Phaikakian land, as the nymph Kalypso had instructed him, guided by the constellation Ursa by night and Apollo's chariot by day. But on the eighteenth day, no bird appears. Then, on the nineteenth day, a bedraggled gull lands on the harbor, followed by a dozen more gulls, snapping their beaks and surrounding him. The bird's feathers are sparse and gray, and one of its wings juts out from its body most unnaturally. I run to him and cry, "Far-flying gull, what has befallen you? Did an eagle tear your wing? If so, thank Zeus himself that you escaped its sharp talons!"

The red-eyed gull shakes its head. "No, loyal one, no eagle

has come near me, nor did any other bird of prey seize my wretched wing. It was a god himself who did it; the earth shaker Poseidon has destroyed me, and perhaps your master as well."

"'Twas Poseidon, Poseidon, Posiedon," his fellow gulls scream.

Hearing this, my heart leaps, yet tumbles when I understand his words. "You were with my master, Sir Gull? What is his fate? Tell me quickly that I might know it!"

"Alas, brave Argos, I know little. But I will tell you what I can. Two days ago I perched on your master's raft as he sailed swiftly toward land. Far off we could see the mountains of the Solymoi and your master's heart was gladdened, for truly the endless sea will drive the strongest man mad. But behind the mountains a dark cloud formed where none had been before, and I knew that we were doomed. It was Poseidon himself who hid in the black cloud, and he sent winds from all directions at us at once. How your master's boat staggered in those winds! Then the earth shaker sent battering waves at us, waves so great that your master tied himself to his raft so that he would not be thrown far from it. I heard him cry, "Woe to me that I did not perish at Troy with my companions and covered in honor!"

"Woe, woe, woe!" his companions cry.

"Oh, say not those words, broken gull, for they tear at my heart!" I whimper.

"You asked to hear my tale, loyal one, and now you must hear it," the gull whispers. His voice is growing weaker, and I fear that he is near his own end.

"Hear it! Hear it, hear it, loyal one," repeat his flock.

"Poseidon sent yet another wave, black and terrible, and your master was thrown from his craft. Had he not tied himself to the mast he would have died then, but instead he pulled hard on the rope, and hand over hand he regained his purchase. Then came the bitter north wind, then the east, then the south, then the north again. The winds tore my wing and I landed back on the raft, near your master, unable to fly. Suddenly, a goddess appeared next to me. It was Leukothea, the goddess punished by Hera, and condemned to the sea.

"'Poor man,' the goddess exclaimed as she surveyed your master. 'What have you done to anger father Poseidon so greatly?'

"But your master could only shake his head and vomit forth seawater. So the goddess said, 'Remove that heavy cloak you wear, mortal one. Untie yourself and dive into the sea quickly, for this raft will soon splinter. Take this veil instead and tie it around your waist; it is immortal, and you will not drown as long as you wear it. Then swim hard with your two hands for the Phaiakian land that is your destiny. When you have reached land, remove the veil, and with your back to the blue sea, throw it behind you, taking care not to see where it lands.'"

"Did my master do as he was bidden?" I ask. "Did he abandon the raft wearing the immortal veil?"

"Alas, loyal one, I cannot say for certain. Just as the goddess herself sank into the wine-dark sea and your master tied the veil round his waist, Poseidon sent his largest wave directly at us. The mast snapped under its weight, and the raft was pitched high into the air. Your master and I were both thrown off, or perhaps he dived, I cannot say, but I flew above the broken raft for as long as I could, and I never saw your master again. Then the west wind carried me here, and it is on Ithaka herself I think I will meet my doom."

"Doom. Doom. Doom."

"But surely that is not your fate, brave gull!"

"Boar Slayer, a man can break his arm and live. A dog can break its leg and live. But a bird cannot break its wing and live for long. An eagle or a seahawk will find me. Why question the ways of the gods? We learn this when we are hatchlings. See? Above us the eagles are already circling."

"They come. They come. They come."

I look up and see what the gull said is true. Two black eagles circle in the sky.

"Go now, Argos," the gull urges. "Perhaps Athena has left a message that your master lives."

"Go! Go! Go!" his flock screeches.

I thank the gull and turn away, bounding up the hill toward my master's home. The shadows in the sky grow larger, but I do not look back. "Why question the ways of gods?" the gull had said. Then, as I trot toward the barn, I see it. A brown owl stares down at me from the peak of the roof. An owl at noon. My hair stands on end. Athena! The great bird stares at me, blinks slowly one time, and then it flies off toward the forest. *Surely my master lives,* I think. And with that happy knowledge, I run down to the goat pasture. Even those stupid creatures cannot spoil my day now.

CHAPTER XXVIII

/©/©/©/©/©/©/©/©/©/©/©/©/©

A boy becomes a man

Telemachos has a burr under his skin. In the morning he
sharpened his short sword until it gleamed, and then he
tested its sharpness on his thumb. The drops of his red blood
dutifully fell to the ground. Then he polished three javelins
of different lengths and, after consultation with Eumaios,
discarded two of his spears, keeping the one with the stoutest
shaft, which I thought strange, because the longer javelins fly
farther. Finally he strung his bow and sent dozens of arrows
thudding into a gourd resting against a tree. Then I saw him
collect water from the cistern and fill three bladders. A servant put figs and honey, along with dried meat, into two
sacks, and then I followed Telemachos to the temple, where
he left one sack as an offering to the gods, although I know

the priests will simply eat it once we leave.

Telemachos wants to hunt; that is the burr under his skin. The days are growing longer, and the deer are leaving the dark valleys and climbing up into the highlands searching for tender leaves. He wants to see if his arrows still fly true and if he has gained distance with his javelin. He wants to test himself after a long winter. As do I.

Finally, as the cook fires have begun to burn down to their embers and the last of the craven suitors have left, Telemachos comes to the barn where I lie. He kneels down so that I can lick his cheek.

"Loyal one, we hunt tomorrow," he says. "We leave early, before Apollo's chariot reaches Ithaka, and we go alone. Are you ready?"

I lick his cheek again. *I am always ready to hunt.*

Then he leaves, and after making a final round, I curl up for the night. I dream of giant stags and fleet-footed does, and they are no match for us.

We set off, as Telemachos had said we would, before dawn's first light. The morning is cool, and the grass is wet on my paws. We move swiftly along the goat trails that lead to Mount Nerito. I know a stream where the deer come to drink, and we will find good hunting there. We reach a fork in the trail, and I proceed north, my nose to the ground. *Oh, to hunt like this every day. To forget about the stupid sheep and the stubborn goats is to be a hunter, and not a shepherd, and that is my true nature!* I move quickly along the new trail, turning my head left and right, looking for new tracks, stopping to sniff the morning air for new scents—the scent of my prey. Suddenly I hear a low whistle. I freeze. Again, I hear a soft whistle. I look back. Telemachos has not made the turn with me. He is headed in the opposite direction, south, to the scrubland. There are few deer there. Still, he is Telemachos, my master's son, and he has called me, so I turn around and run up to him. He pats my head, and we share water from a pig bladder. Then I start back along the northern trail again, raising my tail to show him I have caught a scent. Telemachos doesn't follow me.

"Argos!" he calls. "Argos, come!"

I turn around.

"Argos, come!" he calls again.

What choice do I have? I run back to Telemachos and this time take his mantle in my mouth, tugging it in the direction we should take.

"No, Argos!" he cries.

No?

The boy is young, I think. *He has forgotten how to hunt deer.*

Then Telemachos kneels and holds out his hands. I lick his palms. After a moment he takes my head in his hands and says these words: "Argos, we are not hunting deer. Today we are hunting boar."

May the gods help us.

To track a boar can take days. There are not many left on this island, and they live in the most impenetrable terrain, places where few men will seek them. The boar does not feel the prick of a bramble on its skin or the rocks beneath its hoof, the sting of the wasp, or the bite of the coldest wind. Of all Zeus's creatures, the boar is the shrewdest, the meanest, the strongest, the smelliest, and the most fearless. And I am to help Telemachos kill one.

For two more hours we climb ridges and scramble down slopes, heading deeper into the narrow canyon that bisects southern Ithaka. Telemachos stays right behind me, completely silent except for his deep breaths from our quick pace, his hand gripping his javelin. We stop once to eat and drink quickly, but if Telemachos fears our quarry, he does not show it, because he doesn't linger over his meat and honey. Instead, we press on. I had heard last summer from a fox that a boar had taken over its den near here, killing its kits and claiming the land around it as his own. This is the boar we hunt, and soon I smell him.

Since the boar has no enemies, it does not try to disguise its tracks or hide its spoor, yet at times they can disappear, and not even the best tracker can find them. How many hunters have died thinking they were tracking the boar when it was following them instead? How many hunting dogs have thought they were upwind, only to feel the boar's tusks bury into their exposed ribs? Surely the mischievous gods protect the boar for reasons unknown to me.

Apollo's chariot is high overhead, and I hope the boar is sleeping. Our best chance is to surprise the beast, startle it, and hope it runs from us, so that Telemachos's arrows can find its powerful hindquarters as a target. Then, once it is crippled, we can track it and finish our task with a well-thrown javelin.

That is what every boar hunter hopes for, to avoid a direct charge.

It is no hard feat to find evidence of the boar now. There are broken branches and trampled grass, hoofprints in the soft dirt, bark scraped from trees, and bristles dangling from thorns. Most telling of all, there is the silence. No animal chooses to live near the boar; even the birds hate them.

Telemachos senses the boar too. He crouches low and sniffs the air. Can he smell it as strongly as I can? How quietly we move through the scrub brush! How deliberately we place each step! Telemachos lowers his javelin and holds it at the ready. Ahead of us, I see a low mound supported by the roots of a large juniper. As we step closer, I see that the mound is larger than I first thought, and there is a small opening on one side that leads to a large hollow covered by roots and leaves. It would have made a fine den for a fox family, and now it belongs to a boar. Of that I am certain. I sniff the still air. I smell boar, but where is it coming from? The scent seems to come from two sides, from ahead and behind me. Since I can move more quietly than any man, I step closer to the den and peer inside. It is empty.

Then I hear it. The snap of broken branches, the cries of warning from the birds in their nests, the low grunt of an enraged killer. I bark and spin around. Behind Telemachos stands a boar sow preparing to charge. And then, behind me, I hear the roar of another beast. A male boar, tusks glistening with saliva, paws the ground. There are two boars, and we are between them.

No man—and few dogs—can outrun a boar, and we are on a narrow trail littered with roots and thick with scrub, so we cannot escape. We have to attack to gain the upper hand, and when one is faced with two enemies, it is best to attack the strongest first. There is only one thing to do; I can only hope that Telemachos will follow my lead.

I charge the male boar.

The beast lowers his ugly snout and charges too. Then, just as we are about to collide, I change directions and turn suddenly. The boar follows me, and for that brief moment, just after he turns, his chest is exposed. Telemachos puts an arrow in it. Then the other boar charges. I have turned around again, though, and I run toward the second boar from the side. From the corner of my eye, I see Telemachos lower his javelin, preparing to thrust. I meet the second boar low and raise her front legs, exposing, for an instant, her gray belly. That is enough. Telemachos finds it with his javelin. The boar roars in pain.

Instantly I spin back and see the male boar, wounded but preparing to charge again. I bark, and Telemachos turns around to face him. Again I charge the male boar, but this time I meet him full on. Even with a death wound, his strength is beyond mine, but I only have to avoid his tusks and give Telemachos a target, so at the last moment I roll over onto my back and kick up with my legs. Again I expose his chest, and again an arrow strikes it. Then another. Each arrow weakens the boar further, and soon he collapses. I roll away just in time to keep from being crushed. Meanwhile, Telemachos has turned back to the female boar, and he ends her life mercifully.

We have done it!

I run to Telemachos. There is blood on his leg, but it is boar's blood. He is unmarked. And triumphant. Then, suddenly, Telemachos collapses. I have seen this happen to young hunters. The blood lust leaves them and they faint. I lick the boy's face, and he stirs. Then I carry the sack of honey to him, and he dips his hands in it and licks them clean. Soon he is standing again, and we marvel at what we have done. Even my master never killed two boars on the same hunt! Our names will be sung in the villages and towns all over Ithaka, and honor will flow to the house of Laertes.

But the boars are too large to carry, and Telemachos has not even brought a knife, so we are unable to fashion a sled to drag the smaller one.

"Night is coming soon, Argos," the boy says. "The craven suitors will arrive, and my mother is home alone, with just the servants to protect her honor. We will return tomorrow to collect our trophies."

We hurry back to my master's estate and tell no one of our kill. The next two days, Zeus pounds Ithaka with rain and lightning, so we remain inside. On the third day, Telemachos develops a fever. A week passes before he is strong enough to leave his bed. When he can walk again, he leads Eumaios and a group of servants to the site of our triumph to retrieve the bodies. Nothing of the boars remains but a single tusk. Still, we know what we accomplished.

CHAPTER XXIX

A visit with Aurora

Every few days I leave my master's farm and take the path north to see Aurora. I would like to go more often, but my days are full of hardship and work, and it is not easy for me to leave my home unguarded. But when she can, Aurora will slip away from her farm—for the herds there are small and easily managed by shepherds—and visit me. She arrives in the late afternoon, when the herd animals and the humanfolk nap, and we hunt for hares in the pine forest or lie in the sun.

Sometimes we chase each other through the olive orchards; she is very fast, long-legged and lean, while I am broad of chest and large footed, but I would sometimes catch her—or she allows me to. Other times we take the path down to the harbor and watch the ships as they are rowed into port. They come from far-off places and the men speak languages we had never heard, but the seagulls would tell us where the ships came from: Chios, Thasos, Lesbos, Rhodes, and farther.

The summer passed, and the olive tree branches drooped low, heavy with their fruit. Still, every day the suitors arrived, sometimes in small numbers of ten or fifteen; other times, more than a hundred descended upon our house. When they came, my mistress would greet them, as is the custom here, and then climb the stairs leading to her bedchamber and remain there the rest of the night, weaving and sewing or singing to herself until they left.

How many pigs, sheep, and oxen my mistress was forced to slaughter for them! What barrels of heady wine they drank! My mistress took on new servants and cooks in order to feed them all, and her stores of gold, silver, and bronze were slowly depleted month after month to pay for her forced hospitality. A week ago, one of the new servants asked my mistress why she allowed the suitors to come every night.

"It is only a custom, my lady," she said. "Surely a queen such as you can break a tradition, especially one as burdensome as this," she reasoned.

My mistress stood to her full height and swept back her long

tresses. I thought she might strike the servant for her impertinence, but instead she merely smiled and said, "If a queen does
not honor custom, how can she expect anyone else to?"

Then my mistress left the dining hall and climbed the stairs
to her spinning room and began to sew. I noticed that for the
next seven days the impertinent servant peeled onions from
morning till dusk, and she did not ask another rude question
of my mistress.

It is autumn now, and Apollo's chariot flies faster across the
sky, so the days are shorter and I have even less time to spend
with Aurora. I want to surprise her today with a visit, so I finish
my herding early and race to her farm. I find Aurora napping
under her favorite tree, and I rouse her, saying, "Come, golden
one, let us chase hares while the sun is warm on our backs."

But she is slow to move; instead, she rolls onto her side, pretending to be asleep, although I can see a smile on her muzzle.

"Were you up late chasing sheep, lazy girl?" I ask.

"No, loudest of all four-legged creatures. Sleep did not come,
because I could not find a comfortable position."

And then Aurora stands up, and I can see why she couldn't
sleep. Her belly is swollen, ever so slightly, with puppies.

"You are to be a mother!" I exclaim.

"And you a sire."

"When?" I ask. "How long before you give birth?"

"Another moon must pass, and then I will be ready."

Just then, we both hear her master's whistle.

"I have to go now, Argos. A lamb must have wandered off."

"Let me help you find it!"

"Don't be silly. If my master were to see a half-bear dog near his flock, he would round up the village men and arm them with spears, and my puppies would never know their father! Go back to your master's farm and return when you can. Night is best, when your black coat cannot be seen and the sheep are in their paddocks."

Again we hear the whistle.

"Go quickly, Argos. He will kick me if I don't come right away."

Saying this, Aurora barks once and begins to run toward her master, who whistles a third time from the other side of a small hill. She looks back once at me, but I know she is right. He cannot see me; I am Argos, the Boar Slayer, and men fear my quick jaws and sharp teeth. I turn around and begin to make my way back to my master's farm.

Along the way I skirt Mount Nerito and its foothills and cut through the thick forest that lines my master's fields. It is there I see it: flying just above the tree line, an eagle careening through the sky with a viper in its talons. The snake's jaws are clamped around the eagle's neck, and neither will release its hold. It is an omen. I do not know its portent, but I know the gods are planning ill for me or someone I love. That is their way, for to be immortal simply affords more opportunity to convey misery on those who are not.

I reach my master's farm in time to bring the herds in and to watch from the barn as the suitors make their shameless arrival. As the evening comes in, the wind from the west brings thick clouds that cover the stars, and then Luna herself. The sheep in their paddocks grow anxious over the impending storm, so I bed down in there to keep them calm. Throughout the night Zeus hurls thunder and lightning down upon Ithaka and Poseidon shakes the seas. All night long I think of Aurora. I can only hope that she is dry and safe from Zeus's hammer; that her poor master has given her food to eat so that she does not have to catch a hare; and that the puppies inside her are growing strong, for this is no life for the weak.

CHAPTER XXX

∕◎∕◎∕◎∕◎∕◎∕◎∕◎∕◎∕◎∕◎∕◎∕◎∕◎∕◎

Family matters

Aurora is fat now with puppies. Almost daily I bring her extra food to eat, as she can no longer hunt well enough to supplement the meager rations her master gives her.

"Leave him!" I suggest a hundred times or more. "Come to my master's palace! Come live with me so we can raise our offspring together!"

Each time she replies, "I cannot leave my master, Argos. Though he is poor, it is our fate to remain loyal to one man, just as you maintain your loyalty for brave Odysseus."

"But Odysseus is my master!" I cry.

"Boar Slayer, Odysseus has been gone for more than seventeen years. You are loyal to his memory. I am loyal to a man of flesh and blood who needs me to guard his home and watch his herds."

How those words sting, although she does not mean to wound me.

"My master lives!" I say, though to my own ears I did not sound confident.

"So say the birds, the sea turtles, the bats. And I believe them too, Argos, but my master is inside his house *now*, and I must guard his herds."

"Three old oxen, two sheep, and a goat is not a herd! At my master's farm we have hundreds of oxen, sheep, goats, and swine to shepherd."

"One day he too will own much livestock, Argos. I have heard my master talking about it to a man by the harbor. Then our offspring and I will have plenty to eat and dozens of lambs and kids to guard and lead to pasture. He has said so himself!"

And so my mate will not leave, and I, almost daily, make the trek to her master's farm, watching her belly swell and waiting for her time to come. When it does, it happens at night, under a bush, instead of in a warm barn, where even the lesser dogs on our land give birth.

And I am not there.

But today I race to see her. I find her nursing six puppies and resting in the sun. Aurora's eyes are closed in maternal bliss and exhaustion, and she barely stirs when I lick her cheek. I had carried in my mouth a meaty lamb bone, and I lay it on the ground next to her, and then I stand guard, against what I do not know, but I am Argos, the Boar Slayer, loyal mate to Aurora, and sire of six blind, mewling puppies, five of them black as I am, and one tawny and full of mischief.

What else am I supposed to do?

Three years ago, on a black and storm-tossed night, my mistress promised the suitors that she would wed one of them once she finished weaving the funeral shroud for her father-in-law, Laertes, who grows older and more infirm every day. I have not seen the shroud, but it must be wondrous, as my mistress is the cleverest woman on Ithaka. How she labors on it through the cold, dark nights! She is a queen, and yet I have more freedom; the entire estate belongs to me, as does Ithaka itself.

Tonight the suitors left early. A storm was coming and they did not wish to be caught in it, so they left just after they finished their honey and figs. Luna was covered in clouds, so they had to walk back to their own homes by torchlight. I can only hope they trip and stumble on their way. When the last suitor has left, I enter the hall, and for a moment watch the servants clean the last of the plates. I must admit I hope for a few scraps, and some come my way. Then I climb the stairs that lead to the corridor that ends in my mistress Penelope's room. Across from her bedroom is the room where she sews. I want to see her. I had not licked her hand in several days, nor had she scratched my ears, and I miss her gentle touch.

There is one obstacle before me, though. Melantho, one of her servants, is a jealous older woman; she resents anyone who comes close to my mistress, two legged or four. How many times have I heard her scold a servant girl for simply entering the room where my mistress was sitting. As I am four legged and beloved by my mistress, I am doubly despised. But I have come upstairs for another reason beyond merely a chance to lick my mistress's hand before she retires for the night: when the suitors left to avoid the storm, one had remained. And I smell him upstairs.

Melantho is there too. She has a broom in her hand and tries to block my way, but since when did a stick with straw on one end deter me?

"Back, vile dog!" she cries. "Go back or I'll make you sleep with the pigs!" And then she spits on me.

Argos the Boar Slayer does not heed insults from servants. Or anyone. Still, I wonder why I hear panic in her voice. Does she have something to hide? I lunge at her—never intending to bite, though—and she steps back. As I lunge again, a coin falls from her hand, and she steps on it frantically. Then, just as I press against her leg to make her move her foot, Zeus sends a thunderbolt crashing down near the barn. The storm has come.

A sudden breeze blows through the corridor and extinguishes the two candles lighting the hall, and we are plunged into darkness. I hear my mistress cry out from the sewing room, but is it the sound of the thunder that frightened her, or something else? The breeze also brings the scent of the suitor. I leave Melantho and run down the corridor, but I do not growl. Black death should come silently.

I reach the end of the corridor and stop. My mistress is to my right, in the sewing room. To my left, in mistress Penelope's bedroom, I smell the intruder, but the wooden door is closed. I rear onto my hind legs and press against it, but it will not open. Then I bark to warn my mistress. Behind me, Melantho screams, "The black demon has gone mad! Out, Argos! Leave this house!"

A moment later, my mistress Penelope appears from the sewing room. A small candle in that room adds a gloomy light to the hall.

"Argos, what is it? What do you smell? Who is in my room?" she asks.

Again, I lunge at the door. Again, a bolt of lightning crashes.

My mistress reaches for the latch and begins to lift it. Then two things happen. Melantho reaches us and, taking the latch in her *own* hand, swings open the door. I jump up against my mistress—forgive me, master—and push her down. I hear a bowstring hum, and an arrow hits the wall just over my mistress Penelope's shoulder. Then I turn and leap into the room just as the intruder himself jumps out the window. I hear him cry out in pain from the fall, and then I run out of the room, dodging Melantho and my mistress, and bound down the stairs.

The intruder, if he can run at all, will be heading for the harbor, where he can find places to hide. But he has not gone far. I find him beneath the window from which he had leaped. He cannot run. His leg is broken. I stand over him in the darkness, barking, until my master's guards reach us, followed by my mistress Penelope. Then Telemachos, roused by the commotion, joins us. I stand by him. Lightning strikes again, opening the sky for rain. In the flash, though, I recognize the assailant: Lestorides, an oafish, bald man with a scraggly beard who is quick to use coins to get his way, since he has no charm of his own.

The guards begin to question him. "Why did you attack our mistress?" they demand.

He laughs as only a doomed man can. "Why not ask the queen?" he says. "She knows the truth. And now we do too, for Melantho told us how you weave the shroud for King Laertes every night, and unravel it during the day."

Then he raises his fist toward my queen. "For three years she has done this while we wait like fools for her to finish. Well, I could wait no longer. I wanted to see the shroud myself and bring proof to my comrades that the queen is a liar!"

"Take him from my sight!" my mistress demands.

"But how did he reach your room, my queen?" asks one of the guards.

Then I remembered the coin that fell from Melantho's grasp, and it comes together. Lestorides bribed her to let him into my mistress's room!

Where is Melantho now?

I bark twice and then tug on Telemachos's arm.

"Queen Mother, Argos wants something!" he says.

"The Boar Slayer saved my life tonight. Go with him, Telemachos. You, too," she says to one of the guards.

I lead Telemachos and the guard back around to the front of the house. From there I begin the chase. I find Melantho easily enough. She is running wildly, purposelessly, with thoughts only of escape. From there, it is just a matter of steering her where I want her to go. I cut her off in one direction, forcing her to run in another. Back and forth I drive her, letting her think she has escaped me before I reappear beside her. Finally she has no choice. To avoid my teeth, she climbs the fence and enters the pigsty.

"Sows!" I call. "She is here to steal your piglets!"

Thus did Melantho, who betrayed my queen, sleep with the pigs.

CHAPTER XXXI

/o/o/o/o/o/o/o/o/o/o/o/o/o/o/o/o

Bitter life

For the last ten days I have been shepherding on the farthest reaches of my master's land. Every spring we move the sheep there to fatten on the grassy slopes of the valley, and I have to stay with the sheepherder in a nearby cave, far from my master's palace. And far from Aurora and my children. We spent our last afternoon together naming them. The three black females we called Alloria, Astra, and Zephyrus. The two black males we named Castor and Pollux, after the twin demigods, since neither their mother nor I could tell them apart.

"But what shall we name the golden one?" I asked my mate as the pup tackled his brothers and chewed his sisters' tails. "He is full of fire, isn't he?"

"Let us wait to name him, Argos," Aurora said. "For one day, his name will be known far and wide, as is yours today. Of this I am certain."

"As you wish," I said, placing my paw on No Name's chest to give his sisters a respite. A few minutes later, I left to make the long run back to my master's estate.

To wait ten days without seeing my family is unbearable. Not since the pain of my master's departure for war against the Trojans began to ebb have I felt such loneliness. I have taken out my frustration on the sheep, snapping at them when they wander off and barking at them when they take too long to leave the corral. But soon we will be done here, and I will see Aurora and my offspring. It is time they learn to shepherd and for the golden one to learn to hunt.

I am returning from the farthest sheep pasture when a seagull swoops low over my master's palace. I run to where he circles high above the estate and call out to him, "Seagull, do you have news of my master?"

"Nay, loyal one," he calls back. "But run to the harbor as fast as your black legs will carry you. There is mischief afoot!"

The sharp-eyed gulls have been minding the affairs of humanfolk from the skies since the gods made them, so I run across the courtyard and dash down the path that leads to the harbor. As I draw closer, I hear it: above the noise of the seamen loading ships, the cries of the waterbirds as they dive for fish, and the pulse of the sea crashing against the rocks, Aurora's strangled bark.

I crest the last ridge before the hillside plunges down to the shore, and see her. She is tied around the neck to the mast of a red ship with a thick rope. Men are seated at their oarlocks, waiting for their cadence call, and their sail is inching its way up. It is a yellow sail, and it flaps loudly in the wind. Next to Aurora, my children are piled into wooden chests. I can see only their heads and front paws as they strain to escape. I bark, but the wind carries my words away. As I run down to the harbor, I notice Aurora's owner walking along the shore. I see the glint of copper coins in his hands. He has sold my family!

I run faster than I have ever in my life, slipping and clawing down the trail that leads to the harbor, but I know as I sprint toward the dock that I am too late. Already the ship's rowmaster has set the rhythm, and the sail is catching wind. I can hear Aurora's panicked bark through the crashing of the waves and the shouts of the sailors. A fisherman slings his net at me, but I scamper under the mesh. A jetty runs parallel to the sea for a short distance, and I run toward it. I have to get closer to Aurora!

I am known throughout Ithaka, and so a dozen men or more try to catch me, perhaps thinking there will be a reward for my return. I dodge a few and bite a few more as they try to block my way. Finally I reach the rocky jetty and jump up onto it. I can see Aurora straining at her rope, but it is a thick sailor's rope, woven from many strands. Only the sharpest sword could cut it. One of my puppies has managed to escape the crate and is clumsily walking across the deck toward her. I dash along the jetty, barking for Aurora—just calling her name—for what else can I tell her to do? She is tied tightly, and already there is blue sea between the end of the jetty and the ship. I see her tug against the rope fiercely, even turning around and backing up so she can pull with her strong rear legs. I can see blood on her neck. Her eyes are wild and desperate. She barks something, but I cannot hear it.

"Aurora!" I howl. I've reached the end of the jetty. The next thing to do is jump. Although I know I could never catch the ship, into the depths of Poseidon's domain I plunge.

I dive in from the jetty and begin to paddle, but the incoming tide is so strong that I can barely swim against it. Waves crash around my head. One swell lifts me, and for a brief moment, I can just see the ship with Aurora and my pups barking from the deck.

Then a wave buries my head, pushing me under. I struggle to swim forward, but Poseidon sends wave after wave carrying me to shore, and there I wash up, half dead. A group of fishermen carry me from the breakers and lay me on the sand. They press my chest, and life enters my lungs.

Life without Aurora.

Life without my offspring.

Bitter life.

I close my eyes. Sometime later I hear the swineherd Eumaios's voice and feel his strong arms beneath my head. Then I hear a cry, and I turn and see Telemachos running toward me. What burning shame I feel as he hugs my wet neck and kisses my face. How could I have thought to leave him? Was he not my charge? Did not my master expect me to guard his only son with my life?

I rise unsteadily to my feet. Over Telemachos's shoulder I see the seagull that had called me to the harbor. He will not look at me; his head is buried in his wing.

"Come, Argos," Eumaios says gently. "Let us leave this cursed shore that has taken so many of our loved ones, never to return."

They did not know that my children were lost on this terrible shore as well.

"Don't say that!" Telemachos cries. "My father will come back any day now!"

"Truly, that is so, young Telemachos. If any man can return, it is your father. Tonight we will make an offering to Zeus that Odysseus and his swift ship appear on the horizon soon."

Then together we climb the trail back up to my master's home. At the highest vantage point, we all stop to look out over the blue sea. I see no tall masts; Aurora's ship has already disappeared, and my master is still far away, and I know not where or how or when he will return.

As we turn toward our land, I see a man leading a small flock of lambs in the distance. I sniff the air and confirm what my eyes tell me: the man had been Aurora's master. He sold her and the puppies to buy the lambs, and he is now taking them back to his farm. I freeze.

"Come, Boar Slayer," Telemachos says. "It grows late, and Mother will be worried." He tugs on my neck, and I reluctantly follow.

Later that night, after we have brought all the livestock in and the suitors have left, I run away. Luna is bright, and she guides my steps. Soon I reach Aurora's farm. There is a candle lit in her master's small house, and the heavy wooden door is barred shut, just as I knew it would be.

In a few minutes I chew through the leather cord that keeps his gate closed, and I scatter his small herd in every direction. I care not their fate; most will be taken onto other farms, and those left will meet the wolves. Then I tell one large goat to stand by the window and bleat loudly. After a few minutes I hear the door bar being raised and the door swings open.

Then I go inside.

CHAPTER XXXII

෫෧෫෧෫෧෫෧෫෧෫෧෫෧෫෧෫෧෫

A visitor arrives

A moment ago, a stranger arrived at our gate. He is tall and
beardless, dressed in fine clothes, and carries a long spear of
bronze. I watch the stranger closely because he has no smell,
and I wonder, *What manner of man is this who smells not of
sweat?* I bark once at the man, but I do not bare my teeth, and
then I run to where Telemachos is sitting in the hall, regard-
ing warily the suitors who have already begun to drink my
master's wine, though it is scarcely past midday. Together we
approach the stranger at the entrance, and Telemachos greets
him with courtesy, for he is well-bred.

"Welcome to our house, stranger," Telemachos says, bowing
slightly.

"I thank thee, Telemachos, son of the noble Odysseus," replies the stranger.

Again I sniff the stranger's feet, but he smells not of men or of anything I have known, and yet I am not afraid for Telemachos.

"Tell me," the man says, "is there a wedding today? For I see many men who are not in the fields, nor hunting game. Where is the bride?"

And Telemachos lowers his head so the man does not see his anger and shame. Then he says, "Stranger, what you say is true. There is no wedding today. Nor yesterday or the day before or tomorrow. These indolent men you see here do little work and hunt even less. Instead, they come here to my father's house—my father whose bones some say lie whitening on the mainland or under the waves—and eat his sustenance, making us poorer by the day. If my father were to come back, then they would be light on their feet, running back to their own farms and houses, but he has perhaps died by evil fate and will not return, and they know it."

The stranger shakes his head in sorrow and places his hand on Telemachos's shoulder.

"I grieve for you and your noble mother," he says. "Surely the gods will reward your loyalty one bright day."

Telemachos raises his head. "I thank you, stranger. But tell me, what is your name and where are you from? What ship did you come on, for I have not seen a new one in the harbor? And where are the sailors? And tell me this as well, what brought you to Ithaka? Did you know my father?"

Then the stranger replies, "You have many questions, loyal son of Odysseus, and I will answer them truthfully as I can. My name is Mentes, son of Achialos, and my ship is in the small harbor at the north of your island. Your father and I knew each other from long back. In fact, we are distantly related, and Laertes, your grandfather, would vouch for me if he could, though he is old now and may not remember me."

Hearing this, Telemachos takes the stranger's hand in his and says, "Welcome then, Mentes. My home is yours. I only wish my father himself were here to greet you."

Saying this, my master's son begins to weep, and I lick his hand to comfort him. Then the stranger, Mentes, draws closer and whispers into Telemachos's ear. "Hear me, loyal son of Odysseus. Death has not found your father on some distant land. Listen to my prophecy. He will return sooner than men think, for is he not the Wily One? Already he plans his return, and nothing will delay him long."

My master returns soon? Should I believe this gray-eyed stranger?
I sit on my haunches and wait to hear more. But Telemachos, at these words, falls to his knees, to kiss the stranger's feet.

"Rise, son of Odysseus," Mentes whispers quickly, "for it is not fitting that these men here see you at my feet."

Telemachos stands up and again takes Mentes by the hand. "You are right, stranger and friend. It is not fitting that these men be here at all. But what can I do? The most powerful men on the island seek my mother's hand in marriage, convinced that my father is dead. She has resisted them for many years, but our house is nearly depleted, and soon she may have to enter a hateful marriage to save it."

Mentes shakes his head with indignation. "Shame on these men," he says bitterly. "If only your father were here, standing at that door, wearing a helmet and carrying two spears, as he was when I first beheld him. Then he would bring quick death and make marriage a painful lesson!"

"Alas, he is not here, noble Mentes, and you yourself do not even know where he is," Telemachos replies. "What can I do? My arms are strong and I can shoot an arrow straight, but even I cannot defeat a hundred men."

Again the stranger draws closer. "Here is what you must do, son of Odysseus," he says softly. "Tonight, tell these hateful men to leave and return in one year. At that time your mother will make her choice in marriage to the man best suited for her hand. Then, tomorrow morning, take a fast ship with twenty oars and leave this place. Seek out your father's fate. First go to Pylos, where King Nestor lives, and ask him where your father is. He may know it. If not, sail on to Sparta, where Menelaos reigns. He was the last of the Achaians to return from Troy, and he may know if your father was killed in battle.

"If you hear nothing, then return home and build a tomb in your father's honor. Sacrifice your oxen and sheep so that the gods are appeased, and then let your mother choose her husband. Then, if the gods favor you, plan your revenge on these suitors. Take them on, one by one, until they have paid their price in blood. That is my advice, brave son of Odysseus, though it is bitter to swallow, I grant."

A year, I thought. *Can I live another year with no proof that my master lives?*

Hearing these words, Telemachos embraces Mentes and said, "Your advice is well taken, friend, and I will follow it. Now come inside to our hall and join me for dinner. After that, our servants will see to your bath and give you a fine bed on which to rest."

The stranger nods and says, "That would be most welcome,

loyal son of Odysseus. But leave me for a moment, and then I will join you."

So obedient Telemachos leaves the stranger and enters the house. When he has done so, the stranger pets me once and then instantly turns into a sparrow and flies up to a tree. I bark, and Telemachos comes running out, looking for Mentes. "Argos, where is the stranger?" he asks.

I lift my muzzle up toward the branch where the sparrow is perched. It whistles once and then flies off. I bark again to thank it, knowing it is a divinity who has come to our door, and Telemachos too says a prayer to the gods. Then, light of foot, he turns and makes his way back inside to the hall where the suitors sit eating and drinking. I follow on his heels, after looking back once to see if the sparrow has returned, but it is truly gone.

In the hall, Telemachos whistles so that the boisterous suitors will stop their merrymaking. When they are silent and he has their attention, Telemachos announces in winged words what the deity has told him.

"Suitors of my mother!" he cries. "You have bespoiled my house for too long. No longer is your rapacity endurable; you have scandalized this home and your reputations with your actions, and I beseech Zeus himself to reverse your fortunes!"

Then Antinoos rises, wiping the juice of the ox meat off his lips, and points a finger at my master's son. I growl and stand closer to Telemachos in case Antinoos attacks, but he chooses to fight with words only.

"Telemachos, how dare you rebuke us!" he sneers. "It must be the gods themselves who have put those impertinent words in your mouth. We hundred men are here by custom to seek your mother's hand, as your father, bravest of all men, has not returned for nigh twenty years. If you were my own son, I would strike your mouth for offending a guest in your own house, but since you have no living father, I will spare you that lesson!"

The other suitors cheer Antinoos, but thoughtful Telemachos says nothing until the room grows silent again.

"Hear me, Antinoos, and you other suitors too, for I will not say these words again. This is my offer. Tomorrow I leave on a ship to seek news of my father. I shall return no more than a year hence. While I am away, my mother will marry not. Perhaps on my voyage I will learn that my father is returning; perhaps I will learn that his bones lie beneath the sea. If that is the case, then I will offer my mother's hand for marriage. But if my father is returning, I will bring destruction to your houses. That is my vow to you."

One of the suitors, hearing this, throws a bone at Telemachos, but he ducks it, and the bone lands against the wall. Then Telemachos reaches for his short knife, but Eurymachos runs to him and stays his arm, and he sheaths his weapon. After that, without another word, Telemachos leaves the room.

But I linger.

I lie down under a table, and this is what I hear, though I do not know who says it: "Heed these words, suitors. It is clear to me that Telemachos plans to kill us. Even if he does not find his father, he will bring back men from Pylos or Sparta and visit evil upon our houses. Therefore, I say to you, let us send out our own ship when we learn which direction he sails. Who knows? Might he not perish at sea just like his father?"

The man laughs most foully, and so do the other suitors.

"If we are in agreement then, I shall be the one who spies on young Telemachos, for I know my way around the harbor. I will go there tomorrow and report back to you all, and then we will hire a swift boat to do our bidding," the man continues. "Do you all say aye?"

And they, most treacherous of all men, agree.

I cannot see the man who said this, but I can smell him. From beneath the table I sniff his dirty and yellow-nailed feet. A dog never forgets a scent, and I am Argos, the greatest tracker on Ithaka.

When the suitors are distracted again by a servant bringing more wine, I slip out from under the table. My master's dear son had gone to his room, and I find him there packing for his journey. He takes my head in his strong arms and says, "I leave tomorrow to search for news of our father, Argos, but I dare not tell my mother that I leave, for she would beg me too piteously to stay, and I would obey her. Watch over the household and guard our property, as you have done for so many years, noble one. When I return, with or without my father, we will drive the suitors from our house, if the gods allow it."

I lick his face and settle down on the floor beside his bed to sleep, as I used to do when he was a young boy and I was a pup. Strange dreams come to Telemachos in the night, and he thrashes and moans, though never wakens. But I remain awake as the black evening falls on us, planning my own revenge and thinking of smelly feet.

Dawn's rosy fingers creep over Ithaka, turning the wine-dark sea purple and then blue. After breakfast, I watch as Telemachos and his servants carry his belongings down to the harbor. He calls me thrice to join him as he climbs down the path, but I do not go to his whistle, though it tears my heart to disobey him. Instead, I take my own path, high above the harbor, to a point where the women and children of Ithaka can gaze down at the harbor and far out to sea, watching for ships returning their loved ones. I know Smelly Feet will come there to spy on Telemachos and to learn what ship he hired and which direction he sails, and so I get there first.

I hide in the windswept scrub near the edge of the ridge and wait. Apollo's chariot rises higher, and still I do not move. A young widow from the village climbs the path that I have taken and stands there at the ledge, weeping and cursing the gods. Then two boys come and throw stones down toward the sea, but soon they too leave. Finally I smell him. He is alone. Then I hear his labored breathing as he climbs the path. I think he had drunk too much wine the night before, because he stumbles twice and complains bitterly to no one about his aching head. I crouch lower. Only the gods can see me.

Smelly Feet reaches the top of the narrow ridge, not ten paces from where I lie hidden. His back is turned to me as he stares down at the harbor far below. After a few minutes, I hear him say to himself, "There is his ship. A black one like his father's, with a single white sail. And he sails southeast, toward Pylos, just as he said he would. Now I go quickly to make my report."

I wait for Smelly Feet to turn before I make my move. I want him to see me, his destruction, before he sees no more. When

I charge him, he barely has time to lower his spear, and I easily dodge it. He falls to his doom with my name on his lips.

From the high ridge I look out and see Telemachos's ship entering the bay. He had said he would be gone a year. I think how cruel the ships were that took away the ones I loved: my master, Odysseus, my mate, Aurora, my children, and now Telemachos. I say a prayer to Athena, and then, although my legs are old, I run the rest of the way home. When I am nearly there, I hear Penelope's cry of anguish; she has just learned that her beloved son has left on a ship. I do not leave her side for three days except to growl at the suitors when they arrive each night. Now I alone must protect the honor of the house of Odysseus.

CHAPTER XXXIII

*o
/oo/oo/oo/oo/oo/oo/oo/oo/o*

What the cat saw

The most perfidious of all animals approaches me today as I lie down in the barn to rest. The harbor cat has returned. Only a plea to Athena for wisdom and patience keeps me from crushing that hateful creature in my jaws, for I have sworn vengeance against him. But the goddess favors me and gives me the strength to remain still as he rubs against my side, arching his orange back and lashing his tail around my nose. Finally, though, I can stand it no longer, and a growl escapes my lips.

"Why do you come to Argos, Mouse Catcher? Cats belong on ships and in dirty barns, not here among sheepherders and hunters. If you are lost, I will gladly chase you down to the harbor where you will find your mangy brothers."

"Foul-smelling canine," he purrs. "Do you presume I came here willingly to hear your insults? If Artemis herself had not asked me to come, I would have remained on my swift ship, killing rats and sailing the seas. There are lands far from here where I myself am treated like a god, though this is beyond your imagination. Hear my tale, blackest one, and do not delay me further."

"Tell it, then, Rat Chaser, before you cough up a fur ball."

The cat closes his eyes and then extends each and every claw before he speaks.

"I have just retur-r-rned from Scheria," he says. "Do you know that land? I think not, since, like most dogs, you have probably never left your island."

"Scheria? What of it? Is it a land of rugged men and dogs such as Ithaka? Do they breed warriors there?"

"No, Tail Chaser, it is nothing like Ithaka, I grant you. That land was settled by Nausithoos many years ago, and now it is ruled by Alkinoos, who is learned in building and has erected many great palaces there. There he rules justly and with great honor-r-r, and there your master, Odysseus, washed ashore."

"My master lives? How do you know this?" I demand.

"I was there, Big Foot! I saw the wretched man myself! I live on that island in summer-r-r when the winds are not favorable.

Now, do not interrupt, long-tongued one, or I will say no more. And my story is one you will wish to hear."

I clamp my jaws shut and listen.

"Once your master crawled onto the shore of Scheria, he set out to look for the island's inhabitants, and I followed him. But soon sleep and exhaustion overcame him, and he made himself a bed of soft willow leaves near the banks of a river-r-r and fell asleep. Athena herself covered his eyes and let him rest undisturbed. Meanwhile I returned to the palace, for it was time for my dinner-r-r. That evening, Athena approached the bedchamber of Alkinoos's beautiful daughter, Nausikaa, and whispered into her ear that she must go to the river-r-r to wash her clothes because the men of the island would soon be courting her. To the river-r-r she went the next day, along with her servants and me, for she is a dutiful girl, and there, at the edge of a burbling stream that feeds a deep, quiet pool, she discovered a man she thought was dead."

"Say not those words!" I cry.

"Nay, Boar Licker, I said she *thought* the man was dead, but upon hearing her cry of surprise, the man awoke and jumped to his feet. Imagine her terror-r-r at seeing him, for he was salt crusted and swollen from the sea, but Athena had given the girl courage, and she stood fast."

"Go on, whiskered one," I urge.

"Seeing this girl so fair and resolute, your master bowed to his knees, saying, 'I offer my services, fair queen. Tell me, are you mortal or goddess? For if you are immortal, you resemble most lovely Artemis, but if you are one of the mortals who live on this land, then blessed are your parents, for their spirits must be warmed at the thought of you.' Truly, Tail Sniffer, your master, though nearly dead, still had the wits to charm a young maiden."

I say nothing in reply to this latest insult, for this odious cat still has much to tell me.

"Then Nausikaa her-r-rself answered him, saying, 'You are most thoughtful, sir, for indeed, though we are all mortal here, we are close to Father Zeus, and good fortune follows us.'

"'And what is the name of this land, fair lady, and who are your people? As you can see, I am lost and far from my own home,' your-r-r master said.

"'We are Phaiakians who hold this land, and I am Nausikaa, daughter of great-hearted Alkinoos. But come, it is not right that my servants and I look upon you so poorly clothed. We have mantles here, and oil for your blistered skin, as well as food and wine. Dress, eat, and anoint yourself, then we will return to my father's house, where we will take care of you as is our custom.'

"Then Nausikaa and her servants turned their backs so your-r-r master could prepare himself. While they were thus occupied, Athena came unbidden and cast a spell over him, healing his wounds and erasing the toll of years in battle and hardship, so that he appeared younger and godlike when they turned back to him. Truly, he was magnificent in appearance. For a man."

I think then how my own years of wolf hunting and shepherding have aged me. Would my master even recognize me if he saw me?

"Do you wish for me to continue, old one?" the cat asks, as if he knows my thoughts. Then he yawns, showing me his pink mouth, and stretches his long tail.

"Yes, stealthy one, please finish your tale," I beg.

But instead of finishing the story, the cat slinks over to a patch of sunlight and curls himself into a ball, falling asleep before my very eyes!

After a few minutes I bark at the miserable creature. Finally he opens one green eye and says, "If you wish to hear more, Broken Tooth, you will not make another sound. I will tell the rest of the story when I wake, if there is a saucer-r-r of milk waiting for me, for talking so much makes me very thir-r-rsty. Go now, and retur-r-rn when I wake."

There is a young, kindhearted servant girl who tends to my mistress Penelope and has a soft disposition toward animals. When a lamb is born, she makes sure that it suckles; when a baby bird is found beneath a nest, it is she who climbs the tree to return it. And like many young girls who have not yet learned to think critically, she likes cats.

I find her sweeping the alcove where my mistress often waits in vain for news of my master, and I take her sleeve in my mouth and lead her to the rat catcher still lying asleep near the barn. To hear her cry of wonder and happiness when she sees him lying there, you would have thought she'd found gold, jewels, or a bolt of the finest silk, not a mangy, flea-bitten orange harbor cat. But she squeals with delight and gathers the beast in her arms. To his credit, the cat wakes and plays his part, whining pitifully and hungrily until she realizes he needs milk. She puts him down and rushes to find a goat with a swollen udder.

"Quickly," I say. "Finish your story. And let every word be true, or you will live the rest of your life tailless."

After a series of yawns and a long scratch behind his ears, he continues.

"Once your master-r-r was dressed and had eaten, quick-thinking Nausikaa said to him, 'Follow our chariots back to my father's palace, but stop in the grove of poplars that you will see there, for us to arrive together would cause scandal, as I am to be married soon. So wait some time in the meadow and pray to Athena, for the poplars were grown in her honor. Then go into the city of the Phaiakians and inquire about the house of Alkinoos. Once you are there, enter the courtyard and proceed to the hearth on the other side. There, every evening, my mother and father sit and receive guests. When you arrive, bend your knees to my mother, and if she finds you honest and noble, she will convince my father to help you return to the land of your fathers.'

"Hearing this, your master thanked her most graciously, and soon they left for the palace, with your-r-r master following behind the retinue. I do not know if he prayed to Athena, but I myself was already in the palace, ridding it of mice, when I saw your-r-r master enter the courtyard, approach Queen Arete, and clasp her knees in his arms, as is the custom there."

"What did she say to him? Did she welcome him as her daughter promised?" I ask, desperately, I must confess.

"Aye, Boring one, she did. But fir-r-rst the courtyard grew silent, for never had so godlike a man entered their walls. Then your-r-r master made his entreaty, saying, 'Queen Arete, daughter of Rhexenor, I come to you on my knees after enduring great hardship and suffering. Here, among your friends and family, I ask of you and your noble king, Alkinoos, that you help me return to my homeland, for I am without conveyance, having been shipwrecked and washed ashore.'"

"What did the queen say, orange one? Did she agree to his request?"

"Yes, whisker-r-red one, she did, saying, 'Rise up and sit on this silver-studded chair, sir.' Heralds, bring him wine and supper and let us say a prayer to Zeus, who protects suppliants and grants their wishes when they are just.'

"Hearing this, King Alkinoos also rose and personally took your-r-r master's hand and set him in the shining chair. Then long-suffering Odysseus ate and drank, and the guests let him do so without asking the many questions that sprang to their lips. Finally King Alkinoos said to the audience there, 'Go home now, my guests, to your beds. Tomorrow morning, we shall call the elders in and introduce this man, who appears to me to be one of the immortals, and consider his request.'

"Soon everyone had left the hall except for the king and

queen and your-r-r master. Even the servants retreated to their rooms so that the three of them were left alone, except for me, of course, for I sat in the shadows watching and listening. Then white-armed Arete spoke a question that had been vexing her, asking, 'Stranger and friend, I recognize that mantle you wear. Who are you and where did you come from, and how is it that you wear this mantle?'

"Your-r-r master shook his head ruefully. 'It is a hard thing to tell you in one sitting, O queen, since the gods have given me many troubles, but let me for now tell you from whence I just came and how I appeared at your palace,' he said. 'For the last seven years, I was stranded on the far-off island known as Ogygia, where lives the daughter of Atlas, Kalypso. She lives there alone, but for servants, and my destiny led me to that cursed land after shining Zeus shattered my fast ship with a bolt of lightning. Only I among all my companions survived, floating on the keel of my ship. I was carried on the wave-tossed sea for ten days before the gods brought me to Ogygia. There Kalypso found me and nursed me back to health, even promising to make me immortal such as herself, but I remained steadfast in my desire to leave. Finally, perhaps Zeus took pity on me, for one day she allowed me to construct a raft, and I set sail for your own country, as I had been told that you are generous to strangers and supplicants. I was so happy as I neared your land, but then the earth shaker, Poseidon, threw mighty waves at me, tossing me off the raft. I swam for many hours until I landed safely on your shore, where I fell asleep near the river. There your daughter, Nausikaa, who looked like a goddess, discovered me. All this is true, I swear by the gods.'

"Then Alkinoos replied, 'My friend, from what I understand now, then your first supplication was to our daughter and not us. Is this not so?'

"'Noble Alkinoos,' your-r-r master said, 'do not rebuke your daughter, for she is blameless and sought only to avoid scandal, as she is soon to be married.'

"Then Queen Arete said, 'So she is, stranger. We seek her husband but have not found a man worthy of her.'

"'Until now, perhaps,' said the king. 'You could have my daughter, and I would call you son-in-law. I would build you a grand house, and you would have many servants. But if you want only a swift ship, that I will grant you too. Sleep here tonight, and in the morning, when the winds are calm, you can sail it to your land; my young men are all fine rowers, and they can take you as far as you need to go.'

"Then I saw your-r-r master smile for the fir-r-r-st time, smelly one. Soon a servant arrived and said that a bed had been prepared, and your-r-r master thanked the king and queen most graciously before leaving the room. Then the king and queen left the room too, and a moment later I saw a shadow running across the hall, and I pounced! So we all had good fortunes that night, lop-eared one. Ahh, here comes the maid with the milk! Excellent. I will drink it, and then, with Artemis's luck, this pretty young thing will take me to her-r-r room and I will sleep on a soft bed, while you remain out here with the fleas and the stupid oxen. I shall resume the tale in the morning, Dog Breath, just as your-r-r master did. How fitting, I think."

CHAPTER XXXIV

The rest of the cat's tale

When rosy dawn comes, I run to the barn and find the cat waiting for me.

"Finish your story," I tell him, "now that you have spent a night in the house of Odysseus. It is only right that you do so."

"I will finish the story, black one, but only because the milk-maid will come soon to take me with her-r-r to the market. It seems she has grown quite fond of me. Perhaps we will live here on this estate together-r-r, you and I."

The thought of that odious creature living here sickens me, but I swallow my disgust and bid him continue, which he does after yawning twice.

"King Alkinoos had sent a herald throughout the city, invit-ing all the townsfolk to come and meet your-r-r master, and soon the palace was filled with throngs of expectant men and women, young and old. Then, while we waited for the feast, a blind singer was led into the hall. In exchange for his eyes, the muse had given him the most beautiful voice in the kingdom, and the herald seated him near the king, Queen Arete, and your-r-r master, so that not a note was missed. To the sound of the lyre, the singer began his song, and silence fell over the assembly there. Truly, for a human, his voice was magnificent! But, Big Foot, a wicked god must have moved the singer, for he sang not of lovely maidens and brave young men, but of the war with the Trojans!"

"Surely not!" I cry. "In front of my master?"

"Aye, and he sang of Odysseus as well. He sang of the quarrel between Achilles and your-r-r master, and of all the warriors and their deeds, of Agamemnon and his foolishness that cost so many Achaian lives. Never have I been moved by such a singer. But I was not the only one. Every time the singer paused to breathe, I heard sobbing. *Who is shedding tears?* I wonder-r-red. Can you guess, Hare Breath?"

"Surely it was Queen Arete, or perhaps her daughter, Nausikaa," I venture.

"Nay, Bush Tail, it was your-r-r master himself, though no one could see his face, for he had draped his mantle over it. I myself saw the tears splashing down upon his lap. Finally King Alkinoos saw them too, and heard your-r-r master's lamentations, for once the singer had finished and the audience was demanding another song, he clapped his hands and declared that the time for lyre and song was over, that he wished to show his new friend how surpassingly athletic the men of his island were.

"Oh, how my master has suffered!" I moan. "Surely the games put his mind at rest, though, Rat Chaser, did they not?"

"Not at fir-r-rst, whiskered one. Let me set the scene for you. Everyone went to the fields, newly plowed and marked for competition, and the finest of the island's youth stood forth, including Alkinoos's three sons, majestic Laodamas, stout Halios, and swift Klytoneos. Fir-r-rst, they held the running contests, and Klytoneos was out in front by a farrow's length, and he brought honor to his mother and father. Then they wrestled, and Eurylaos won his matches, as he was best among them all at that hard sport. For the jumping, Amphialos outleaped them all, while with the discus Elatreus threw it the far-r-r-r-thest. Finally, in boxing, it was Laodamas who was the last man standing, and he too swelled the chest of his father, the king. Then, after they had finished all the contests, Laodamas said, 'Come, friends, let us ask the stranger if he would like to enter a contest. He looks strong enough for sport; his thighs are muscular, as are his arms and his mighty neck. Surely though he is no longer young and has suffered much, he has some skill left in his body!'

"So with encouragement from his companions, Laodamas approached your-r-r master and said, 'Father Stranger, come and try these contests with us. You seem to know athletics, and there is no greater pleasure than testing one's speed or strength against another, and surely it would lift your spirits to compete with us before you set sail!'

"Then your-r-r master reproached Laodamas, saying, 'Young man, son of Alkinoos, why do you urge me to play your games? My mind is occupied with my own cares, not athletics. I long only to return to my home; I seek not glory in this kind of sport.'

"Then Eurylaos, the haughty wrestler, approached and spoke rudely to your-r-r master: 'I understand, stranger. You clearly are not a sportsman, as we are. You are just a sailor, a commander of rowers and mariners, perhaps even a profiteer. Your legs and arms are stout, but you do not look like an athlete, if the truth be told.' And then he spit on the ground near your-r-r master's feet!"

"He did *that*?" I ask.

"Aye, Black Nose. I was close by, in Nausikaa's arms, and I saw everything."

"Did my master smite him? He was a guest, but none would have blamed him, surely!"

"Nay, but he clenched his fists. Then he said, 'Reckless boy, that was not well said. You may be strong, but the gods did not bestow upon you good graces or eloquence. Now you have stirred my anger by your insults, and though I have been at war and at sea for many years, I think I shall try your contests.'

"Then your-r-r master, still wearing his mantle, took up the heaviest discus there, heavier than any of the Phaiakians had used, and he spun with such speed and fury that it hummed in the air and all who stood nearby, brave mariners themselves, threw themselves on the ground.

Finally the discus landed, overflying the marks of all the others by twice again! Then your-r-r master said words that bit: 'Try to reach that mark, men of Phaiakia, and I will throw it again even farther. And if you want to wrestle or box me, then have at it, except for Laodamas, for he is the son of my host. If you wish to contest me at archery, then lend me a bow, but be warned, only the great Philoktetes shot more Trojans than I, and if you wish to see me throw the javelin, you should know that I can throw the spear as far as most men can shoot an arrow. Only in a footrace do I fear you would surpass me, for I have been battered at sea, and my legs have lost their conditioning. What say you all?'

Oh, to have seen my master issue this challenge!

"Did anyone dare approach him?"

"Nay, Tail Wagger-r-r, only clearheaded King Alkinoos spoke. He said, 'Forgive this one his graceless talk, stranger. In truth, we are not as excellent as you in boxing and wrestling, but we are fine sailors and lovers of song and music. That is how I hope you remember us when you return to your land and sit again with your family, as men who feasted you well and did not insult a stranger. Now come, let us bring up the singer again, and we will show you our customary dances, for we are light on our feet and excellent dancers.'

"Then Nausikaa carried me back to the palace, and the townfolk returr-r-ned there too. Soon the lyre players were seated and the music began. Your-r-r master sat beside the king and queen in a place of honor while dancers moved back and forth among themselves, streaming red ribbons, and clapping their hands. Such a racket! Truly I thought I had gone to Hades itself, but the townfolk spun and spun. Finally, when the music had stopped for a moment, your-r-r master leaned over and said to King Alkinoos, 'Truly, it is as you boasted;

none anywhere can match your dancers. I sit here in wonder at them.'

"That pleased the king. He rose and proclaimed loudly, 'Hear me, leaders of the council! We have before us an honorable man, a man of good character and a friend. Let us each give him a gift of friendship, as is our custom. I say we each give him a fine tunic, a robe, and a talent of gold. Come, let us assemble these gifts at once and present them soon, for his departure is imminent.'

"So he spoke, and heralds went running back to their master's homes to acquire the gifts. Then Antinoos continued, saying that Euryalos himself must make amends for having insulted your master. Hearing this, Euryalos rose and approached the king, bent his knee, and said, 'O great Alkinoos, thank you for the opportunity to make amends to your guest. To him I gladly give this sword, with its silver handle, along with its ivory scabbard.'

"Then, turning to your-r-r master, Euryalos said, 'Take this sword, Father and stranger, as a token of my esteem. May the winds carry away my rude language, and may the gods grant you safe passage to your home, for I know you suffer from longing to be there.'

"Then he gave the sword to your-r-r master, who took it with great solemnity, answering, 'Farewell to you also, my friend, and may the gods give you many prosperous years. And thank you for this gift. I will carry this sword as a reminder of your kind words to a stranger.'"

"Such a great and noble man," I say softly.

"Truly, Argos. Even I was moved by his sentiments, as was Nausikaa, whose tears fell across my back. Then your master embraced all who were there, lifting the children high above his head and clapping the shoulders of the athletes who had competed. Finally King Alkinoos announced that the singer would sing one more song in his guest's honor. Everyone was seated, and again the lyre was brought forth. The blind singer was led out into the middle of the square, and he seated himself beside the musician. Silence flew over the court. Then the singer said, 'Bring forth the honored guest that I might read his face and know what song to sing.'

"Your master stepped forward, and the blind singer placed his hand over your master's face, touching the strong brow, the proud nose, the scarred and bearded cheeks. Then your-r-r master returned to his place between the king and queen while we waited for the singer to find his words.

"Athena herself must have spoken to the blind singer, for he seemed to be listening to someone, though no one stood beside him. Finally the lyre player strummed a note, and the singer began. I thought he would sing a tale of distant homelands and widowed wives, of seafarers and doomed mariners, or young lovers kept apart by warring families. But he did not."

There the loathsome creature stops and yawns.

"What did he sing, Long Tail?" I demand. "Was it a song of praise to the gods?"

"Leg Lifter, I am too exhausted to continue. Let me sleep for some time, and then I will resume."

The creature stretches his skinny front legs twice, and then his eyes began to close. Gods! Can a cat not stay awake for more than hour without requiring a nap?

"But surely you can stay awake a few moments longer, enough to finish the tale!" I plead. "What of my master? Has he left their island yet? You must tell me!"

"I cannot continue without a nap, flea-bitten one. Now, away with you while I find a sunny spot high in yonder-r-r barn. Return in a few hours with something juicy to eat, and I will finish my story."

Apollo's chariot flies over the western sky, and I have sheep to paddock. Soon suitors will be coming, and they will be expecting me to greet each of them with a snarl. There is no time to acquire another mouse. So, putting my muzzle right next to the cat's ear, I inhale as deeply as my old lungs will allow, and bark.

Oh, how that cat jumps!

When he lands, I speak in winged words. "Listen to me, most distrusted of all creatures. Your ship sails at dawn. If you wish to be on it, you will finish the story, or you will spend the rest of your short life eating skinny field mice and hiding from me, as well as every eagle that soars over Ithaka. Are my terms clear enough?"

"Yes, Boar Slayer," he mutters balefully. "Now where was I?"

"The blind singer was about to begin his song," I remind him. "Was it a love song?"

The cat laughs. "No, Sheep Breath, it was a song of war. He sang of your master, Odysseus, and how he built the giant horse and hid in it with his most trusted men. How the Trojans brought it into their city, not knowing it bore death and doom for them. He sang of how your master left his hollow hiding place in the belly of the wooden beast and sacked the city, killing many Trojans. That was the song that issued forth from his lips."

"And what of my master? What did his face reveal when he heard it?"

"He wept most piteously, though none saw it, for he covered

his face, except for King Alkinoos."

"The king saw my master weeping?"

"Aye, and finally he raised his hand and cut off the singer, saying, 'It is not right, stranger, that our most accomplished singer causes you such grief. Even though we have given you many fine gifts, your heart must surely hold great sorrow. Yet how can we be proper hosts if we cannot help you? Tell us what your father and mother called you. Tell us your land, your city, your citadel, so that our ships can sail you there, even though there is a prophecy that we will one day convey a stranger to his home and great Poseidon will punish us for it by hurling rocks onto our city.'

"Then your-r-r master removed the mantle that covered his face and looked out among the throng of people there. He raised his chin and gazed at them with clear eyes. Truly, all who were there knew him then to be a king."

Then the cat pauses.

"What did he say, Green Eyes?" I demand.

But the cat does not answer. Instead, with a sudden leap, he jumps into the air and lands high on a rafter, too high for me to reach him with my jaws, though I try three times.

"Here is what your master said, you buffoon!" the cat calls down at me. "He said, 'I am Odysseus, sacker of cities, son of Laertes. I hail from sunny Ithaka, where in the center rises a mountain called Nerito that can be seen from many miles away. The land is rugged, but it breeds good men. My wife, if she lives, is called Penelope, and I have a son named Telemachos. I have not seen either for twenty years, but at one time they were guarded by a fearsome dog named Argos. Now, I ask you—'

"Stop!" I cry. "My master said my name? He remembered me?"

"He did, indeed, Boar Kisser. I cannot say otherwise. Now may I continue?"

My master remembered me! After twenty years!

"Finish the story, please, Sir Cat," I say. "I will not interrupt again."

After a long pause while he licked his feet, the cat resumes his story.

"Your master said, 'Preeminent King Alkinoos, since I have revealed myself, will you grant me a ship so that I may sail it home? And in return, may the gods grant you and your wife and children great comfort and success in every endeavor.'

"'It shall be so,' Alkinoos said, and then he loaded the ship with gifts, treasure greater than Odysseus had won even sacking Troy. Then, your-r-r master boarded his new ship, oared by the sea-loving Phaiakians, and laid down to sleep, for he had promised that he would not try to learn his location, and Alkinoos had said if he did so, then the gods would not harm him while he slept, but instead send a great following wind to speed his ship to Ithaka.

"That is when I jumped on board my own ship, and together both ships sailed toward this wretched place, though my ship was not laden with treasure and thus was the faster. I lost sight of your-r-r master's ship several days ago. Per-r-rhaps it sank."

Just then a bell peals. The ship in the harbor—the cat's ship—is setting sail. We both hear it. The cat leaps from the rafter onto a bale of hay, then leaps again and lands near the door of the barn. I am an old dog and the cat is still young and swift, so he eludes me at first. I chase him across the grounds and down the trail leading to the harbor, across the black rocks that form a barrier against the sea tide, then down to the moorings where his ship is docked. Artemis herself gave that cat wings, and I know I can't catch him.

But others can.

I bark three times. That is my signal to the gulls, and from out of the very heavens they come.

"The orange harbor cat!" I cry. "Avenge your fallen brothers as I cannot."

The birds descend on the ship with their sharp beaks, but I turn away and look out over the sea one last time.

Is my master at this very moment sailing toward Ithaka? Only the gods know.

CHAPTER XXXV

ᘒᘒᘒᘒᘒᘒᘒᘒᘒᘒᘒᘒᘒᘒᘒ

Homecoming

My master has landed! He is here on Ithaka!

Here is what I know. I was down at the harbor, looking for signs that my master's boat had arrived, when I heard a pelican and a small group of gulls arguing.

"I say twenty!" the pelican said.

"Not a day more than nineteen!" the largest gull replied.

"It's twenty, because my mother was just a hatchling when he left!"

"My father saw his black ship personally," the gull said. "He perched on its mast. *Nineteen* years ago!"

"Nineteen! Nineteen! Nineteen!" his brothers squawk.

"Gentle birds!" I cried. "Why do you argue? What subject

vexes you so that you disturb this calm morning with your squawks?"

The pelican pointed his strange long beak at the gull and said, "This gull says your master left nineteen years ago, and I say twenty. Settle our dispute, Argos. How long ago did your master leave?"

Such impertinence!

"Why do you torment me with such a question, Fish Swallower? Do you think I have not counted every day that he has been gone? It is twenty years and more, for my master still has not returned!"

"But, Boar Slayer, haven't you heard?" the gull said. "Odysseus arrived three days ago on Ithaka. His ship ran up the beach on a small harbor that the men of Ithaka seldom use. There the Phaiakians carried your master, still asleep, onto the bank, near an olive tree, but hidden from the road, and placed around him his many gifts, bronze, gold, and fine linens. Then they themselves turned their way homeward, leaving him to be awakened by the gods. A tree owl saw the whole thing."

Then, I confess, Argos the Boar Slayer whimpered like a puppy. But just once. Master Odysseus was on the island! But where? I didn't know the harbor where he slept. Was it nearby?

Was my master even now striding toward his home? The birds did not know.

"Find him!" I commanded the gull, which was the smarter of the two. "Find him and report back to me, or I'll tell the barn cats where you make your nest."

The gull screeched at me, but did as I bade, and was soon flying high over the island, in search of my sleeping master, and the pelican flew off to fish.

Later that afternoon the pelican returned and told me a story of great woe: Poseidon, angered that the Phaiakians had conveyed my master home, turned their ship and sailors into stone, just within sight of their home.

So do the vengeful gods extract their dues.

Night has fallen and there is no news of my master. The gulls could not find him, and I think I have been deceived. Then, just as I am herding the last sheep into its paddock, I hear a tree owl's call. I find him perched on a juniper branch. This is the tale he tells.

"When Apollo's chariot reached its zenith, your master stirred and woke. But he did not know where he was, for Athena, daughter of Zeus, had made everything on the island look strange to him, so that he was not certain he had even reached home. 'Ah me,' he lamented. 'Where am I now? The Phaiakians promised to bring me to sunny Ithaka, but this land is shrouded in mist! Are the people of this land savage and violent or hospitable to strangers? And what shall I do with these gifts? Where should I hide them until I know the true nature of these people?'

"Then with great sorrow, your master hid the treasures and then set along the beach to look for the island's inhabitants. Along the beach he met a young man clothed in a shawl and armed with a spear.

"Know ye who that young man was, Boar Slayer?" the owl asks me as if he were a tutor himself speaking to a student.

"No, Sir Owl, I do not," I answer.

"Thick-headed pup! It was Athena herself disguised as a young man!"

Athena!

"Tell me, wisest of animals, what did my master say to the goddess?"

"Pay attention, grizzled one, and I will tell you all. Seeing the young man, your master rushed over to meet the goddess, saying, 'Dear friend, what land is this and what people live here? Is it an island or part of a mainland, jutting out toward the salty sea?'

"The gray-eyed goddess Athena answered thus: 'You are a stranger, no doubt, for this is a land with a name. Here there is grain for bread and grapes for wine, goats, cattle, and timber as well, and streams that run all season. Why, even the Trojans have heard of this land, for this is the island Ithaka, stranger.'

"Ahh, Boar Slayer, most men would have rejoiced boldly upon their homecoming, but your master is wily and trusted not this stranger. Instead he checked his words and said, 'I heard the name Ithaka when I was on Crete, far across the sea, and now I myself have come here. I fled wide Crete and am an exile now, having killed Orsilochos, a man swift of foot, with whom I fought against the Trojans, and who tried to rob me.'

"Then Athena changed herself into a woman again and took your master's hand. 'Truly you are ever contriving, clever one,' she said. 'But I know you, Odysseus, and now you know that I am Athena.'

"Your master fell to his knees then, Pink Tongue, crying, 'It is hard, O goddess, for a man such as me to recognize you, for you take every shape. But is it true that I am back to my dear country? It looks nothing like Ithaka!'

"And then the goddess chastised your master. 'Wily One, most men, upon arriving home after enduring such great suffering, would have run to their wife and children. But not you.

Why do you ask so many questions? Here, let me prove to you that this is your island.'

"Then, with a wave of her hand, she scattered the mist, and your master began to weep as Ithaka was revealed to him.

"'Daughter of Zeus,' he cried. 'Truly you have answered my prayers. I brought with me many treasures, which I have hidden, but now I wish to give them to you as gifts, for gold and jewels are not as dear to me as my own country.'

"Smiling, the goddess lifted your master from his knees and said, 'What need I of gold and jewels, brave one? Instead let us plot the destruction of the suitors who, even now, would steal your land and corrupt the heart of your loyal wife.'

"Truly, O goddess, with your help I would fight three hundred men."

And would I, alongside you, master.

"So the goddess and your master entered a nearby cave to make their plan."

Hearing this, my knees give way. *My master is so close!* I thank the tree owl and then ask, "Tell me, wisest of birds. Where is this cave? Can you lead me there? I can leave this moment!"

"I can take you there, Boar Slayer, but I will not. It is more than a day's walk for an old dog such as yourself, and you would be missed here. The suitors might grow suspicious and make their own plan to kidnap Penelope, or worse, for your master's son is still away, is he not? It is better for you to stay here and wait. I will tell you what I learn, so that when the time comes for your master's return home, you will be ready."

I have to admit the tree owl is right. He flies away after saying this, and I return to my watch. Twenty years have passed; I can wait another day or so to smell my master again, to feel his strong hand stroke my fur, to put my muzzle next to his knee. But I do not know his plan, and I cannot take the risk of spoiling it.

I will wait, though my bones ache and my eyes dim.

I will wait.

The next night the owl returns as he had promised.

"I watched the cave all day, Argos," he tells me. "And late in the afternoon, your master emerged from the entrance with gray-eyed Athena.

"'Now make your way to your faithful swineherd, Eumaios,' she commanded your master. 'Wait there for me. Eumaios is loyal and will accommodate you, for he is a good and noble man and friendly to your son and steadfast Penelope. While you are there, I shall go to Sparta, where your son is seeking news of your fate from Menelaos. I have heard that men are lying in wait for him, seeking to do him harm, but I shall not let evil befall him.'"

"'Please protect him, fair goddess,' your master said. 'For I have been gone too long to have my son taken from me at this late juncture.'

"'Do not worry about Telemachos, brave one,' the goddess replied. 'Instead think of the vengeance you will have over the suitors if you follow our plan. And remember, do not reveal yourself yet.'

"And upon saying this, she took her wand and tapped Odysseus on his shoulder. Suddenly his handsome flesh began to wither on his bones. His bright eyes dimmed, and his black hair turned gray and sparse. Then the very clothes he wore fell off, and she put a vile and dirty tunic over his body. Finally, arming him with a crooked staff, she bade him farewell, and your master began his journey across the island to find his loyal swineherd. No man would know him now," the owl says with a snap of his crooked beak.

Argos will, I think. *Argos will.*

CHAPTER XXXVI

With the swineherd

The owl, not wishing to be seen while Apollo's chariot still flew, sent a kingfisher to follow my master as he ascended a rugged path that led through pine-covered hills and then down into the valley where the loyal swineherd lived, tending to my master's land and herds. According to the kingfisher, the brave one found the swineherd Eumaios sitting on his porch, watching the fields from three sides, ever vigilant and keen of eye.

Inside the enclosure, scores of pigs wallowed and rutted, though their numbers had diminished, I know, because the suitors keep ordering more pigs to roast to feed their craven stomachs. The swineherd keeps four dogs nearby (slow-witted curs, really, but loyal to the swineherd), and when they saw my master coming along the path toward them, they ran at him with teeth bared. A cowardly man would have swung his staff at the dogs, but my master, instead, lowered his staff and sat down on the path to show he meant no harm. Seeing this brave act, the swineherd ran to my master, shouting at the dogs and driving them back with stones and kicks.

When the dogs retreated, the swineherd said, "Old one, you are either brave or foolish. The dogs might not have heeded me and instead attacked you, as you are defenseless. That would have brought shame on me."

"Surely your dogs are loyal, and there is no shame in that," my master said, and offered his hand.

Then Eumaios reached down and pulled my master to his feet. "My dogs are loyal, as am I, for I too seek nothing more than to protect my own master and his herds."

"And where is your master?" Odysseus asked. "And what is his name?"

"Alas, I do not know where he is—if he is alive and looks on the sunlight while he wanders strange lands, or lies dead. I know only that I mourn him, and I grieve for his family, who miss him most."

"That is a sad tale," my master said, his eyes watering as he learned of his servant's honor.

"Indeed, but I think that you too have sad tales to tell. Come, old man, enter my shelter and I will give you food and wine, for no man is a stranger under Zeus."

The kingfisher followed the men and hopped onto the porch to listen while the swineherd and my master shared goat stew and wine, but not before making offerings to the gods. After they had eaten, my master said, "Tell me your name that I may remember you for your loyalty to your master, should I meet him."

"My name is Eumaios, but alas, I fear you will never meet my master, thanks to cursed Helen, for many brave men died on her account. In Agamemnon's cause, my master went to Ilion, there to fight the Trojans, and he never returned, but perished perhaps. In his absence the land is overrun by cowards who would seek my master's land and steal his loyal wife. They demand his fattest pigs for their stomachs and steal his sheep and goats. They despoil his land and neglect his vines and olive trees. Truly they are savages and not fit to live among clean and noble men. Even yourself, old and tattered as you are, are more noble and honest, I can attest."

My master said nothing for a time and let the swineherd grieve. Then he said, "Dear friend, tell me the name of your master. You say he perished in Agamemnon's cause. Tell me his name, for I have wandered many places and perhaps met him along the way, for a man such as that would have stood tall among other men."

Eumaios stirred his fire and said nothing for some time. Finally he spoke. "Old sir, I fear you will never meet him. The dogs and the vultures have yanked the skin from his bones by now, or else the fish have eaten him, out in the great sea, and his bones lie buried in the sand upon a beach. So he must have perished, leaving his loyal wife and brave son to mourn him, and for me, most of all, for I will never know a lord as kind again as he. How I long to behold his eyes again, on this, his island. You asked me his name, sir, but I have some modesty naming it, for in his heart he loved me, and so I call him my master, though he is dead."

Moved greatly by his servant's loyalty, my master said softly, "Dear friend, on my oath I tell you that Odysseus is on his way home. Within days he will return, and he will take his revenge upon any who deprives his wife and son of the honor they are due."

But the swineherd only shook his head.

"I don't know if what you say is true, my friend," he said. "But I pray to the gods that brave Odysseus comes soon, for his stalwart son Telemachos left this fair isle many days ago to seek news of his father. And even now the dread suitors, I hear, are planning to ambush him upon his return, so that his name is never heard again on this island."

Hearing this, my master, the Wily One, said nothing. Then faithful Eumaios fed my master again and gave him wine, and they talked of ships and faraway islands and said nothing more of Odysseus's return. When it grew late, my master thanked the swineherd and said, "I have but one more request, dear friend. My clothes are nothing more than rags, and winter approaches. Do you have a mantle and tunic I might wear tomorrow? I shall return it if it pleases the gods."

"Yes, old sir," Eumaios said. "I have only a few cloaks and mantles, but you shall have my finest as a reward for keeping an old, lonely swineherd company."

Saying this, he laid out a mantle and tunic, simple but clean, and spread out another mantle on which my master would sleep.

"Thank you, kind friend," my master said. "And where will you sleep tonight?"

"I am but a lowly swineherd," the old man said. "I sleep with the pigs."

I still cannot believe that my master is here in fair Ithaka, and I have yet not seen him. I have been patient for so long, and now it is almost too much to bear. I have turned and begun to walk toward the sheep paddock when, suddenly, my back legs give way. After a few minutes I manage to stand and walk again, but I totter on my feet like a newborn fawn. *Hurry, master!*

CHAPTER XXXVII

Telemachos returns

This morning a seagull circled high above the sea cliff, calling me to come down to the black-rocked beach to hear his tale. I gathered my stiff legs beneath me and made my way down to the beach. The gull, a large female, perched on a large rock, above a small flock of her sisters.

"What do you have to tell me?" I call up to the gull.

"Only this," she says. "The goddess Athena found Telemachos three days back at the court of Menelaos. She came to him at night while he half dreamed and told him to return to Ithaka at once. She warned him that some of the suitors had hired a ship and lay in wait for him between here and Samos, so he must sail the long way around and land at the first promontory on Ithaka. Then he must find the loyal swineherd, and tell him to go quickly to Penelope and tell her in private that her son has returned."

"Telemachos returns! Returns! Returns!" squawk the other gulls.

"What of the suitors who would seek to ambush my master's son? Won't they give chase?" I ask.

"No, loyal one, fear not. Gray-eyed Athena has said that the earth will swallow those men, for they have no honor," the gull replies. Saying this, the gull rises and swoops above my head. "I will tell you when I espy his ship," the seagull calls, and then she dips one wing before turning and soaring back over the gray sea.

"Ship. Ship! Ship!" her flock cries, and then they too rise and, forming a delta, fly along the shore until I can no longer hear their cries.

Hearing the gull's words, my heart is gladdened so much that I bound up the sea trail back to my master's estate. When I arrive at the barn, Apollo's chariot is high, and I turn around three times before curling up on my bed of straw to nap for a few minutes, for I am old now, and old dogs must sleep before they fight.

There is great stirring on the isle of Ithaka. The birds will not stop their incessant chatter long enough to tell me the news, but I sense that there is joy in their whistles. Finally a raven descends on black wings, and I ask that he tell me what fortune has brought.

"Just this morning I saw-aw-aw a black ship beach near the promontory on the west of the island. I flew down to see if marauders were trying to land there, for it is sheltered and the cove is little known. But only two men disembarked, loyal Ar-Ar-Argos. One of the men was armed with a bronze-tipped spear. And then the ship turned back and sailed away."

"Telemachos has returned!" I cry, and shake all over, as we dogs often do.

"Yes, it was he. But why did he land there? Only the swineherd lives near there. Telemachos should have brought an ar-ar-army, for surely he alone cannot overthrow the suitors!"

"There is a reason to it, Sir Raven. Fly back, cleverest of birds. Fly back and follow my master's son. I would hear tell of his arrival at the swineherd's cottage."

"I will, noble Ar-ar-argos." He snaps his beak three times, which is how a bird smiles. "Surely the evil that has reigned on our island since your master left is about to end," he cries as he flies away.

I spend the rest of the day guarding sheep and resting. In the afternoon, two suitors come and demand the shepherd give them three lambs to be roasted. My master's flock grows ever smaller, but there is little I can do. For now.

In the late afternoon the raven returns. He lands on a branch outside my master's palace and calls out to me, stretching his black wings.

"Ar-Ar-Argos! Telemachos has landed safely on Ithaka, along with his loyal friend Theoklymenos."

My ears have not deceived me. Telemachos is safe! I stand too quickly and can feel my old bones creak. "Do go on, intelligent one."

"Not long after they landed on the black-rocked beach, a falcon swooped overhead; in his talons, a pigeon struggled. The falcon flew between Telemachos and his ship while tearing feathers from the pigeon. As the feathers floated down, Theoklymenos fell to his knees, crying, 'This is a great portent, Telemachos. Surely it means you are destined to win Ithaka!'

"'The gods make many promises, loyal one,' thoughtful

Telemachos responded. 'For now, we must go our separate ways. You will go to my house and seek out Eurymachos, who is the noblest suitor, and the most eager to marry my mother and take my father's land. Befriend him and learn his plans. The rest of my men on the ship will sail back around to the port and seek lodging there.'"

"And what direction did Telemachos take?" I ask the raven.

"After that, I saw-saw-saw that the falcon had dropped the dead pigeon on the beach near the breaking surf. So I flew over to eat it before it got wet."

I remain patient, as one must be when talking to ravens.

"But where did Telemachos go?" I ask again after a few moments. "Is he on his way here?"

"It was a wood pigeon, you see. The plumpest kind. And it was about to get wet. I'm not a seabird. I don't eat fish."

The raven seems quite pleased with himself, hopping around on his thin legs. If I were younger, I could have charged him. I'm sure I would at least have bitten some tail feathers before he could fly away. But instead I wait. Eventually, the raven hops back over to where I sit.

"Where did Telemachos go? That was your question?"

"Yes, Sir Raven, most intelligent of all the birds."

That compliment pleases the black bird. He ruffles his

feathers and preens for a moment.

"Telemachos lifted his spear, a powerful one with a bronze tip that caught-caught-caught the sunlight, and then he took the trail that leads to the swineherd's hovel."

Then the raven flies off, but he circles back and hovers over me for a moment.

"I fly now to the swineherd's cabin, Ar-Ar-Argos. The boy should be reaching it soon. I shall return in the morning with tales of his arrival."

I bark once to show my appreciation, and then I set off to make my evening rounds. How my sides ache and my feet throb as I do this. How dark the pastures look to me, how dimly I see the sheep.

Come soon, master. Soon.

CHAPTER XXXVIII

/∂/∂/∂/∂/∂/∂/∂/∂/∂/∂/∂/∂/∂/∂/

A father's embrace

This morning one of the mongrels that watches the swine-herd's pigs comes bounding up to me, his pink tongue lolling from his mouth.

"B-B-Boar Slayer! I have n-n-news for you!" he sputters.

In truth he smells as bad as the pigs he guards, but I simply maneuver myself upwind and say, "Catch your breath, noble friend, guardian of my master's swine, and tell me what you saw this morning."

Hearing this, the dog first slurps great gulps of water from my bowl and then tells me what he saw.

"M-m-m-my master woke early, as he always d-d-d-oes, brave Ar-ar-ar-gos, and so did the old m-m-man staying with him, a strang-strang-stranger. They made b-b-b-b-breakfast and began to eat it w-w-w-when a young man appro-appro-appro-appro— Came up the road to our house. When he got closer, I and the other dogs ran up to him. Then I sm-sm-sm-smelled him. It was Tele-Tele-Tele-Telemachos, returned from his journey seeking Ody-Ody-Ody— His father. We all barked for happ-happ-happ— Joy!"

"Calm down, young pup," I say as gently as I can. "I won't bite you! Put your tongue back in your mouth and slow down!"

I let the pup drink more water and rub his belly on the stiff grass. Meanwhile, my old dog heart is kicking like a goat. Finally he is ready to resume.

"My mast-mast-master and his old guest came outside to see why we were barking. Telemachos ran up to my master and kissed his face, his shining eyes, his hands. Oh, it was noble sentiment, brave Argos! Then my master began to w-w-weep with joy."

"'You have returned, Telemachos, sweet light of my life!' he cried. 'I thought this old man would never see your face again. Come into my home and tell me of your trip to Pylos. Did you hear word of your father?'

"Then tall Telemachos and my master and the stranger went inside. I snuck in just as my master closed the door, so I could hear his tale. There were only two chairs, and Telemachos said to the stranger, 'Sit, sir, for I am still young and your legs have carried your weight longer.'"

Oh, how gentle and polite is my master's son, I think.

"The old man smiled at this sign of respect, and he and my master took seats while Telemachos propped his sharp spear against a wall. Then c-c-c-courteous Telemachos said, 'I heard nothing about my father, loyal Eumaios. There are rumors and whispers, but the gods alone know his fate, for no man alive has seen him since he won victory at Troy. But now tell me, does my father's bed still hold spiderwebs, or has one of the suitors taken it over?'

"'No, brave Telemachos,' my master, the shepherd, answered. 'Your mother is steadfast, but still weeps away her wretched days and nights.' He sighed deeply, and then said, "Come, young master. We have eaten, but there is bread and honey for your repast, and figs to round out the meal. It is but simple fare, I admit, but you are welcome to it.'

"And hungry Telemachos thanked my master and ate, then he drank cool water from the jug. Finally he turned to my master Eumaios and asked, 'Uncle, who is this stranger, for he is not like any man I know on Ithaka. What ship brought him here?'

"Then my master said, 'He is an old man who has seen

much. He fought with your father against the Trojans and now has landed on Ithaka as my guest. Take him to your home and treat him as such, for I am poor and can offer this most honorable man little.'

"'Alas, stranger,' Telemachos said. 'I would gladly give you a mantle, sandals, and a sharp sword, but I cannot admit you to my house, for the dreadful suitors there are laying waste to it.'

"Then the old man spoke, saying, 'Your gifts are much appreciated, noble Telemachos, but tell me, do you not have brothers to help you against the suitors? Are there not men in the village who would follow your command against them?'"

Hearing this, I smile. *Ah, master, even in front of your son, you remain the Wily One, do you not?*

"Should I continue, ancient one?" the pup asks.

"Please do," I say.

After scratching his ear, he resumes his tale. "'Let me put it plainly, sir,' Telemachos said. 'The first god Kronos had but one son, Arkeisios. He had but one son, Laertes, and Laertes had but one son, Odysseus, and in turn Odysseus had but one son, myself. So I have no brothers, nor uncles to help me. And the men in the villages, those who did not leave with my father, are the very ones seeking to take my father's land and bed his wife. These men have followers as well, so that they number more than one hundred. That is why I cannot offer you respite as a man should to his guest, for I too am a stranger in my own home.'

"This tale moved the old man to tears, and he sat heavily against the wall. Then Telemachos turned to my master and said, 'Loyal Eumaios, go quickly to my dear mother Penelope and tell her I have returned. Tell her I am safe and will stay here. Give her this letter and tell no one else, for there are many there who plot against me.'

"'And should I go on from there and send a message to your grandfather?' my master asked. 'For poor Laertes also weeps for his son and grandson.'"

"Tell my mother to send a loyal servant to Laertes, then come back here swiftly. The Fates' threads are winding tight, my loyal friend, and though no mortal knows if and when my own father returns, I believe I am destined to see him again soon.'

"Th-th-then my master Eumaios put on his sandals and left. I followed him out the door, hoping he would feed me, but alas, he was in too great a hurry. But just as he turned down the path to come here, a tall and beautiful woman clothed in a gold-thread mantle appeared."

"Athena!" I exclaim.

"Yes, b-b-brave one, it was the goddess herself. I turned back and followed her. She approached the door of the cottage, but only the old man saw her, for Telemachos had turned his back. The old man came out to greet her and . . ."

"And what? What did the goddess say to the old man? Tell me, little one!"

"She-she-she said, 'It is time, brave Odysseus, to reveal yourself to your son.'

"And then she struck the old man with a wand, and he changed before my eyes! Brave Argos, the old man grew tall and stalwart. His jaw firmed and his skin turned to bronze. His beard changed from white to black, and the old mantle my master had given him fell away, revealing a mantle of the finest silk threads. I have never seen anything like it, noble one!"

Yes, I think. *To see my master in his glory is unlike anything else.*

"Th-th-then Athena herself d-d-d-disappeared, leaving your master alone to greet his son after twenty years."

"What did brave Telemachos say? Did he fall to his knees or rush to embrace his long-lost father?"

But the young pup looks at me with something like pity.

"B-b-brave Argos, Telemachos had not seen his father since he was a babe. Every pup knows that. He didn't recognize him. Instead he stepped back and said, 'You have changed, my friend, from what you were formerly. Surely you are one of the gods. Be gracious to us, for we have little here, but what we do have we offer to you.'

"Then your master, the long-suffering Odysseus, rushed to his son and embraced him, crying, 'I am not a god, but your father, for whose sake you have been grieving.'

A whimper escapes my lips then, but fortunately the mongrel does not hear it, so excited is he to finish the tale.

"Brave Odysseus kissed his son's face, his hair, while tears streamed from his face. O Argos, it was a sight to behold! But still Telemachos did not believe him! He pulled away and said the most hurtful words, 'No, you are not my father, but some divinity who seeks to trick me, as if I have not grieved enough! Only one moment ago you were an old man, and now you resemble a god!'

"Then Odysseus spoke. 'It is I, truly, my son. No other Odysseus will you ever see. But here I am as you see me, and after terrible suffering and hardships, I have returned to my own country. And to my family.'

"When he spoke those words, young Telemachos believed him at last and sank into his arms, shedding tears and crying pitifully."

I too lower my head at the thought of their misery, for joy cannot yet be theirs while the suitors remain in their home and Penelope mourns.

"Should I continue, brave one?" the pup asks.

I nod, for I cannot speak at the moment.

"Th-th-then mighty Odysseus said, 'Come, Telemachos, tell me of the suitors. How many are there and what are their names? I have pondered this matter for many years and would know if you and I together can defeat them.'

"Telemachos shook his head. 'O father,' he said, 'I have heard of your prowess, your fame as a fighter and your cunning, but what you speak of is impossible. No two men could face that number alone, for there are more than twice ten. Indeed, they now number more than one hundred, though at least four were killed by wolves or some similar beast.'"

I am that beast, I think.

"'No, Father,' Telemachos continued. 'I fear your revenge will be bitter upon us, though I am willing to taste it. Yet, if you can think of someone to stand by us, our odds would increase.'

"Then, brave one, your master smiled.

"'There are two who would aid us, my son, and they are gods. For Athena and Zeus the father may come if we call, though they sit high in the clouds. Now, listen close to my plan.'"

Suddenly the pup rolls over onto his back and begins to wriggle with his legs in the air.

"What was the plan, pup? Did you hear it? Get up and tell me!"

The pup rolls back over, but looks at me with shame. "A-a-alas, brave Argos, I can not. At that moment a flea bit me in the pink of my ear and I had to scratch it, so I know not what he said."

Pups these days are the most foolish of creatures. Still, praise is due.

"You did well, young pup," I tell him. "Now run back to your home and keep your ears clean of fleas. If you learn the plan, come back and tell me. I will remember your loyalty when my master is returned safely home, and you will be given a large flock of sheep to guard."

"Th-th-th-thank you, brave Argos. Farewell."

We touch noses, and then the mongrel scampers off.

How desperately I want to run to the swineherd's hovel to see my master! But I know I must wait here, and my legs are too wobbly to carry me. The gods are weaving destruction, and I am but one of many spiders in the web.

CHAPTER XXXIX

౸౸౸౸౸౸౸౸౸౸౸౸౸౸

Comes a beggar

Dawn comes, and the raven swoops low over the barn where I lie resting. In truth, my legs are weak today, and I cannot yet rise.

"Noble raven," I call. "Did you come from the home of the swineherd?"

The raven does not answer, but alights on the fence and ruffles his feathers.

"What news do you bring of my master and his son? Have they devised a plan?" I ask again.

Still the raven speaks not.

"Noble raven, did you hear me?"

Finally the bird speaks.

"Is it true, brave Ar-Ar-Argos, that you called the kingfisher 'most intelligent of birds'? Did you say that?"

I realize then what I had done; ravens are the most vain of all birds. Even a peacock has more modesty.

"I did say that, noble raven. But only a bird as silly as a kingfisher would believe it, thus proving the opposite, yes?"

The raven turns his head sideways and regards me for a moment.

"Haw-haw!" he laughs. "You are very clever, Ar-Ar-Argos. Truly, you understand the mind of my cousin. They are-are-are quite susceptible to false praise."

"Indeed. Now, what of my master and his son? What did they say this morning upon rising?"

"Ahh, brave Ar-Ar-Argos. A plan is under way, I think. Overnight, Athena changed your master back to an old man, and this morning young Telemachos rose and took up a shar-shar-sharp spear in his grip, saying to the swineherd, 'I am going to my home so that my mother will know I have returned. You should take the stranger to the city and let him beg there. You have been gracious enough to him, but he must not be a burden upon you any longer.'

"Then your master agreed, saying, 'The young warrior is right, my friend. I am too old to be of use here. Take me to the city so that I might find a purpose there and charity from the city folk. You have served me kindly, and the gods will reward you if they are just.'

"Then did brave Telemachos leave, carrying his stout spear, and after breaking their fast, the swineherd and your master also left, on their way to the city."

"If they are on their way to the city, then they will pass by here!" I cry. "After twenty winters my master returns to his land!" If I were younger, I would have run in mad circles at the prospect of seeing him, but alas, now my legs will not carry me in such a fashion.

"Calm yourself, loyal Ar-Ar-Argos," he says. "Your master is still in disguise. The moment is not yet at hand for revenge."

The raven is right. I do not know my master's plan, and until I do, I will have to be careful not to give any clues to the suitors that my master has returned, for they are a suspicious lot, and would kill even a beggar if they suspected he was loyal to Odysseus. And kill me too.

I thank the raven, praising him again for his surpassing intelligence and wisdom, and he flies off with puffed feathers and a dip of his wing. I know it will take several hours for Telemachos to arrive, so I struggle to my feet and make my rounds, checking the sheep and the goats, one of whom gave birth to a kid last week, and so I must be vigilant about the eagles who like nothing better than tender young goats, enough, even, to risk my wrath.

After Apollo's chariot passes its zenith, I trot slowly down to the swineherd's path and see, dimly, in the distance, a tall young man carrying a spear. Telemachos has returned! I bark and run up to him on tottering legs, letting him rub my belly and scratch my ears. Then I follow him up to the house, but not before I smell, far off, but upwind, the suitors, who will be arriving within the hour. A growl escapes me.

Inside his father's palace, Telemachos props his spear against the wall and bounds up the stairs to see his mother, sweet Penelope, who begins to weep loudly. I could not follow him up the stairs as my legs are too weak, but I hear her thank the gods that he has arrived safely home.

Telemachos tells his mother of his fruitless journey, how no one had heard if his father had perished or still lived. *How it must pain my young master to deceive his mother.* I can hear his voice catch as he tells her this tale of woe. As his mother weeps, I hear Telemachos ask, though he knows the answer: "Tell me, Mother. Since I have been away, do the suitors still come daily to court you and eat from our table?"

"They do, my son," she answers bitterly. "They come daily

and court me, telling me tales of shipwrecks and destruction, that no man returns after twenty years, even godlike Odysseus, as they deplete our herds and beat our servants."

Then my young master whispers so that none but his mother and a loyal dog can hear, "Truly, Mother, just as when a doe while grazing brings her fawns too near the den of a wolf, so shall my father, Odysseus, bring destruction upon those men."

It takes all my will not to bark in agreement at my young master's words, but just then I hear the suitors approaching the gates. For the next few hours, they distract themselves with games of spear throwing and hurling disks while my master's servants prepare their dinner. The servants roast lamb and goat and bake loaves of bread in the hearths. Others roll grape leaves stuffed with rice and set bowls of salty olives on the tables. Still others pour flagons of wine and honey mead into cups, for the suitors will be thirsty after their games. Then Medon, the head servant, calls the men inside, and they take off their mantles and prop their spears against the wall before sitting down to eat. As they enter, I leave the banquet hall with my tail hanging low, as if I were afraid of them. My master has taught me well: one should never let an enemy know that he is not feared.

Outside I manage to climb to a small ridge and sniff the air.

How I have longed for that scent! My master, Odysseus, sacker of cities, is near. What indescribable joy I feel! Then I have a terrible thought: *What if my master has forgotten me?* I was just a whelpling when he left, barely a year old. What hardships he has endured! What despair he has known! *Why do I expect him to remember me, a faithful dog, now sunken ribbed, broken, and nearly toothless?* I could not bear that. So instead of running down the goat path to meet him, I lie down near the barn to wait, turning myself around and around until I am in a position to see the path.

A few minutes later I see them. The old swineherd Eumaios walks side by side with a stooped, ragged beggar—my master. I creep closer but remain hidden, for I smell another man approaching. Just then the goatherd, Melanthios, a proud and vicious man, driving his goats from the far pasture, comes upon them. Seeing Eumaios, whom he has always envied for his friendship with my master, he curses the swineherd, crying, "Why do you bring a beggar around here? He's just the kind of wretch who spoils the fun of feasting, begging for handouts and wine to drink! You'd better not bring him near the house of Odysseus, for he will feel the weight of heavy blows from the heroes within!"

Then Melanthios raises his cudgel, as if to strike my master!

I jump to my feet and run toward them, growling and barking, but I am still too far away to do more than bark. Then Melanthios swings his club, but my master catches his arm, and the blow never lands. The goatherd curses and draws away. "May the gods strike you down, beggar, along with you, Eumaios," he sneers.

Eumaios raises his own hand to strike the goatherd, but my master steps between them. "We mean you no offense, sir," I hear my master say. "Please pardon us. We are on our way to the city and will not stop to beg at your master's palace."

This was brave Odysseus? Had the goddess stolen his pride as well as his form? Then I see it. My eyes are old and tired, but I see my master wink at Eumaios, as if to say, "Follow my lead!"

Of course! My master is not yet ready to reveal himself. Now I have a part to play. I advance upon them, growling, with my few remaining teeth bared and hackles raised.

"That old dog will see that you don't come near the palace!" The goatherd laughs. "Now be off! And thank the gods I have more important things to do than beat you!"

Melanthios continues on his way, while I, still growling, approach Eumaios and my master. *Oh, forgive me, Odysseus, for showing you my teeth, worn and broken as they are!*

I advance slowly, waiting for Melanthios and his goats to descend into the valley. Once they do, I bark once, loudly, for effect, and then I run limping toward my master.

I hear Eumaios say, "Don't worry, friend. The dog will not bite as long as you are with me. He was well trained once, by his owner, the noble Odysseus."

Then my master puts his hand out with his palm up for me to smell it. *Oh, words cannot describe that smell.* His hand smells of the briny sea and the blood of Troy, the sulfur of Hades and the honey mead of Kalypso, the smoky ash of a spear hardened in the fire. He smells like a king. Then I lick his hand, though only once. My master looks me in the eye, as if to say, "Don't reveal who I am, faithful one!"

Still I wag my tail and fold both of my ears back. May the gods strike me if I did not see a tear form in my master's eye.

"Eumaios, my friend," my master says. "Whose dog is this? He has a splendid shape, though he is ancient. What a broad chest he has, and a sturdy muzzle. He looks as if he could have once outrun a deer. What is the old dog's name?"

Then the swineherd answers. "This is the dog of a man who perished far away, my master Odysseus. You should have seen him in his youth, friend. Such strength and speed he had! Never could any wild animal escape if he pursued it, and he could track anything, even the wild boar, which he and his master hunted, fearing not their size and cunning, but ridding Ithaka of their destructive ways."

"You have not named him, but I shall, for I have heard his legend and that of his master, Odysseus. His name is Argos, is it not?" my master asks deceptively.

"Aye, this is loyal Argos, once a great boar hunter and wolf killer, but now death stalks him, I fear, for even one such as he is not immortal. It is strange to see him lick your hand, friend, for only Telemachos and my mistress Penelope has he let near since his master left. Come now. We have reached the palace, and Telemachos awaits us."

My master takes my head in his hands and looks deep into my eyes. "Can it be that you still live? Truly the gods are good, bravest of all dogs," he whispers. "Now you may let go of your duty to me and hunt the wild stag and the fearsome boar on Mount Olympus. They wait for you on the other side, most loyal of all creatures."

Then he gives me a final pet, and the two men stride toward the palace. I try to follow them, but my legs will not move, and so I lie down. I close my eyes for a few minutes and feel a cool wind ruffle my fur.

Outside the hall where the suitors feast, I hear dogs growling.

I open my eyes slowly and see several small shepherding dogs, all of which belong to the house of Odysseus and its herders, coming onto the estate. I had told them to remain close to my master's estate this day in case any suitors should try to flee. I know them all by sight, and some by name. I had taught most of their fathers how to guard their flocks, and I have outlived them too. Still, these younger pups show respect, rolling onto their backs, or at the very least, lowering their heads as they approach me.

All but one does this, I notice, but I say nothing, as he is a stranger to me, and I have not the strength to admonish him. He is very large and sturdily built, with a coat of thick, tawny fur. His muzzle is black, his ears erect, and his eyes sparkle. I force myself to my feet, and we touch noses, as is the custom when two alpha dogs meet. "Greetings, stranger," I say to the dog. "Where are you from, and what is your name? I know most of my brothers on fair Ithaka, but know you not."

I do not introduce myself, as there is no need; my name is known throughout Ithaka.

"I am from the north of the island, sir," he says, "and I have never come to this part of Ithaka until now." His voice is pleasant and well pitched. "Alas, I have no name, Uncle, being orphaned while young, and living not among men but in the wild."

I lie down again before my legs give away, but I remain upright. "What brings you here to my master's palace, then?"

The handsome dog steps closer to me so that only I can hear his answer.

"I learned that Aristratus, one of your mistress's suitors, has returned. I wish to see him for he wronged me once."

Aristratus? That name is familiar to me, yet I cannot place it.

"The chance for revenge will come presently, my friend," I say. "Stay close, and soon your fine jaws will find their target. Destruction is coming, and dogs such as we will play our part. If you are hungry, there is food near the kitchen, where the cooks throw out old meat and water too."

"Thank you, noble Argos," the dog replies. "I caught a hare on my journey, and it was enough for now."

We touch noses again, and this time he lowers his tail to show his respect. My head begins to swim, and I realize that I have begun to pant, although the day is not yet hot.

"Young one," I say, "tell me your lineage. Who was your father? Your mother? Where did they live? I would surely know of them if they were from here. And you must have brothers and sisters, do you not?"

For a long time my companion does not speak. Then he says, "Alas, brave Argos, as I said, I am orphaned. I do not know my father's fate, and my mother is long gone. I know not even if my brothers and sisters live. They were taken away from me when I was a pup. I alone escaped, only to watch helplessly as they, along with my mother, were carried aboard a red ship to be taken to a far-off isle. That was the last I saw of them, although I heard their howls of fear for many months afterward in my sleep."

Could it be?

"Did you say it was a red ship?" I ask.

"Yes, noble one. With forty oars. I counted them."

"And this ship. Were its sails yellow? Not white?"

"As yellow as Apollo's chariot," the dog says bitterly.

I have seen red ships in the harbor a few times in my life, but all but one was rigged with white sails. "Tell me of your mother. What color was her fur? Was it tawny like yours? Was her muzzle golden as well? Do you remember?"

"Aye, I remember her perfectly. Both her fur and her muzzle were the color of meadow flowers in spring, as yellow as the solidago plant that covers the mountain sides."

"We call that plant goldenrod. And it is beautiful."

I close my eyes. I can see her. My golden mate.

"Noble Argos, do you faint? Should I fetch a servant?"

"No, I was merely thinking and remembering. The man you

seek—he was the one who bought her?"

The dog whimpers. "Yes. I have thought for many years that revenge would bring me peace, but I know now it will not. I have no brothers, no sisters, no mother, and no pack. Not even a flock of sheep to guard. Nor do I have a master to guard, having lived in the wild for many years as a wolf might. Seeing you reminds me I am more alone than before."

He has her eyes, I think.

I lie down on my side. I can no longer hold my head up. How heavy my eyes feel.

"You are *not* alone. Lie close to me, my son, offspring of Aurora," I said. "Lie close to your father and know that you belong to me."

I feel him lick my ear.

"I will remain by your side, noblest of creatures," he says softly.

Then Athena herself places her hand over my eyes. I sense her there beside me.

"My son," I begin.

"Rest, Father."

"I will rest soon enough," I gasp. "But first you must listen to my charge. My master, noble Odysseus, has returned after many years to retake his home. He is the one dressed as a beggar, but soon he will be king again. His only son is brave Telemachos. Telemachos is your master now, and Queen Penelope your mistress. Guard them both well."

Then Athena closes my eyes.

I am Argos, the Boar Slayer; dog son of Odysseus, sacker of cities, dog brother of noble Telemachos; mate of golden Aurora, now father to a noble son, and here my story ends.

BOOK III

CHAPTER XL

ᔆᔆᔆᔆᔆᔆᔆᔆᔆᔆᔆᔆᔆᔆᔆᔆ

I find a master

*No blind poet has sung my story, as they did my father, noble
Argos, but I will tell it as it happened—though roughly, I confess,
for I never lay at night beside a tutor or a philosopher, and my
words are ill formed, I fear. Still, I am the son of Argos, guardian
companion to Telemachos, and my tale will be remembered by
some, I think.*

Brave Telemachos was in the dining hall when Odysseus, still
disguised as a beggar, and Eumaios entered, and I followed.

"Eumaios," Telemachos said. "Whose dog is this? I have not
seen him before. Surely he belongs to some noble, for his bearing is proud, as if his sire were Herakles himself, so large and
well-formed is he."

"I know him not, Telemachos," the swineherd said. "He belongs to no shepherd on this island, or farmer, I believe, for I would have heard of him if so. Perhaps he escaped from a ship. A few have landed recently, and their sailors drink our prized wine and forget themselves often."

I approached Telemachos and licked his hand.

"I think he has found a new master," Odysseus said. "I too once had a loyal dog, worth more than gold to me. You should take him, sir, for a companion like that is hard to find on this island or any other."

"I shall indeed take him, for one day I will hunt boars again, and he looks to be a fine tracker, and fearless, too," said Telemachos.

"Aye, not even a lion would he fear, I venture," said Eumaios.

Telemachos laughed and stroked my head. "Thank you, Eumaios, that is what I shall call him. Leander, the lion hunter."

Leander! That is to be my name. I licked Telemachos's hand again to thank him. I was his now, for life. My father's command was fulfilled.

I sat beside Telemachos, and with one hand on my neck, he said quietly to the two men, "Forgive my manners, friends. Take this bread and this meat, freshly carved, sirs. Sit at this small table, where I break my fast, and fill your stomachs, so I do order. Then, when you have finished the meat, old beggar, go into the dining hall where the suitors are eating, and ask them each for bread, for I would see who is generous and who is not."

Brave Odysseus nodded, and after eating, he, Eumaios, and I entered the great hall. In the hall Odysseus saw Athena (I saw her also), though no other man divined her presence, and he knew she was there to see which of the suitors she would spare from disaster. So Odysseus approached every man, and with his palm extended, asked for spare coins and bread to fill his sack. They all but a few denied him even a crust of bread, and one scoundrel spit on brave Odysseus's outstretched hand! How Argos would have shown his sharp teeth then, but I could not. Not yet.

Then, among the suitors, Antinoos spoke disapprovingly, castigating Eumaios for bringing a beggar into the hall, saying, "Foolish swineherd, why did you bring this old man here? Are there not enough beggars and vagabonds in the city? Let him beg there rather than here among us!"

The Eumaios replied, "Antinoos, though you are noble, you are not well-spoken. Why begrudge a poor beggar food and coin? Although I would expect it, for you, among all the suitors, treat the servants the worst here, me, most of all."

Hearing this insult, Antinoos raised his hand to strike the swineherd, but my master, Telemachos, cried sharply, "Enough! What he says is true, Antinoos. You treat the servants cruelly, and you are more eager to eat than to give to another."

Enraged, Antinoos lifted a stool and threatened to hurl it at the swineherd, but Odysseus stepped between them and said, "Won't you give to an old beggar? You, among all men here, are the most kingly. Therefore, you should give me a better present of food than all the others. And if you do so, I'll sing your praises wherever I travel, for I wander many places and would sing your fame over the endless earth."

Then Antinoos said, "What spirit brought this pain among us? You are nothing more than a shameless beggar. You already went around the entire circle asking for bread, and some gave to you generously! Do you require more, shameless vagabond?"

Odysseus shook his head. "No, the shame is on you. Your wits do not match your handsome face. For you would not give salt to a servant or bread to a beggar, even though it is not your house and there is food in abundance!"

Hearing this, Antinoos threw the footstool at Odysseus, striking him in the shoulder! But Odysseus did not move, nor was his body shaken by the missile. Instead he strode to the windowsill and sat there as if gathering his thoughts. Then he shook his head and said, "It is one thing to be struck in battle, or in a fight to protect one's belongings from a thief, but to strike a man simply because he is hungry and asks for food is a terrible thing. Therefore, if there be any gods or furies who look gently upon beggars, they will surely strike you dead before you are married!"

But Antinoos was not chastened. Rather, he cursed Odysseus in return. "Go now, beggar, on your own feet, before we drag you out from this house and tear the skin from your body!" he thundered.

It was then that loyal Eumaios intervened, for surely Odysseus and Antinoos were close to attacking each other, saying, "Come outside, friend. It is better to eat your bread in the fresh air than to suffer the foul curses of an enemy."

Hearing that, Odysseus took his crust-filled sack, and he and Eumaios and I left the room to join Telemachos. Sometime later, a servant girl came outside and said, "Kind sirs, I bring a message from my mistress Penelope. She says that you, loyal Eumaios, may return home to your pigs before it grows too dark, and that your friend should come to my mistress's chamber, for perhaps he knows news of long-suffering Odysseus."

How did Odysseus not betray his joy then? To see his loyal wife after such long suffering! But noble Argos's master is known as the Wily One, is he not? Instead of doing as he was bidden, he told the servant girl this: "Tell your mistress, fair Penelope, that I will come to her after sunset and when the suitors have left."

The servant girl left with her message, and Eumaios stood up as well to leave, but before doing so, he whispered into my master Telemachos's ear, "Dear boy, I go now to guard the pigs. Watch yourself and the old beggar tonight, for there are men here who would do evil upon you both."

"Thank you, loyal friend," Telemachos said. "I will see to things here tonight, as will the gods. Return in the morning, though, if you can, and we shall see what the new day brings."

Then loyal Eumaios left, following the narrow path to his home, while Odysseus drew his cloak near in the cooling evening and built a small fire. Telemachos remained outside with him. I lay there beside Telemachos, and he stroked my back.

It was the first time I allowed a man to touch me.

Later that night, I put my teeth around Telemachos's mantle and led him to where my father, Argos, lay, but his body was gone. All that remained was a tuft of black fur glistening in the moonlight. Telemachos picked it up and returned to the fire, giving the tuft to noble Odysseus.

"The gods have taken your most loyal companion to Mount Olympus, Father," Telemachos said softly. As he said this, a cloud passed over the moon, although the sky was clear and star filled.

"Truly, Argos was like a brother to me," brave Odysseus said.

"And to me, a father," said noble Telemachos.

Then did I see a king and his son weep.

CHAPTER XLI

A wrestling match

I smelled him first, then heard his curses and oaths as he trod up the path to our estate. His cloak was made of fetid animal skins, and he had not bathed for many days. Iros, it was; a local beggar known for his strength and his large belly, who apparently came often to the palace when the suitors were there, to beg for coin and food. I growled and raised my hackles, but Telemachos called me to his side and made me sit between him and his father.

"Greetings, sir," Odysseus, still also clothed as a beggar, said.

"Not greetings, but farewell, I think," Iros replied. Truly, the smell of his breath was worse than a boar's. "Leave this court now, or I shall be forced to drag you out. So say the suitors who hired me to dispatch you. Suitors!" he called. "I have come to do your bidding!"

The door to the palace opened, and the suitors passed through it. Having feasted, they longed for sport.

"Stranger," Odysseus said calmly, "there is no need for such talk. There is plenty of food here, and the door is wide enough for both of us. You are a beggar as I am, so don't threaten me, for though I am old, I may still bloody your face."

Then Iros called out to the suitors, "Did you hear that? The old man threatens me!"

Then Antinoos, most haughty of the suitors, called out, "Friends, let us wager on this contest. I say to the combatants, whichever of you wins shall come here every night for dinner and sit among us as equals. What say you, men?"

And the suitors all cheered this wager. Then Odysseus, the Wily One, spoke, saying, "Truly, though I am an old man, I agree to this. For though I bear this vagabond no harm, my stomach drives me to it. But you must all swear that none of you will take the side of Iros and strike me with a heavy hand so as to give this man the advantage. Swear you this?"

Laughing, the suitors all swore their pledges. Then brave Telemachos stepped forward and said, "Stranger, fear not these men. I am your host, and whoever should strike you would find himself outnumbered. So I swear!"

The men all jeered Telemachos, which brought a snarl to my lips, but Telemachos kept a strong hand on my neck. Then the suitors made a circle around Iros and brave Odysseus, urging them on. Then did Odysseus remove his outer tunic, displaying powerful thighs and broad shoulders. Athena herself came down (though only I saw her) and magnified my master's limbs so that the suitors were astonished.

Iros himself paled and began to back away, but Antinoos cursed him, saying he would be fed to the dogs on a forgotten island if he did not fight, so he charged Odysseus, trying to gain the upper hand. But Odysseus was too quick. He spun out of Iros's grasp and struck him just below his ear. Iros fell to the ground, and the suitors erupted with laughter. Then Odysseus took Iros by the foot and dragged him outside, propping him against a tree.

"Sit here and scare away the dogs and pigs," he said to Iros, "and never again claim to be king of the beggars, or worse than this will befall you!"

Then a suitor called Amphinomos by the others brought Odysseus a loaf of bread and a cup of honey wine to eat inside the great hall.

"To your health, Father and stranger," he said, raising his own cup. "May you be prosperous in the future, for you have been, until now, most unfortunate, it would seem."

Odysseus raised his cup and answered, "Truly, you are very wise for a young man, and well-spoken, so let me tell you what I know. Surely, of all the creatures that walk this earth, man is the most helpless, for when he is young and full of life, he believes the gods are with him, and when he suffers misfortune, he then blames it on them too. I myself was once promised by the gods a life of prosperity, but look at me now. So I say do not take the gods' gifts for granted, but offer thanks whenever they are come your way."

They each drank from their cups, and Odysseus continued. "I look around and see so many suitors devising evil and showing no respect for the wife who lives here. They take for their own possessions of a man who I think will return soon. When he does, I hope your destiny has led you far from here."

Hearing this, the suitors became silent.

"Perhaps what you say is true," Amphinomos said finally. "And perhaps it is not," he sneered. Then he took another drink and returned to his seat. I looked over to Telemachos, and he was staring at Amphinomos, as if to remember his face for another day. Then above me, I heard footsteps: three pairs of feet crossing the floor. Telemachos heard them too. "My mother will be down soon," he said to Odysseus, who nodded once.

None of the suitors heard this; they continued feasting, raising their cups and cursing the servants if they were too slow to refill them. But Odysseus and his son, my master, ate quietly, watching, and saying nothing. Then my nose twitched and my ears stood up, for my mistress Penelope had descended the stairs, and she approached the great hall, but such was their noise and revelry that the suitors did not see her as she stood in the door, watching their actions. Never had a woman looked so bewitching, though she held a sheer veil over her face to protect her modesty. My young master Telemachos was the first to see her, and he approached her as a loving son would do. Beside me I heard Odysseus inhale sharply, but he could not betray his identity.

"Tell me, son," my mistress said. "Was there a struggle down here?"

Then noble Telemachos said, "Yes, Mother, there was. It shames me to say that under our roof the suitors wagered on a struggle between two beggars. How low our house has fallen. If only I had twenty men as strong as the stranger who defeated Iros, then the suitors would be driven away and honor would be restored here."

So the two were lamenting their fate when suddenly Eurymachos noticed fair Penelope, and he rose to his feet, while slamming down his empty cup with force to draw attention to his announcement.

"Daughter of Ikarios," he said. "Loyal Penelope, your beauty tonight outshines the goddesses. Surely tomorrow there will be even more suitors here, for there is no one among the Achaians whose beauty and stature surpass yours."

Trembling with terrible emotion, Mistress Penelope answered him thus: "Eurymachos, my beauty and my stature were ruined by the gods when my husband, Odysseus, set sail for Troy. Before he left, he took my arm and said, 'Dear wife, not all of us will return from this war. The Trojans are men who can fight in battle, and they can throw spears and shoot arrows as well as any Achaian. I do not know if the gods will spare me or if I will be killed there in Troy. But if I do not return, then let everything be in your hands, and when our son, Telemachos, is grown, you may marry any man you please.'"

Hearing this, the craven suitors cheered. But my mistress had not finished.

"Be silent, guests. Thus did my husband speak," she said gravely. "And now, wretched me, my son is grown and custom demands that I remarry. But I tell you all, my husband would not have released me to such as you. In the past, suitors would have come to my home bringing gifts of cattle and fat sheep to feed the family of the bride; glorious gifts would have filled the hall. They would not have eaten up their bride's livelihood, nor abused her servants."

As she said this, Telemachos smiled, as did noble Odysseus through his beard, and shame colored the faces of some of the suitors, but not all. Cowardly Antinoos rose then and said to my mistress, "Noble Penelope, forgive us our actions. When we have finished our meal, we shall depart, and in the morning we will return with gifts worthy of your good name."

But my mistress did not answer Antinoos. Instead she turned to Telemachos and kissed him on the cheek before retiring to her bedchamber. Telemachos watched her as she departed, then he took a leg of lamb and a loaf of bread and left the hall to sit outside. I followed him there and sat beside him. He took pieces of meat from the bone and offered them to me.

Oh, to be fed by hand from one's master is a sweet thing!

CHAPTER XLII

ᗡᗡᗡᗡᗡᗡᗡᗡᗡᗡᗡᗡᗡᗡᗡᗡᗡ

Odysseus meets my mistress

Once the suitors had left and Odysseus's palace was dark, with
only a handful of servants still cleaning, Telemachos turned to
Odysseus and asked quietly, "Noble father, do you have a plan
to overcome the suitors? We are but two still, and they number
more than one hundred."

I snarled at the mention of the suitors, and noble Odysseus
said, "There are three of us, I believe. Is that not so, pup?"

I licked my lips, baring my sharpest teeth, and they both
laughed.

"Truly, I say to you, I believe this loyal one is ready to send
more than a few of them to their fates," Telemachos said.

"We shall see soon enough," Odysseus said, turning serious,
and scratching my ears. Then he said, "Tonight, my son, go

through the house and make sure all of my armor and weapons are hidden. When the suitors return in the morning, we must ensure they leave their spears and swords outside. That will give us the advantage. Now it is late and I must make more plans tonight, as well as give thanks to Athena, for she is my protector."

Noble Telemachos rose and left to do Odysseus's bidding. I stood with him, but he said, "Stay, loyal one. I have no enemies here, but my father does. Guard him tonight, for the servants may think him only a beggar."

And so I remained with Odysseus. Some time later, a servant girl appeared in the door and called out to us. "Stranger," she said. "My mistress would speak to you if you are still awake."

"I am," Odysseus said, rising. "Take me to the lady."

I followed them into the palace. The servant girl took Odysseus into the sitting room, where Penelope waited for him, and I entered too. A fire warmed the room, and a fleece had been spread out over a chair for Odysseus to sit upon.

"Stranger, welcome, and please make yourself comfortable," Queen Penelope said, smiling. "And who is this lion that accompanies you?"

How unlike dogs did the gods make men! No dog could resist wagging its tail upon seeing his mate after twenty years, and yet Odysseus revealed nothing, but said, "My queen, this is Leander, a loyal dog sent by your son to guard me against the suitors who bear me ill."

When he had seated himself, and I beside him, Mistress Penelope said, "Please do not take offense, but I have some questions for you, stranger. First, who are you and where are you from? Where is your city? Who are your parents? I think I see in you noble lineage, but it is covered in rags and torn clothing."

Then did Odysseus answer, "Lady, no man could take offense to these questions. Your faithfulness is known as far as the farthest islands and goes up into Olympus itself. But ask me not my name and lineage, I beg you, for the answers will fill my heart with grief, and it is not right that it should do so in a house in mourning such as this."

"Stranger, your words are fine and well said," my mistress replied. "Truly, this is a house of grief and has been since my husband left for Ilion. As you saw tonight, the suitors, all powerful men, lords of their estates across Ithaka, wear my house out. For years now they have pressed me to marry one of them, but I weave my own plans. I set up a loom here in this room and said to them all, 'Young men, my suitors, it may be that great Odysseus is perished, and his father, King Laertes, lies near death himself from grief. When I finish weaving this shroud for him, then I will choose one of you.' And so each day I spin and weave at my great loom, and each night I burn what I have woven. I did this for three years, but last year a disloyal servant saw me burning the shroud and told the suitors. They forced me to finish it, and now I cannot escape my marriage."

Saying this, my mistress began to weep. I walked over to her and placed my head in her lap, and she stroked it gently. Then she said, "I have confessed much, stranger. Now, won't you tell me your name and city and relieve a widow of her anguish for a short time?"

After a few moments, brave Odysseus said, "O loyal wife of Odysseus, son of Laertes, since you ask so plainly, I will tell. You may not know it, but there is a land called Crete, a beautiful country with good harbors, fertile soil, and tall pine trees for shipbuilding. There was I born and given the name Aithon, son to greathearted Deukalion, and grandson to Minos, who conversed with Zeus himself. And there did I meet your husband, noble Odysseus, when a strong storm forced him to take shelter on the way to Ilion. I took him into my home for twelve days and entertained him with proper hospitality, and on the thirteenth day, the wind relented and he set sail with his men on a fine black ship."

Hearing this, my mistress gasped. "Surely this is untrue and designed to ease a grieving widow's mind!"

Great Odysseus placed his hand on his heart, saying, "Nay, lady. It is true that I knew your husband and knew him well."

"My friend," my mistress said. "I think I shall give you a test to see if what you say is forthright. Tell me, what sort of clothing did my husband wear on his body, and what sort of man was he himself and his companions as well?"

My mistress began to stroke my head for she was truly vexed by the stranger's tale. How soft her hands were, how gentle!

Noble Odysseus answered thus, "Lady, many years have passed since then, and look at me now, how I have fallen from high place. But still I will tell you what he wore and who his men were. Great Odysseus wore a woolen mantle of purple hue with two folds, but the pin that held it was golden and artfully made: a hound much as this one at your lap, holding a deer in its paws. It was much admired. Of his men, their faces are a blur to me but one—his herald. He was a little older than your husband, round in shoulders and dark complexioned, and wooly haired. His name was Eurybates, and Odysseus valued him among all his companions. Is this so what I have told you?"

But my mistress could not answer because she was weeping.

Bitter tears splashed onto my forehead. Dogs cannot cry, thank the gods, but her tears fell from my own eyes as if they belonged to me. Finally my mistress collected herself and said, "Stranger, while before you had my pity, now you have my friendship and a place of respect here in my palace. The clothing I gave my husband is as you described it, and all who saw it shine admired the pin. But I know now that I will never welcome my husband into this house again."

Then my mistress buried her face in my neck. Now, I am a brave dog and have seen many things, but nothing except for the loss of my mother on that red ship moved me like this. How I wished then that I could say words of comfort to my mistress, but the gods severed human talk from us when Kronos first strode the earth.

For a time Odysseus said nothing; truly, he is the wisest of men. How many husbands would have taken their mourning wives in their arms and said, "I am here, O wife, but in disguise"? But instead he said this: "O respected wife of Odysseus, son of Laertes, let not your lamentations spoil your famed beauty. Mark what I tell you, for this I say in all honesty. Your husband is near."

My mistress raised her lovely head and said, "Now that I have called you friend, you say this cruel thing? To give false hope is to give no hope, stranger, so regard carefully what you say."

Then great Odysseus knelt beside us and put his hand on my shoulder and said, "Loyal Penelope, I am as faithful to you as this dog is to your son. I know this to be true. Although brave Odysseus has suffered much and lost all his men, he is close at hand, I swear to Zeus."

My mistress rose from her chair and made her way to the door. Turning then, she said, "I do not doubt that your words are true, if you believe them to be so. But I cannot believe them. Still, you are my friend and honored guest. I will tell the maidservants to bring a basin to wash your feet and new clothes for you to wear. They will prepare a bed too, for that is fitting in this house. Tomorrow you will dine at our table, seated beside brave Telemachos in a seat of honor, for you have sought to bring comfort to a grieving widow, and I thank you for that."

Then Odysseus said, "Noble wife of Odysseus, I am not accustomed to beds, so I will sleep here on the floor beside the fire. Nor do I want some young servant girl to wash my feet. But if you do have an old nurse or servant, one who has suffered as much as I, then I will allow her to do so."

"Dear friend," my mistress said, "truly you are as thoughtful as any guest who has come to my palace. There is such a woman here, an old nurse who once comforted my unhappy husband as a youth. Her name is Eurykleia, and I shall call her at once."

My mistress departed, leaving Odysseus and me alone in the room. He put his hands on my head and drew my forehead to his, looking into my eyes.

"You remind me of another great and loyal companion," he said to me. "One whose name will be known as long as men treasure loyalty and courage."

I licked his hand in honor of my father. After a few minutes, the old nurse Eurykleia entered the room, carrying a basin and a cloth, and sobbing.

"Why do you weep, kind nurse?" noble Odysseus asked. "Is this request loathsome to you?"

"No, stranger, it is not the task that brings my tears," she said softly. "I saw you when you entered the palace, and my old eyes thought they had seen noble Odysseus himself. But then I learned from the servants that you were just a vagabond and not the king he was. Still, there is something about you that reminds me of my master Odysseus, and my ancient heart is moved to tears, though I know not why, except that I miss him greatly. Please forgive me, stranger, and I will gladly wash your feet."

"Do not be troubled, loyal nurse, by your tears for your master, for they bring even more honor to this house," the Wily One said to her.

The old nurse came around to where Odysseus sat and placed his feet in the basin. Slowly, gently, she washed his feet and legs until suddenly, when her hand reached the area just above his knee, she let his foot go, and it fell onto the side of the basin, tipping the vessel and spilling the water onto the floor.

"It is you!" she whispered. "You have the scar from your first boar hunt, just above the knee. My master has returned!"

The old woman jumped to her feet and began to run out of the hall to proclaim the news. But I knew this was not brave Odysseus's plan, so I too sprang to my feet, and I am faster than an old nurse, and I was able to leap between her and the door, blocking it. A moment later, Odysseus had the nurse in his arms. "Nurse, do you want to kill me?" he whispered fiercely. "I tell you straight out, if you say anything, that will be accomplished!"

The old nurse sank to her knees. "Master," she said, "forgive this old nurse. I raised you from a child, and though you are not the same man in aspect who left twenty years ago, the gods have favored me and brought you home. But fear not, I am as stubborn as stone and will tell no one. But if it pleases you, I would retrieve another basin and anoint you in oil, as befits a king."

This she did, and when she had finished, she swore again to Odysseus not to reveal his identity, and after she left, we settled down to sleep. I lay on the floor near the divan where he slept, and occasionally brave Odysseus's arms would slide toward the floor and brush my back. When he turned over, he would reach down and pat my head, and I would lick his rough, oar-callused palm. I am sure he was dreaming of his beloved Argos.

Later that night, though, I heard sounds from the rooms above, and I rose to investigate, careful not to wake Odysseus. Creeping into the great hall toward the stairs, I saw a dim light growing brighter. I sniffed and caught the scent of my mistress Penelope, holding a candle as she descended the stairs. She seemed to be dream walking.

I followed her as she entered the room where Odysseus slept. Running ahead of her, I licked his face, waking him just as noble Penelope reached the divan. Then Odysseus jumped to his feet, drawing his dagger! My first thought was that only the cruelest gods would let a man kill his wife by accident after so much suffering. I barked and jumped in front of Odysseus. Truly, the gods favored me! My bark woke my mistress from her dream walk. I heard a gasp behind me, and then her gentle voice, asking, "Where am I?"

Brave Odysseus lowered his dagger and took my mistress by the arms. "You have been dream walking, noble Penelope. Tell me, what spirits possess you and torment your sleep?"

He guided her to the divan, and she sat there for a moment, pale and speechless, until her senses came to her.

"Friend, forgive my intrusion. My days are tormented by grief and my nights are tormented by dreams. Come, listen to my dream and see if you can interpret it, for I can find no message in it, yet it comes round every night."

I do not understand human dreams. Dogs—when they dream—dream of the hunt. Sometimes we hunt alone and sometimes we hunt with a pack, as our ancestors did and our cousins the mountain wolves still do. That is all. I have dreamed of my brothers and sisters many times, hunting alongside me. Together we are tireless and can track any prey. Those are fine dreams.

But this was my mistress's dream: "I have twenty geese who swim in the pond and scratch about the house. They feed on grains of wheat and drink from our trough. But in my dream, a giant eagle with a carved beak swooped down from the mountaintop and killed them all with his sharp talons. I began to weep—in my dream—and the ladies of the village tried to comfort me, but they could not. Then the eagle landed on the jut of the roof and said aloud in a human voice, 'Do not fear, daughter of famed Ikarios. This is a blessing, not a dream. The geese are the suitors who eat your food and drink your wine, and I, the eagle, am a portent of your husband come home. He will destroy the suitors just as I slew the geese.' And then I wake and look outside, and there are the geese feeding on the grain and drinking from the trough, as always. What say you of this? What is your interpretation, friend?"

Noble Odysseus shrugged his broad shoulders and smiled. "Lady," he said gently, "it is impossible to see this dream in any other way, since Odysseus himself, in the form of the eagle, told you its meaning and how it will end. The suitors are doomed, one and all, upon his return."

But my mistress did not believe Odysseus. "No, honored friend," she said. "Although my son and I would like nothing more than your version to be true—for it would mean my beloved husband is still alive—some dreams are deceptive. Such, I fear, is my dream of the geese. No, what the dream has told me is this: tomorrow dawns an evil day. It is time that I assent to marriage."

I growled then; I could not help it. But my mistress continued, "Before my husband left for Ilion, he would practice his archery on the grass outside our home. He would set up twelve axes and, standing far away from them, shoot an arrow from his greatest bow through all twelve handles. I will set up these axes as a contest for my suitors, and whoever is able to string my husband's bow with the greatest ease and shoot an arrow through the ax handles will win my hand, and I will go away with him, forsaking this house where I once found love."

This time a whimper escaped me, but neither Odysseus nor my mistress paid heed. Instead, he took my mistress's hand and said, "O faithful wife of Odysseus, the gods themselves could not disapprove of this contest, for they will strengthen the arm and steady the hand that draws the bow."

"No one can say what the gods desire, my friend," my mistress replied. "But having decided this, they seem to have lifted a weight from my shoulders, and now sleep falls heavily upon me. I must return to my bedchamber. Forgive my waking you, and may the dawn find you rested."

Saying this, she rose and left the room. I followed her to the stairs, where the night servant met her and took my mistress up to her bedchamber. I returned to find Odysseus preparing to sleep again.

"We must both rest, loyal one," he said, petting my head, "for tomorrow King Odysseus returns."

CHAPTER XLIII

/◎/◎/◎/◎/◎/◎/◎/◎/◎/◎/◎/◎/◎/◎

To string a bow

Bright dawn came and woke us both. Above me, in my mistress's bedchamber, I could hear her weeping, for it was the day she must choose a husband. Brave Odysseus heard it too. He lifted his hands and said, "Father Zeus, you who led me over dry land and dark seas to my home, do not abandon me now. Show me an omen that you are with me this day."

Then immediately we heard thunder rolling above our heads, though the morning was clear, and Odysseus smiled. A few minutes later, Telemachos, followed by Eumaios, strode like a god into the room. He was wearing a fine silk tunic, and a sharp sword was slung over his shoulder. In his strong hand he gripped a spear. He clicked his fingers once. I ran to him and positioned myself by his side.

"Did you sleep well, friend?" Telemachos asked Odysseus, maintaining their ruse. "Did my mother grant you hospitality? A bed and a warm fire?"

"I slept well, noble Telemachos," the Wily One said. "And while sleeping, my mind devised many things." I saw him wink at his son, but before Telemachos could reply, several servants entered the room. One rekindled the fire, while another rolled up the blanket on which Odysseus had slept. Several more entered the kitchen.

"The house wakes early. Dawn has just risen," Odysseus commented.

"There is a public festival today," Telemachos replied. "The loathsome suitors will be arriving soon, I think. Even now the shepherds are bringing pigs and goats to put on the spit."

Just as he said this, Melanthios, the goatherd, appeared at the door. He looked at Odysseus and spat on the floor. "Stranger, are you still here?" he sneered. "Do you intend to stay all day, pestering the gentlemen with your begging? If so, you and I shall come to blows!"

Brave Odysseus said nothing, but I saw him clenching his fists. Then Melanthios left the room, and I lifted my nose and smelled another herder enter the yard. By his scent, I knew he was an oxherd. He entered the hall and I knew instantly—the way that dogs always do—that he could be trusted. Telemachos greeted the oxherd as Philoitios.

"Who is this stranger?" the oxherd asked Eumaios after greeting Telemachos. "What are his origins and who were his ancestors? Unlucky man, he is dressed like a beggar, yet has the bearing of a king."

Saying this, he approached Odysseus and offered his right hand. "Welcome, stranger. May prosperous days befall you, for I can see now that you are in the grips of misfortune. May Father Zeus take pity on you, though alas, he did not pity the master of this house, Odysseus, who is dead and gone to the house of Hades."

Then Philoitios began to weep, for he had loved Odysseus and served him loyally, I could tell.

Seeing this, Odysseus put his hand on the cowherd's shoulder and said quietly, "Noble oxherd, you seem like a good and honorable man. I tell you this, and even swear it as Zeus is my witness: Odysseus will come home again soon, to this very house, and you shall see him with your own eyes as he rids this house of the despicable suitors who reign here."

Hearing this, Philoitios placed his hand on Odysseus's shoulder and said, "How I wish that day comes soon. When it does, you will see what kind of strength my hands have."

So then did Eumaios, Philoitios, Odysseus, and my master Telemachos sit and begin to devise their plan. I left the house then to learn more of its surroundings, and as I crested the rise that leads to the sheep pasture, I saw a band of suitors sitting on the ground in earnest discussion. I approached them downwind so that I could hear them more easily, yet remain unseen.

One of them, whom they called Amphinomos, argued forcefully, "Friends, this plan of ours to kill Telemachos is too difficult for now. Let us think of our feasting instead, for today's festival will ensure that we eat well. We have time to do our deeds on another day."

Just then an eagle flew over, carrying a trembling pigeon in its talons. The men took this to be a portent and agreed with Amphinomos to forestall their evil plan. Rising, they brushed their tunics and started down the path that wound to mighty Odysseus's palace.

I growled as they passed, and then went to round up the stray sheep for my sire, noble Argos, who, alas, was no longer there to do so.

When Apollo's chariot reached its zenith, the suitors took their seats in the great hall to await their feast. Servants filled their wine cups and cooks brought huge slabs of meat to the table and began carving them. I sat just outside the hall, waiting for Odysseus and Telemachos to arrive. After a few minutes they did, side by side, Odysseus still disguised by Athena and dressed as a beggar, and Telemachos looking strong and stalwart in a fine golden mantle.

I followed them inside the great hall, and the boisterous laughter ceased immediately as Telemachos seated brave Odysseus at an empty chair near his own honored place and filled both of their cups with wine. Never have I seen a hundred men so silent!

Then noble Telemachos spoke. "Gentlemen," he said. "This man is my honored guest. I ask you to share your meat with him and fill his glass accordingly. Most of all, bear him no insult, for to do so would be to insult me the same."

Telemachos looked about at the men seated at the table, but none would meet his flashing eyes. Only when he sat and began to cut his own meat did the suitors resume their eating, never looking at Odysseus, or at noble Telemachos, who had defied them. Instead they feasted and made toasts to their own valor, forgetting to thank both the gods and the house of Penelope for their food. Such uncouth men! Even I, living in trash heaps and fields, recognized this.

I myself ate meat passed to me under the table by my master Telemachos, and I licked the juices off his fingers. Then, as the feasting began to wane and the cups were drained, one of the largest of the suitors rose to his feet. His name, I gathered, was Ktesippos, and from under the table I saw my master clench his fists when he stood up.

He tapped his cup until everyone was silent and addressed them. "Hear me, friends. This stranger has sat among us as our equal, as he should, for he is a guest of Telemachos. But come, let us too give him a gift, so he can give it as a prize to the woman who washes his feet, or to the other servants who dress him or make his bed."

Then Ktesippos grabbed the hoof of an ox that lay in a basket and hurled it at Odysseus!

But Odysseus avoided it by turning his head slightly, and the hoof hit the wall. All around, the suitors inhaled sharply, but stalwart Odysseus smiled and said nothing. Then Telemachos rose to scold Ktesippos. "Sir," he said, "it is good that your missile missed its mark, for had it struck my friend, then you would have met my sharp spear, and your father would be planning a funeral instead of a wedding."

Then another suitor said, "Your words and temperament serve you well, young Telemachos, and it was wrong for Ktesippos to insult your friend in such a manner. But let me offer some counsel. It has been ten years since anyone heard news of your father, has it not? For ten years you and your loyal mother have held off these suitors here in hopes that your father should return to his rightful place. But now the temper in this house has changed from one of hope to despair, for even the most loyal blood of Ithaka can no longer think that Odysseus will ever return."

Around the table the suitors grunted in assent, nodding their heads like cows. The suitor continued. "Now it is time, dear Telemachos, to counsel your mother. Sit with her and explain that she should marry the suitor who is the best man among us and can provide the most for her. In that way, you can control your father's inheritance while she looks after the house of another."

Then the suitor sat, and several men around him clapped and pounded his back for saying what they did not have the courage to speak. *Courage? I am certain Telemachos had more courage as a suckling babe than these men!* I looked over to brave Odysseus, but he said nothing. What nerves he had! To remain silent when a hundred men proclaim you dead at your own dinner table! But beneath the table, his fists clenched again and again.

Then my master, noble Telemachos, answered. "It is not for me to tell my mother where her broken heart should lean, and

I will not force her to choose a husband if she is not ready."

Suddenly the strangest thing happened! Athena came down, invisible to all but me, and stood at the entrance to the room. With a nod of her head, the suitors began to laugh uncontrollably. Their eyes burst with tears as they crammed the sizzling meat from the spit into their jaws. Soon they had covered themselves in meat juice and wine, and they began to insult one another—and even Telemachos—crying, "Woe to your house, Telemachos, for the gods have brought this worthless vagabond to your door. He will never leave, yet he can do no work to earn his fare. Better to sell him to a slave ship than to have his dead weight around your house!"

So they spoke, but noble Telemachos said nothing. Instead, he looked at his father, and they shared the same thought as I did: that the suitors, with those words, had begun their undoing. I sat on my tail to keep it from twitching.

A moment later I heard my mistress descending the stairs. Yet she did not enter the great hall where the suitors grunted and howled like swine. Instead she, along with her servants, went to the far corner of the house, to a locked chamber. Telemachos sent me then to guard her, for indeed the suitors had grown mad and could not be trusted near her.

Taking an ornate, ivory-handled key from her gown, she

unlocked the door and entered the chamber. Inside were shields of bronze and gold-tipped spears lying next to gifts from many other islands. At the back of the room, hung on a peg, was a splendid bow. It was a powerful bow, as tall as a man, and made of the strongest yew wood. Hanging alongside the bow was a quiver full of arrows, which my mistress took as well. Then with the bow and the quiver in her hands, my mistress suddenly sank to her knees and began to weep. The servant girls—stupid creatures—did nothing, but I went to her and put my muzzle against her cheek and let her bury her face in my neck.

"I shall have to marry one of them, my new friend," my mistress whispered. "The gods demand it."

I could do nothing but lick her tears and nuzzle her cheek, but perhaps that helped in some small way. After a few minutes, my mistress rose to her feet, and with her hand on my shoulder for support, she left the chamber, carrying the quiver and majestic bow, after locking the door behind her. Together we walked back to the main hall where the suitors sat, quarreling now and boasting of their prowess with weapons and battle strategy. They did not see us at first, so lost in argument were they. But my master Telemachos and his father, noble Odysseus, now sat off to the side, watching the suitors carefully.

My mistress stood beside the pillar that supported the roof. On either side of her, servant girls held opposite ends of the veil in front of her face so that she might retain her modesty. Then she spoke, not loudly, but in a commanding voice, so that the suitors stopped and listened immediately.

"Hear me now, haughty suitors, you who have filled your bellies daily at my table, drunk my wine, and insulted my servants in this house of a man far greater than yourselves! Never have you said one word in his honor; instead, you talk incessantly of marrying me without even proof that my husband is dead and that I am a widow. But now it is time for you to claim your prize!"

The uncouth suitors began to cheer. "Pick me, choose me, I am the one for you!" they crowed.

"Silence!" my mistress cried. "Here is the contest before you. This is the bow of godlike Odysseus. The one who is able to string it with ease and send an arrow through twelve axes shall become my husband. I shall go away with him and forsake this house, though I will never forget it in my dreams."

The men began to clamor again, arguing who among them had the strength required to win the contest. Then my mistress beckoned to the loyal swineherd, Eumaios, who was watching from an anteroom.

"Here, Eumaios, let them see this mighty bow and feel its stiffness. They will not boast for long."

Eumaios took the bow from her, but he, too began to weep, when he saw the bow of his master. Still, he carried it among the suitors and let them marvel at its strength. I sat and watched the suitors. Some were in awe of the polished weapon and some scoffed at the notion that it could not be strung. Beside me, my mistress still wept, but silently.

Then handsome Telemachos rose and addressed the men in the hall. Surveying them, he cried, "Come, you suitors. There is the prize before you: a woman like no other and this wealthy estate. Surely it is time for the contest!"

The men cheered and began to rise from their seats. I heard my mistress inhale sharply, for truly they sounded like an army in battle. Then noble Telemachos continued, shouting over the furor.

"I too will seek to string the bow, and if I am able to do it, then my mother will remain here, in the house of Odysseus."

Then, drawing his sword, Telemachos left the hall, striding out into the yard, where he dug a trench and set up the axes as straight as a string. When the men had approved of his work, one of them yelled, "Yours is the first attempt, son of Odysseus. After that, we *men* will try our skill."

They formed a wide circle around noble Telemachos as he stood on the threshold. He took the bow in his strong hands and three times bent it nearly enough to string it. Each time he failed, the men called out insults and scorn. I growled but took no action. Instead I watched and waited.

Odysseus had carefully made his way into the circle of men and stood near Telemachos. I watched as he pretended to enjoy the spectacle. He too jeered when noble Telemachos failed to string the bow on his third attempt. But I saw his eyes too. They were full of cunning.

Then, pulling the bow for the fourth time, Telemachos, with shaking muscles, curved the tips and inched the loop closer. The men jeered loudly, taunting him. Then I saw Odysseus shake his head ever so gently—a signal to his son—and Telemachos gave up.

"Shame on me," Telemachos said. "I must be a coward or a weakling. My hands shake too much, and I have now sapped my puny strength. Come then, you who are willing, there must be many of you stronger than I."

So he stepped aside, laying the unstrung bow against the side of the palace. Then a suitor named Antinoos stepped up to the threshold and cried out directions. "Take your turns in order, from my right to my left, my friends. This bow will be strung soon enough, I grant you."

The first to attempt to string the bow was Leodes, but he failed quickly enough. Most of the other men tried also, but they all failed too, and they began to grow dispirited. Then Antinoos had Melanthios build a fire and heat the bow, thinking that would make it pliant.

Meanwhile, brave Odysseus, who had been watching from outside the circle of men, with Telemachos and me at his side, walked into the courtyard and found there Eumaios, the swineherd, and Philoitios, the oxherd, standing together talking. Approaching them, Odysseus put his hands on their shoulders and said, "Oxherd, swineherd, let me ask you both a question that vexes me. Would you fight for Odysseus if he returned to his home, or would you support the suitors, who may be able to offer greater rewards than a man gone for twenty years?"

Eumaios, the swineherd, answered first and without hesitation. "Friend, if Odysseus returned, he would see what kind of strength these hands have. I pray every day to the deities for him to return."

"And you, oxherd? Where do you fall?"

"I stand with my brother in the fields, stranger," Philoitios said. "Should he ever return, noble Odysseus would have me at his side."

Then Odysseus stepped even closer to these loyal servants and said, "I am he. I am here in front of you, disguised by the goddess Athena. See, here is the scar that the boar inflicted on me."

Odysseus pulled aside his mantle and showed them his scarred thigh. Seeing this, Eumaios began to kneel, but Odysseus pulled him to his feet.

"Loyal Eumaios," he said, "do not kneel here in the courtyard! Others might see you and ask why. Among all my servants, you two men do I trust. Let me say this quickly, for the contest will soon be over. When we have overthrown the suitors, I will reward you both with houses along with many fine possessions. Now, here is my plan."

CHAPTER XLIV

∕∽∕∽∕∽∕∽∕∽∕∽∕∽∕∽∕∽∕∽∕∽∕∽∕∽

The king returns

After a few minutes, brave Odysseus and my master Telemachos entered the yard where the suitors stood, struggling to string the bow, and sat down not among the suitors, but under an olive tree. They watched and said nothing, and I lay near Telemachos, watching too. The bow had passed to many men, all of whom had failed to string it. Finally it was passed to Eurymachos, he of broad shoulders and sinewy arms. He took the bow, turned it over the fire, and then, placing one end on a stone bench, he pulled down with his right hand from the top while lifting the string with his left. How red his face turned, then purple, then nearly black! Still he could not string it. Stopping then to catch his breath, he shook his head and muttered, "Shame on us that we fall short of godlike Odysseus. Unborn men will be told of our sorrow here today."

Then Antinoos said, "Worry not, Eurymachos. We shall leave the axes in a row overnight, and in the morning say prayers to Apollo, and he will aid us in our contest. For now, let us wash our hands and renew our libations. Have the servants bring more wine."

Hearing this, the suitors were cheered. They entered the great hall and began to eat again. After some time had passed, during which Telemachos combed burrs from my fur, brave Odysseus and Telemachos rose and entered the great hall. I followed at their heels. Knocking on the wooden joist with a staff, Odysseus quieted the men.

"What do you want, beggar?" one of them, a shriveled, gray-bearded man, asked.

"I ask a favor of Eurymachos and Antinoos, sir," Odysseus said loudly. The suitors grew silent. How it must have pained him to show such deference to those men, I thought.

"What is your request?" Antinoos demanded.

Wily Odysseus nodded. "I ask only this. You are correct to wait until morn and after your prayers to attempt a second time to string the bow. But for now I ask that you give the bow to me and let me test my arms against it, for I used to be strong and would know if my wanderings and begging have weakened me."

How indignant the suitors were at this proposition! They jeered brave Odysseus and threw bones at him. Oh, the shame he endured! My hackles rose and a growl formed on my lips, but my master Telemachos placed his hand on my shoulder, and I sat down. Watching.

Then Antinoos rose and pointed a fat finger at Odysseus, saying, "Wretched vagabond, isn't it enough that we let you sit here among us? Now you want to enter the contest? Let me tell you this: you may try to string the bow, and you may even succeed, but if you do, you will still be a beggar and not our equal. Sit and be quiet if you know what is best for you!"

Hearing this, my mistress Penelope, who had been sitting with her servant girls in a side room, entered and rebuked Antinoos. "Antinoos, it is rude to speak thusly in front of my son's guest. Do you really think this stranger could string my husband's bow and then take me home to be his wife? Just ignore him and return to your feasting."

Then Eurymachos stood and apologized to my mistress. "Forgive us, loyal Penelope, for our vanity and wounded pride. We are all ashamed that we could not string the bow, and for this man to claim that he could stings our hearts."

Queen Penelope shook her head and laughed bitterly. "There is no glory among you anyway, for you eat away your honor at the home of a great man, so why should you care what other people think about this man's request? Still, this stranger is a big man and claims to have a noble father. Give him the bow and see what happens! I tell you this: if he strings it, then I will give him fine clothing to wear and a sharp javelin to ward men and dogs away. And I'll send him anywhere he would like to go, on our finest ship."

When she said this, I began to fret. My mistress did not know Odysseus's plan, and I was afraid she would spoil it with her promises. A whine escaped me, but Telemachos stroked my head and calmed my heart. Then noble Telemachos stood and approached his mother, and placing his hand on her arm, said gently but firmly, "Mother, no one has more authority over the bow than I do, and I can give it to the stranger as a gift or never let him touch it. It belonged to my father, after all, and has passed down to me. Now take your servants and retire to your room. Finish the tunic you have been sewing and make sure that your servants are engaged tonight as well. I ask you this with deepest respect."

My mistress looked deep into noble Telemachos's eyes and nodded. After kissing him on the cheek, she said, "It is true, son, that I am very tired tonight and have no patience for these men. Come, girls, let us retire and leave this room. Perhaps in the morning they will be gone."

Saying this, she and her servants left the hall and climbed the stairs to her bedchamber. Then Eumaios, the loyal swineherd, brought the bow into the room.

"What are you doing with that bow, pig herder?" one of the suitors yelled. "If you touch it again, I'll feed you to the dogs!"

Then Telemachos raised his hand and said to Eumaios, "The bow belongs to me, my friend. And I say let the stranger hold it."

So Eumaios went to Odysseus and handed it to him. Then Odysseus whispered something to the swineherd, which only he and I could hear. It was this he said: "Tell the good nurse Eurykleia to lock the doors to the great hall from the outside, and no matter what she hears, she must not unlock them."

Eumaios nodded and left the hall.

Brave Odysseus took the bow and turned it this way and that, inspecting the tips and making sure that the horns were still strong. This was a charade; he knew the bow was still unbroken, but his actions caught the attention of the suitors, who watched with scorn on their faces. Then, with all eyes upon him, he took the strongly twisted sheep's gut and effortlessly strung the bow!

A great sorrow fell upon the suitors, and the color drained from their faces. Outside a cloud passed over the sun, and Zeus sent a portent of rolling thunder heard throughout the cloud-darkened room. My master Telemachos touched my shoulder and said, "Stay, Leander," and then he left the hall quietly while the suitors were dismayed.

Then, notching an arrow onto the tightened string, mighty Odysseus strode over to the open window, where all could see the axes lined up in a row. As the suitors rushed to the window, he pulled back the string and let fly the bronze-tipped arrow. It passed through all twelve axes and lodged in an oak on the other side. Even I, who can hear a bat's wings, heard nothing from the suitors as the arrow found its mark. At that moment, Telemachos returned.

Turning then to his son, Odysseus said, "Telemachos, your guest has not missed his mark, and my strength is still sound within me. Now it is time for the final course and then the dance and the lyre, for this is the end of the feasting."

Then did noble Telemachos show the suitors that he had returned armed. He raised his javelin, and with the other hand gripped his sword. Both were tipped in shining bronze. Then he tossed the quiver full of arrows to his father.

CHAPTER XLV

/◐/◐/◐/◐/◐/◐/◐/◐/◐/◐/◐/◐/◐/◐/◐

Honor restored

Father, perhaps you could see from Mount Olympus itself the destruction we brought. The suitors all perished that day, some bravely, some with cowardice in their hearts. I myself slew many, and prevented others from escaping out the window, though some feared my master's bow more than my snapping jaws and tried to pass me. They all failed. Let it be sung, Father, that four men—two who are godlike, two who are shepherds—and I defeated a hundred that day and suffered not our own grave wounds until the end.

We had stopped fighting, for our foes were vanquished. Brave Odysseus looked about the great hall, seeing if any man had escaped black doom. None had. Among his companions, only Eumaios and Telemachos bled, but not fatally so.

Odysseus placed his arm on my master's shoulder and said, "Now go summon the nurse, Eurykleia, for I have questions only she can answer."

Telemachos turned to go, and just then one of the suitors, who had hidden under the bodies of his comrades, rose and hurled a bronze-tipped spear at Telemachos! I leaped in front of him and took the spear in my shoulder.

Not even the tusk of a boar brought death as close as this. I saw with failing eyes Master Telemachos throw his own spear at the man, catching him in the chest and pinning him to the wall. Then I felt my master's arms around me, lifting me and putting me down gently onto a mantle spread over a table. I looked down and saw red blood staining the silk cloth. I did not even whimper. Leander, the lion slayer, remained silent while his life slowly eased from him.

The next thing I heard was the old nurse entering the great hall. When she saw the destruction there, she cried out in triumph, for she hated the suitors and what they had done to her master's house.

"Nurse, keep your joy in your heart," Telemachos cautioned. "These are slain men who have met a shameful death, yet there is no glory in their doom. Now, come here and see to my loyal companion, for he is grievously wounded."

The nurse ran to me and placed her ear next to my chest. "His heart is still strong, noble Telemachos, but his wound is fatal. I cannot save this dog, but I can give him herbs to hasten his final sleep."

Telemachos pushed her aside and placed his own great head on my chest, listening.

"Disloyal nurse!" my master cried. "This dog saved my life many times this day. Treat him as if he were my son!"

Then Eumaios came up to the table and said, "Noble Telemachos, let me tend to him. I am skilled at healing all things with four legs."

Saying this, Eumaios tore great strips of cloth and tightened them around my shoulder, staunching the blood. Then he withdrew a sharp knife and cut around the wound until he could reach the point of the spear. The nurse put cool water on my tongue. Father, I think then the gods were very close, because I felt a warm hand passing over my eyes, yet it belonged not to the nurse or Eumaios.

Although I was blind, I heard brave Odysseus ask for his wife Penelope, but the nurse Eurykleia said, "Master, Athena, or some god, has put your loyal wife to sleep. She knows not what has transpired here this evening, nor that you have returned, nor that her monstrous suitors are dead. Come, you must wake her."

"No," Odysseus said. "She should not see such destruction in her house. When the house is cleaned and in order, I would see the servants brought before you, and you will tell me who was loyal and who was not, so the disloyal ones can be banished. Then I will waken sweet Penelope."

"Master," I heard Eumaios say, "this loyal one grows cold. We must move him near the hearth."

I felt their strong hands beneath me as they lifted me gently to a cushion near the fireplace. How warm the fire felt, as if I had been cold all my life until that moment.

"I can do no more for him, sirs," I heard Eumaios say. "If the gods desire it, he will live."

"Then remain with him, Eumaios. I must see to my wife, fair Penelope," Odysseus said.

But just then I heard footsteps descending the stairs. One had the light bearing of my mistress. Then, for a long moment, I heard nothing.

Finally I heard Telemachos say, "Mother, why do you not greet your husband, who has suffered much, and after twenty years has returned?"

"My son," she answered finally. "I am too full of wonder to speak, and I cannot even look him in the face, if he is truly Odysseus. Too much has passed for my winged words to ask questions. Where would I even begin?"

Then I heard brave Odysseus say, "Come, my love. It is not right that you should see me covered in blood and filth as I am. And the gods have changed my appearance as well. Let us go upstairs and pray to Athena to return my form and shape; then you will believe I have returned. Eumaios, remain here with noble Leander. Attend to me if he worsens."

They all agreed to this. My master Telemachos came up to me and stroked my muzzle. Then he kissed my forehead. How I wish I could have seen him, but gray death was too near! I grew cold and began to shiver. Eumaios draped a mantle over me, and Telemachos tucked it in. Then, Father, I closed my blind eyes and surrendered my body to the will of the gods.

On the third morning I woke and found that I could see. Dimly at first, but then with greater clarity, I saw Telemachos sitting watchfully by the fire. Beside him were bowls of water and food.

"You are awake, noble Leander?" he asked quietly.

I barked, although it pained me some.

"Athena be praised. You must be thirsty, loyal one. Drink from this bowl. I'll help you."

Telemachos dipped water into his hands, and I drank.

We sat quietly. Apollo's chariot rose higher in the east, flooding the room with light. Each passing minute I felt stronger. Telemachos looked out the window, shaking his head.

Surely there is no more danger to us? I thought.

"It is a strange thing, Leander," Telemachos said. "For the last three days, hundreds of seagulls have flown in circles just outside, swooping and diving. Should they not be at the shore?"

I could not answer him, but later that day a crow told me why the gulls were flying so close to us. They were seeking to honor one who had been their friend. When I am stronger, I will go to the harbor and thank them on behalf of Argos, the Boar Slayer, most loyal dog son of Odysseus, sacker of cities, dog brother of noble Telemachos, mate of golden Aurora, and father of Leander, the lion slayer.

ACKNOWLEDGMENTS

To my detriment I tend to keep my writing close to the vest, but a few people were instrumental in bringing *Argos* to print, and I wish to acknowledge them here. My children, Kabir and Shalini, never rolled their eyes when I told them about my idea for *Argos*, and for that I thank them. Jonas Horwitz and David Hardy read early drafts and made useful suggestions. Tom and Laura McNeal, two fine writers I admire tremendously, introduced me to my agent, the late George Nicholson. If there is a pantheon for young adult publishers, George stands alone on Mount Olympus. I deeply appreciate the efforts of Erica Silverman and the fine people at Sterling Lord Literistic, who continue to support my writing. To my editor at HarperCollins, Toni Markiet, I extend my most sincere gratitude. She took a chance on a fledgling writer with a strange idea for a book and let me remain true to my vision for *Argos*. Finally, my wife, Anu Kumar, never wavered in her support of my writing habit, encouraging me through fallow periods and rejections and making my successes all the more sweet, and for that I could never say thank you enough.

A note on sources: I think I first encountered the story of Odysseus through Tennyson, in the great poem *Ulysses*. I then read Robert Fagles's version sometime in junior high, and in college I read Richmond Lattimore's *The Odyssey*. Since I don't read ancient Greek, I dipped into all three again as I wrote *Argos* and found them just as good as I remember.